# PAUL, BIG, AND SMALL

# PAUL, BIG, AND SMALL

DAVID GLEN ROBB

SHADOW
MOUNTAIN

*For Ruth,*
*who taught me to jump*

Visit us at shadowmountain.com

Library of Congress Cataloging-in-Publication Data
Names: Robb, David Glen, author.
Title: Paul, big, and small / David Glen Robb.
Description: Salt Lake City, Utah : Shadow Mountain, [2019] | Summary: Paul, a
    talented rock climber despite his very short stature, becomes friends with six-foot-tall
    Lily and Hawaiian newcomer Big to navigate the high school halls filled with bullies.
Identifiers: LCCN 2019014114 | ISBN 9781629726021 (hardbound : alk. paper)
Subjects: | CYAC: Friendship—Fiction. | Bullying—Fiction. | Rock climbing—Fiction.
    | High schools—Fiction. | Schools—Fiction. | LCGFT: Fiction.
Classification: LCC PZ7.1.R579 Pau 2019 | DDC [Fic]—dc23
LC record available at https://lccn.loc.gov/2019014114

Printed in the United States of America
Lake Book Manufacturing, Inc., Melrose Park, IL

10  9  8  7  6  5  4  3  2  1

# Chapter 1

When I first met Lily, she burped in my face. We were seven at the time, and it was disgusting. I squeezed my eyes shut as if that could protect me from the warm, moist air that erupted from her stomach and spilled over me. It smelled like peanut butter and Fritos.

It happened at a small park near my house. I'd gone to get a drink, and Lily was leaning against the cinder block wall next to the drinking fountain with her arms folded and ankles crossed. I thought she looked a little suspicious because she appeared to be trying too hard to look casual by staring off into the sky. Plus, all her friends were nearby, giggling.

I knew something was up, but I stopped to get a drink anyway. Lily was cute, and I figured it wouldn't be too bad to be the victim of a cute girl's prank. She was long and gangly with big brown eyes and her hair in a big Afro. I was also intrigued by the fact that she was black. There weren't a lot of black kids where I lived. I'd only met two or three in my life up to that point.

Just before I got to the drinking fountain, Lily cut me off, leaned over, and took a big drink. I was puzzled. Why were her friends giggling so much? Then she lifted her head up from the fountain and leaned toward my face. There was a long, strange moment where I thought she was going to kiss me. I was thrilled and terrified at the same time. Then, only an inch from my lips, she opened her mouth and let out a deep, gaseous belch.

Lily smirked at me while her friends burst into an explosion of laughter. I tried to pretend it didn't bother me and gave her what I hoped was a "you're so immature" expression. She still stood between me and the drinking fountain, so I said, "Could you please move? I'm trying to get a drink."

Lily simply folded her arms and continued to smirk while her friends laughed even harder. I wasn't sure what to do. I didn't want to look like a wimp by backing down. On the other hand, I didn't dare push her out of the way. She was taller than I was, and if she punched as hard as she burped, I was really in for it. Just before I decided to walk away, she stepped aside.

As I was drinking, she asked, "What's your name?"

I wiped the water from my mouth with the back of my hand and said, "Paul. What's yours?"

"Lily," she said.

I looked up into her face. The first thing I noticed was her smile. It was crooked, and she didn't have either of her two front teeth. Just glistening pink gums where they had once been. The second thing I noticed was the dark-brown spot on the side of her chin.

"Is that a mole?" I asked, pointing at it.

Her friends quit laughing and watched.

Lily's hand went to her chin, and her smile vanished. "Yeah, so?"

"Is it cancerous?"

2

"What's that mean?" she asked. She sounded mad. I don't think she liked me pointing out her mole or that I knew a word she didn't.

I took a step back and said, "It means you could die from it."

"You can't die from a mole," she said.

"Yes, you can. My mom did."

Lily's expression made me step back again. "No, you *can't*," she said. Her hand dropped from her chin and became a fist.

I should have shut up at that point, but I couldn't. In my seven-year-old mind, I felt it was my duty to warn her of the danger she was in. If Lily had a mole, then she might have cancer. The doctors said my mom would have been fine if she had known about her cancer sooner. I said, "It's true, and you could have cancer, and you could die."

Then Lily punched me in the face.

That mole was the reason I recognized Lily on my first day of high school eight years later. Being punched in the face had lodged the exact size, shape, and location of that little mole into my memory like a handprint—or in this case, a fist-print—in setting cement.

I fought the current of students in a congested hall between classes. No easy task when you're only four feet, ten-and-a-half inches tall and weigh ninety pounds. When you're as short as I am, it's hot, humid, confusing, and claustrophobic to be trapped in a crowd. I felt like a baby calf separated from its mother in the middle of a wildebeest stampede. I tried to cut out to the side, aiming to duck through a doorway before I was trampled to death.

When I reached the doorway, I looked up and saw a silver

women's bathroom sign. I panicked and tried to veer away, only to be knocked to the ground by somebody's chest.

Now, I'm short and all, but this guy was way over six feet tall. He stood like a tree in the middle of the stampeding students. Sprawled in the shadow of his towering form, I somehow managed not to be crushed.

"Sorry, man," I said.

"Man?" a distinctly female voice said.

In my defense, I generally navigated school hallways with my head down and my eyes on the floor. It was safer that way. No eye contact meant I was openly submissive and less likely to catch the attention of a passing alpha male. Teenage guys are a lot like dogs in that way.

But that meant I hadn't actually looked at the person I had run into. I just assumed she was a guy due to her height. When I finally looked up, I saw that the lamppost-sized person standing above me was definitely a girl. A black girl. And that's when I saw the mole. She loomed over me, looking down with an expression of disgust, her hands on her hips, but I couldn't help but think she was still kind of cute. But she was *so tall*.

"Watch where you're going, twerp," Lily said as I struggled to get to my feet.

"Sorry," I mumbled, my face burning. I didn't know whether Lily was angry or amused, because I didn't dare look at her. There was a long, awkward moment of silence. I felt like a minnow squirming in the shadow of a long-legged crane, waiting to see if I would be deemed worth eating.

She finally let out a huff, stepped around me, and continued on her way.

Stumbling to the side of the hallway next to the bathroom

door, I put my back to the wall and watched Lily stroll off. She towered over all the other students, and they scrambled to get out of her way. I let out a sigh of relief. That was close. The last thing I needed on the first day of school was to get beat up by a girl.

I waited next to the bathroom until the crowd thinned and it was safe to continue. I was late to my next class, and the only seat left was on the front row. I hated sitting on the front row. I liked the back row. It wasn't because I was a troublemaker or anything. I just needed to stay invisible.

Staying invisible is how I survived school. I didn't talk in class unless absolutely necessary, all my clothes were neutral in both color and style, and my hair was ordinary and unremarkable. Besides the fact that I was abnormally short, I didn't stand out in any way, good or bad. I was like the human equivalent of one of those stick bugs that look like the branch of a tree: people could step right on me and never know I was there. I had mastered the art of social camouflage.

But to get to my seat on the front row, I had to step over these long, smooth, black legs. *Very* long, smooth, black legs. I glanced up, and there was Lily, looking at me. Even sitting in a desk, she was still taller than I was standing up.

She smirked and said, "Hey, twerp."

"Hey," I said. It came out as a pathetic squeak. I felt my face heat up again.

Lily looked me up and down. I would like to say she was checking me out, like she thought I was hot or something, but it wasn't like that. I'd grown used to people looking at me like she did. Usually it was when I told them my age, and they were like, "*You're* fifteen?" and then they looked at me again as if trying

5

to decide if a fifteen-year-old guy could really fit into a body so small.

I sat down next to Lily, feeling the eyes of thirty-five other students giving me the same appraising look. I heard someone say, "Who let the kindergartener in?" Then a guy wearing at least three items of clothing that violated the school's "gang safety" dress code said, "Maybe he's really smart, and he skipped a bunch of grades." The first person was being a jerk, but the other guy seemed to be genuinely wondering if I was some kind of kid prodigy. I wasn't sure which was more embarrassing.

The teacher started roll call. "Paul Adams," he said and tilted his head down to scan the class over the top of his glasses.

"Here," I said like a choking mouse.

The jerk in the back of the class said, "Oh, how cute, he's finally going through puberty. Maybe he'll hit a growth spurt." A bunch of people laughed.

If only that were true. The fact was, I was pretty much through puberty. Body hair? Check. Voice change? Check. Obsessing about girls 24-7? Check. Growth spurt? Unfortunately, check. As much as I hated to admit it, I was done growing. My dad was only five foot two, and my mom had been four foot nine.

The teacher, Mr. Teller, said, "Knock it off, Mr. Dolores." He made a mark on his tablet and continued calling names. Then he said, "Lily Small," and I let out a snort, thinking the whole class was going to erupt in laughter again. I mean, a girl well over six feet tall named "Small"? She was a walking cliché like "Little John" or some giant biker everyone called "Tiny." It was funny.

Not a single person laughed.

Mr. Teller looked over his glasses at me and scowled. The rest of the class stayed dead silent. I didn't dare look at Lily, but I could *feel* her looking at me, like red rays of heat were coming from her direction. I spent the rest of the class staring at the graffiti scratched on the top of my desk.

When school was finally out, I grabbed my skateboard from my locker and rode home. Once there, I ditched my board and books, grabbed my climbing gear, and hopped a bus into Ogden. My dad didn't usually get home from work until six or seven each night, so I'd talked him into getting me a membership at the climbing gym in town.

I loved rock climbing. Not that I'd ever climbed a real rock before. Just the fake climbing walls meant to mimic the real thing.

The first time I'd climbed had been at the county fair two years before. The local climbing gym, the Ogden Climbing Center, had a portable wall they'd set up to promote their gym. It was ten bucks to climb, but if you made it to the top and rang a bell, you could have your money back.

My dad looked up at the climbing wall and said, "That doesn't look so hard."

We watched a middle-aged guy with a goatee try to climb it while his wife cheered him on from below. He grunted, and his bald head glistened with sweat. He swatted for a handhold, and one foot popped off. He kicked at the wall, causing deep, hollow booms to echo as he struggled to get his foot back on a hold. The muscles of his arms and shoulders bulged under his black Harley-Davidson T-shirt. He growled and swore as his wife yelled for him to hang on.

"Looks pretty tough to me," I said through a bite of a churro.

"Don't talk with your mouth full," my dad said without looking away from the wall. "He's making it harder than it needs to be. Look, why doesn't he grab that yellow hold on his left and put his foot on the big blue hold by his right knee?"

Baldy's wife must have heard my dad because she turned to him and sneered, "If you think it's so easy, *shrimp*, why don't you try it?"

I felt a surge of anger at the crack about my dad's height, but he didn't even flinch. My dad was like a tiny Zen master. Nothing could touch him. I'd never once seen him get angry at people's rude comments. He was always calm and in control.

"You know, I'd really like to." He smiled up at her. "Unfortunately, I'm out of commission." He held up his right hand, which was wrapped in a bandage. He'd burned it a few days earlier while cooking a pot of spaghetti. Climbing was definitely out of the question.

Baldy gave another loud grunt. All of us looked back up in time to see him fall. The rope went taut at the harness around his waist, and he was lowered to the ground, shaking his head.

"This is a total rip-off. It's impossible," he said as his feet hit the ground.

The guy running the climbing wall started unbuckling him from the harness. "It's not impossible. I've had at least half a dozen people make it to the top today."

"Yeah, right," Baldy said. "This whole thing's a scam. No one can do it."

The guy working the wall frowned. "I'll climb it for you right now if you want. If I don't make it, I'll give you your money back."

"Sure *you* could do it," Baldy said. "You probably know some trick or something. That's how you scam people out of their money."

"Sir, I've seen kids as young as ten make it to the top of this wall. We're not scamming anyone." His voice sounded strained, and he talked through his teeth like he was trying to bite back what he really wanted to say.

"Alright," Baldy's wife said, "if this isn't a scam, then have this kid do it." She pointed a long finger with a fake pink nail straight at me.

I looked at my dad for help, but he was still staring up at the wall as if studying his next move in a chess game.

"Uh, I don't think—" I started.

"Yeah," said Baldy. "I'll tell you what, if this scrawny kid here makes it to the top, we'll pay you another ten bucks. If he falls, you give us our money back and admit this is a scam." He squinted down at me. "What are you, like nine or ten?"

For a moment, I considered lying and telling him I was ten. Then he wouldn't think there was anything abnormal about me. Unfortunately, my dad was standing right there, so I mumbled, "I'm, um, thirteen."

"What?" Baldy asked.

I wasn't sure if he hadn't heard me, or if he couldn't believe what I'd said. "I'm thirteen," I repeated, then waited for what I knew would come next.

Baldy didn't disappoint. He gave me the up-and-down look, then burst out laughing, and said, "Like father, like son, huh?" Without waiting for an answer, he turned back to the guy running the wall. "Well, do we have a deal?"

The guy working the wall looked me in the eye, then down at my shoes, shrugged, and said, "Deal. Come and give it a try."

"What? I don't know how to climb." I turned back to my dad. "Dad?"

Everyone looked at him. I wondered if he hadn't heard what was going on, but after a long moment, he turned from the wall and said, "Why not? You'll do fine. If you ring the bell at the top, I'll buy you dinner."

"If you ring the bell," said the guy working the wall, "I'll buy you *both* dinner."

"That's right," said Baldy. "Give it a shot."

"I don't think so," I said, backing up.

"Don't be silly," my dad said in his calm, Zen-master voice. "Get up there, and give it a go." He grabbed what was left of my churro and gave me a gentle push forward.

"I really don't want to, Dad." That wasn't entirely true. I would have enjoyed trying to climb the wall, just not with the pressure of strangers watching. Of *anyone* watching.

"You'll do fine," my dad said.

I started to object again, but I saw something beneath the calm surface of my dad's expression. He raised his eyebrows just a little. There was a kind of cool intensity in his eyes. I realized that the rude comments of Baldy and his wife had not gone unfelt. He nodded toward the wall, and it was as if he said right out loud, *Get up there, and prove you can do this.*

I stepped up to the wall, and the guy started helping me buckle into a harness. After a moment, he realized the harness was too big, and he had to switch it for a kid-sized one. It had pictures of monkeys on it. I felt my face heat up with embarrassment.

The guy must have noticed because he whispered, "Don't worry about it. No one can tell it's a child's harness."

Right then, a little girl called out, "Look, Mom. His has monkeys on it." I knew the girl wasn't trying to make fun of me. She was just excited about the monkeys, but everyone else started laughing, especially old Baldy. He burst out with this deep, bellowing laugh like a bloodhound baying.

The guy putting on my harness moved so he was between me and the crowd and said, "My name's Andy. What's yours?"

"Paul."

"Okay, Paul, here's what you need to understand. Everyone thinks rock climbing is all about muscle and strength, but it's not. It's about finesse and balance."

"What?" I said. I had no idea what "finesse" was.

"Never mind," Andy said as he finished clipping me into the rope. "All you have to do is climb with your feet. Think footholds not handholds, think balance not strength, and . . ." He must have noticed I wasn't understanding anything because then he said, "Just enjoy yourself and forget about everyone else. Now go."

Easy for him to say. He was tall and lean. His tan face had a week's worth of scruff, and his wavy, brown hair was sunbleached. He looked like he'd just gotten back from climbing Everest.

I stepped up to the wall. There seemed to be plenty of holds to choose from, so I grabbed one with each hand. I looked down and found a hold for each foot and stepped up. So far, so good. I looked up and found two more handholds and repeated the process. It wasn't so bad. In fact, it was pretty easy.

I did the same thing again, only this time, when I stepped up with my feet, I found an even higher foothold. It was bigger, and I thought it would help me make extra progress. It seemed to work at first, but then I realized I was off-balance. I couldn't let go with either hand or I'd fall. Now what? The sun was beating down on me, and my hands were starting to sweat. I had gotten myself into a scrunched-up position, and my muscles were starting to feel the strain. I looked down to see I was only five feet off the ground. How pathetic.

"See that," I heard Baldy say. "He's already about to fall. Just give up now, shorty. It's impossible."

A shot of anger coursed through me, and I renewed my determination. I looked from handhold to handhold, but I couldn't make up my mind which one to go for. There were three of them only a foot or two from my face, easily within reach, but I couldn't let go long enough to grab any of them.

I was about to make a desperate slap for a hold when Andy said, "Think about your feet."

My feet? My feet weren't the problem. My feet were fine. I couldn't move my hands, and they were starting to sweat off the holds.

"He's right, Paul," my dad said. "Your feet are so high up, you've gotten yourself off-balance. Step back down, and you'll be fine."

"Hey," Baldy's wife said, "you can't help him."

"Oh, let 'em. He's not going anywhere," said Baldy.

Baldy was right. They weren't helping. What did my dad know anyway? He'd never climbed in his life. He wasn't the one stuck only five feet up, wearing a child's harness with cartoon monkeys on it in front of everyone. I looked at my handholds again. I rocked to the right, and then to the left, trying to find a way to get enough weight off my hands to move them.

Nothing.

I figured if I was going to fall anyway, I might as well look down at my feet. I saw an okay-looking hold not far below my right foot. It wasn't as big as the hold I was on, and it didn't make any sense to move from a great big foothold up high to a significantly smaller one down low, but I didn't see any other options. I pressed my cheek to the wall, removed my foot, and slowly let it slide down. Once it hit the hold, I was shocked to feel half my weight shift off my hands. I was almost comfortable.

I had enough balance to let go with one hand, wipe the sweat off my other hand on my pants, and move to one of the higher holds. I suddenly understood Andy's advice: climb with your feet, use balance not strength. I still didn't know what this "finesse" thing was, but at least I was moving again.

"Nice work, son," my dad said.

"That's it," Andy said. "Just keep that up."

I started up the wall again, looking down at my feet more than I was looking up. I always made sure I was balanced before I even thought about moving my hands. I realized why Andy had looked at my shoes before agreeing to the bet. So much depended on your feet. If I'd been wearing flip-flops, I'd never have made it this far.

As I neared the top, I heard Baldy say, "He just got lucky. He won't get past my high point."

"He's already higher than you got," his wife muttered.

The holds were getting smaller and were spaced farther apart, and I was getting tired. I wasn't sure if I was going to make it, but I was really starting to enjoy myself. As the holds got smaller, I could focus more. I imagined I was some kind of super-precise machine, like the ones that put cars together on assembly lines: every movement exact, no wasted energy.

I watched each foot until I'd placed it exactly where I wanted it on each foothold. I found the best possible way to grip each handhold, no matter how small. Every time I moved, it was as if the only thing that existed in the whole world was the hold I was reaching for. I felt almost weightless. Everything disappeared from my mind. I was a single point in the universe.

Then there was a shiny brass bell in my face. I was surprised to see it, and it broke my concentration. I heard Baldy and his wife chanting, "Fall, fall, fall."

I looked down at them, confused. Why were they yelling at me to fall? Then the strange spell of the climbing lifted, and I remembered the bet and the insults. I smiled.

My strength was draining fast, but I wanted to show them that just because they were bigger, it didn't mean they were better. I put on a show of pretending to stretch and yawn like rock climbing was so easy it was boring. I patted my mouth with one hand and then, as casually as I could, I reached out to ring the bell.

Just before my fingers touched the string, I fell.

# Chapter 2

When I arrived at the gym, I immediately looked for Andy. He was the manager of the Ogden Climbing Center—or OCC as we called it—and he was nicer to me than some of the other people who worked there. Plus, he always complimented my climbing technique, which was nice to hear since I didn't often get a lot of compliments from anybody about anything.

The gym was huge. Some of the climbing walls were three stories high. I liked climbing those the most, but that meant I needed a rope and, more importantly, someone to hold the end of that rope. "Belaying" is when a partner runs your rope through a device clipped to their harness so they can catch you if you fall. If I wanted to climb the bigger walls, I had to find a partner to belay me, and I didn't exactly have people lining up.

I usually stayed in the bouldering section unless Andy could belay me. The bouldering section was made up of walls that were only ten or twelve feet high. The floor was padded, so there was no need for a rope. If you got into trouble, you just jumped off and landed on the soft pad. It was fun, just not as exciting as the big stuff.

On my way to the bouldering area, I saw Andy teaching a half circle of students.

I heard Andy say, "It's overhanging, right? While not all overhangs are necessarily harder than vertical climbs, they do require a few additional skills. This one happens to be harder than anything we've climbed in this class so far. Knowing that, what do you think is the most important quality you'll need to climb it?"

I stopped to watch. I figured maybe I could learn a thing or two if I listened in.

A slender girl with her blonde hair pulled into a tight braid said, "Strength?"

"All right," Andy said. "Who's the strongest person in our class?"

Practically in unison, everyone said, "Hunter."

Andy said, "You've been volunteered, Hunter. Get up here."

A guy who looked to be seventeen or eighteen walked over to the wall. He was tall, muscled, and moved with a confident swagger. "Should I tie into the rope?" he asked. Despite his size, he had a strangely high-pitched voice. Even my voice was deeper than his.

"No need to tie in," Andy said. "You won't be going all the way up just yet."

I edged my way closer, trying to stay unnoticed. I wasn't sure how Andy would feel about me sort of stealing a climbing lesson. I knew the classes were expensive because I'd wanted to take one, but my dad wouldn't pay for it. Instead, he bought me a *How to Rock Climb* book I'd never bothered to read.

I slid up behind the students and peeked between their

shoulders. I was pushing my camouflaging ability to its limits, but no one gave me a glance.

Andy said, "Okay, Hunter. Start right here, and see how far you can get."

Hunter gave the class a self-assured smile, revealing two rows of gappy teeth in his big, square jaw. "I got this."

He stepped onto the wall and started climbing. Well, at least he tried. Once he was on the wall, he couldn't seem to move. He kept trying to reach for the next hold, first with one hand and then with the other, but each time he let go, he would start to swing off the wall like a door on its hinges. His muscles bulged with the effort.

"Focus on your footwork and body position," Andy said.

Hunter tried looking for different footholds. The only one was high and way to the right. He took his right foot off and stretched for it. A few of the students made sounds of awe, and the blonde girl said, "Nice job."

I was pretty impressed, too. I looked at Andy's face to see what he thought. He had a subtle smile that said he knew something we didn't. I looked back to Hunter. He managed to get his foot on the hold, but there was no way he could put much weight on it. He wasn't going anywhere with that move.

With his cheek pressed to the wall, Hunter looked back up at the nearest handhold. It was blue and looked like a golf ball-sized mushroom. He let out a few quick puffs of air and then lunged for the hold. The instant he let go with his hand, both feet blew off the wall, and he slid to the ground. Everyone let out a moan of disappointment.

"Good effort, Hunter," Andy said, giving him a pat on the back. "Go ahead and sit down." He turned and addressed the class. "Sometimes it doesn't matter how strong you are. Physical strength will only take you so far. Strength dwindles as you climb; strength is a gas tank that, sooner or later, is going to run dry." Andy let that sink in for a second and then asked, "If strength isn't the quality we need to climb something like this, then what is?"

No one said anything. They just looked at each other like there might be some kind of clue in all the different body types standing around. I looked at the ground and tried hard to remain invisible.

Finally, Hunter said, "Maybe if I was taller I could have reached that hold. I'll bet Lily can do it."

Alarms went off in my head. Lily? *The* Lily? How could I have missed the towering black girl with the cornrows in this sea of white kids?

"What do you think, Lily?" Andy asked. "Will you give it a go?"

"Sure, I'll give it a shot." Her voice was strong and confident. She stood up and up and up. She was a head taller than everyone in the class except Hunter, and even he only came to her eyebrows. She had been sitting in the front, so all the standing students had blocked my view of her. With two long strides, she was at the base of the overhanging wall. She reached up and grabbed the blue mushroom Hunter had worked so hard for without even taking her feet off the ground.

Everyone groaned, and the blonde girl said, "That's so unfair."

Lily grabbed one of the lower holds with her left hand and stepped onto the lowest two footholds. Her gaze locked on a sharp red edge up and to the left of the blue mushroom. It was far enough away even she couldn't reach it. Then she seemed to remember Hunter's high foothold out to the right. Lily cranked on the blue mushroom with relative ease and stretched her right foot out to the hold. It wasn't difficult for her long leg to reach it, and she appeared fairly comfortable.

Hunter said, "Good job, Lily."

That surprised me because guys like him didn't usually like being outdone by anyone—and especially not a girl.

A smile spread across Lily's face. The kind of smile a boxer has when she's circling a wobbling opponent and knows she's about to land the knockout punch: confident and certain. It was strangely attractive on her.

Then Lily looked back to the red edge to her far left, and the smile disappeared. It was no closer. In desperation, she grabbed the blue mushroom with both hands. It was too small, and she had to wrap one hand over the other. She started to bring her left foot up to the hold where her left hand had just been. The intensity in her eyes was almost scary. The toned muscles in her shoulders and arms tightened.

Lily let out a fierce growl. It wasn't a pretty move at all. No finesse, that's for sure—I had learned the word by then—but it was working, and I admired her determination. Just as her foot reached the hold, everything blew off the wall at once. She would have landed flat on her back if Andy hadn't been there to spot her.

"Wow, Lily, that was fantastic," Andy said.

Lily steadied herself and then looked down at him with eyes narrowed in anger. She must have thought Andy was being sarcastic.

He continued, as if he didn't notice the death stare she was giving him. "It's not often you see someone try that hard at anything. People usually give up before they reach their real limitations. They simply *think* they've hit their limit and let go. I love to see a climber explode off the holds. It means they didn't quit. Well done."

Lily must have realized he wasn't making fun of her, because her eyes returned to normal. She mumbled, "Thanks," and sat down.

Andy turned to the class. "Lily's height gave her a distinct reach advantage in the beginning, but there are times when even she will not be able to reach the hold she wants. And, in rare circumstances, height can actually work against you. So if Hunter's strength will not get you to the top of this overhanging climb, and Lily's height will not get you there either, what quality are we missing?"

He scanned the group until his eyes landed on me. I don't know how he saw me with only my one eye peeking from between two sets of shoulders, but he did. "Paul," he said, and his look was like a spotlight. Everyone turned and stared at me.

"Uh, sorry, Andy," I stammered. I'd been so focused on what Andy was saying, I'd forgotten I wasn't supposed to be there. "I'll head over to the bouldering wall. I didn't mean to, um, interrupt."

"You're not interrupting. You're just the person I need. Get up here."

"Me?"

"Yeah, you. Come here."

"Um, okay." I made my way to the base of the wall. My heart was thumping, my hands were sweating, my face was burning, and I knew I must have looked even smaller and more pathetic than usual compared to Hunter and Lily. Andy knew I hated being the center of attention. What was he trying to do to me?

"Paul is not as strong as Hunter nor as tall as Lily," Andy said. "Let's see if he can show us our missing quality."

I made a mental note to thank Andy later for pointing out all my physical shortcomings to everyone. I put on my climbing shoes, then stepped onto the lowest holds, but Andy stopped me.

"You better tie in," he said.

I hesitated. Why would I tie in if Hunter and Lily hadn't?

"We don't have all day," he added with a smile when I didn't move.

I put on my harness and tied in. I considered just giving the route a cursory attempt and running off to hide as fast as I could, but then I thought about what Andy had said to Lily. About how he respected it when a climber blew off the holds because it meant they'd tried their hardest. I didn't want to lose what little respect I might have earned. I decided to try my hardest.

I grabbed the lowest handhold. It had been head-height for Hunter, but I could barely reach it even standing on my tiptoes.

"He can't even reach the other starting hold," I heard someone whisper.

"There's no way he'll even get off the ground," someone else said.

They said it as if to defend me. Like Andy was picking on a little kid, and they didn't think it was funny.

The second starting hold really was out of reach. I had to step onto the low footholds and really crank on my lone handhold to get it. This was it. I took a deep, slow breath and focused. It was like someone turned the volume down on the world. Somewhere, way in the back of my head, I knew people were still talking, even encouraging me, but I no longer heard them. They didn't exist anymore. There was only the next hold, which was not, I realized, the blue mushroom—at least not for my four foot, ten-and-a-half-inch body. Nor was it the foothold way out to the side like

Hunter and Lily had chosen. It was a tiny dime-edge at my waist level. It was so small, Hunter and Lily hadn't thought it worth noticing.

Continuing to breathe slow and deep, I managed to lift my foot up to the tiny edge. Because of the hold's size, I had to be precise. I set my foot down like I was a brain surgeon and my patient's life depended on my accuracy. Satisfied, I looked up at the blue mushroom. It was easily within reach, but something else was wrong. I couldn't move. If I let go with either hand, I would fall.

What needed to change? My feet. I looked down, and then adjusted my feet so they were both facing the same way. That allowed me to twist my right hip into the wall. There it was: balance. It took a lot of effort, but I reached up and grabbed the blue mushroom with my right hand.

I'm not even sure what happened after that. I just let instinct take over, and I quit thinking at all. The next thing I knew, I was at the top with nowhere else to go. It felt strange and wonderful, like snapping out of a trance or waking up from a dream.

As Andy lowered me to the ground, I heard him say, "Did you see the way Paul turned his toe in, dropped his knee, and put his hip into the wall? Here's what I want you to remember: height will help most of the time, but it can also hinder you sometimes, and strength will slowly run out, but technique—if you can maintain your focus—will always be there for you, indefinitely."

After I hit the ground, I untied from the rope and used my camouflaging skills to sneak away. I was almost around the corner when something made me glance back at the class. Years of being made fun of and bullied had helped me develop an instinct for sensing danger.

Right then, my "spidey senses" were tingling. The most

obvious source was Lily. Against my better judgment, I glanced at her. She wasn't hard to spot, towering head and shoulders over everyone else. She was supposed to be spotting her partner while they practiced drop-knees, but instead she was staring straight at me. Her look was cold and calculating, as if she were deciding between assorted possible tortures to determine which would hurt me the most.

She saw me looking. She folded her arms, causing the lean muscles of her shoulders to flex, and stood up straighter—as if that was even possible. I shrunk down smaller—as if that were possible.

Hunter stood next to her with his back to me. Lily elbowed him and said something in his ear that made him turn around and look my way. This was bad. What were they plotting? I made a quick exit before I found out.

# Chapter 3

I decided to fake sick. "Dad," I said, "I can't go to school today. I'm sick."

My dad looked up from his bowl of Froot Loops and squinted at me, suspicious. "You're not sick." He said it just like that. A statement of fact. Undeniable.

I decided to go for it anyway. "I think it was something I ate yesterday. I was up a few times in the night with diarrhea. I'm not feeling that bad, but I'm afraid to get too far from a toilet, you know?"

"It's only the second day of school." Another fact.

"I know. It's really terrible. I hate to miss a day already."

My dad studied me for a minute, and I tried not to squirm. I put on my most pathetic and convincing face. I knew he knew I wasn't sick. The question was if he was going to call my bluff. He put down his spoon and leaned back in his chair. Not a good sign.

"You said you had a good day at school yesterday."

"I did."

He stared at me, waiting.

"I mean, it wasn't without its hitches. You know, first day of high school and all that, but yeah, it was good."

He continued to stare.

"I mean, I ran into this girl, literally, and she hates me from like first grade. Punched me in the face, even, back when we were seven or eight. Then, yesterday, I learned her name is Lily *Small*, and I kind of laughed at that, because she's really tall, and now she hates me."

He kept looking at me, and it was like he was using psychic powers to keep me talking.

I wanted to shut up, but I couldn't help it. I had to fill the silence with something. "Then, when I went to the climbing gym after school, she was there, and I think I might have accidentally embarrassed her and this other, like, bodybuilder guy because I climbed something they couldn't, and now I think they might want to kill me so . . . yeah, I have diarrhea."

"You need to apologize."

"What?"

"You need to apologize. You shouldn't have laughed at her name or her height."

He was right. Of all people, I should have known not to make fun of someone's height. It'd never occurred to me that the rule might apply to tall people, too.

"Yes, sir," I said, and went and got ready for school.

Fairfield High was surrounded by middle-class and upper-middle-class neighborhoods that all seemed to be playing a game of who could build a house higher on the mountainside. The higher the house, the more prestigious or something like that. It's in a suburb of Ogden, Utah, and for most people, it's not a bad place to go to school.

But I *hated* school. It wasn't a place I could go to learn. It was something I had to *survive*. It was Darwinism in action. When I was in fourth grade, my dad bought me a big collection of wildlife documentaries. I watched them a million times, and it didn't take my nine-year-old brain long to figure out that, in the animal kingdom, you were either predator or prey. Then one day it occurred to me that the students at my school were exactly the same.

Just like the animals in my documentaries, the prey students had adapted to survive by moving in herds, running away, or hiding, while the predators stalked the school in packs like hyenas, laughing and cackling as they tore into their quarry. Technically, hyenas live in clans, not packs, but the point is, I was the smallest and the weakest of the prey animals in a school crawling with hungry predators. I had to be constantly on guard. It was exhausting.

I navigated the halls full of dangerous animals better on the second day of school than I did on the first. I found a few side halls with less traffic. I was only knocked to the ground once by a guy who had to be upwards of 300 pounds. He lumbered down the hall with a big, friendly smile on his face that made me think he was imagining himself on a beach, holding a drink with an umbrella. His Polynesian looks and the bright-red, flowered Hawaiian shirt supported my theory.

I followed in his wake like a dolphin behind a cruise ship. It was a technique I used sometimes: I got on the tail of the biggest guy around and coasted along in the gap he left behind him. The trick was to stay close because the gap closed fast. So I was right on this guy's heels when he must have remembered something he'd forgotten or made a wrong turn because he suddenly stopped and turned around. The next thing I knew, I bounced off his big, soft belly and fell to the floor.

"Oh, I'm sorry, little dude," the huge Polynesian said. He reached out a hand to help me up. Normally being called "little dude" would have bugged me, but he had such a friendly, spaced-out smile on his face, I knew he didn't mean anything by it. In fact, I wondered if he was high. "You okay?" he asked. He managed to both smile and look concerned at the same time.

"Yeah, I'm good. Thanks."

"Sometimes I don't know my own size, yeah?" he said and laughed. Then he lumbered away. I was pretty sure he had no idea where he was going.

That was the only issue I had until fourth period—Language Arts. The class with Lily. I figured my best strategy would be to come in just seconds before the late bell and be the first to leave when class was over. I'd apologize right before I left, and then hope she didn't decide to make my head explode with her death ray.

I kept a close eye out as I worked my way through the halls to class. I spotted Lily slamming her locker shut from practically a mile away. Now I knew where the den of at least one predator was, and I could avoid the area in the future. Bonus.

I tailed Lily from a distance and learned some valuable information. First, I confirmed that she really was quite pretty despite her ridiculous height and frightening presence. Oddly enough, the fact that she wanted me dead didn't make her less attractive. Unlike a lot of tall girls who slouched, pulled their shoulders in, or lowered their heads in an effort to look shorter and smaller, Lily stood straight and threw her shoulders back, proud and haughty. She reminded me of a warrior.

The second thing I noticed was that she was alone. I assumed she would have been surrounded by an entourage of obnoxious jocks. She was so tall, she had to be an athlete. I had no idea what sports she liked besides rock climbing, but I figured she was the star of them all. Where were all her teammates, high-fiving her? Where were all the guys vying for her attention?

Then I saw the looks people in the hall gave her. I knew that look. It was the one I got all the time. The up-and-down look. The one where they take you all in, their eyes go wide, and then they snicker and whisper to each other. I got the look because I was so short; Lily got it because she was so tall. As I watched, an acne-faced kid stopped right in the middle of the crowded hall and said, "Whoa, you're tall." Like Lily might not have noticed.

Suddenly it hit me—there were only one or two guys in the whole school as tall as Lily.

Also, Lily was black. Being one of only three or four black kids in our entire school made her stand out even more.

And, as dumb as it sounds, it seemed like a lot of the white kids looked nervous to be around her. Not because they were racist, just because they hadn't met many black people.

It turned out that Lily was a loner . . . like me. Well, not exactly like me, because she was still clearly a predator while I was most certainly prey. But she was a predator without a pack.

Instead of waiting until the late bell was about to ring, I decided to follow Lily all the way to class. I stepped around her legs without looking at her and sat in my desk. I could feel her laser-beam eyes on me again. I took a long time to organize my folder, papers, and textbook as I tried to find the courage to apologize. Finally, just as the bell rang and Mr. Teller made his way to the front of the class, I blurted out, "Sorry I laughed at your name yesterday, Lily." It came out in a mumbled jumble, probably because I had my chin against my chest and was looking at my lap.

"What?" Lily asked, sounding irritated.

"Nothing."

"You're so—" Lily started to say, but Mr. Teller cut her off, calling for the class to quiet down.

What was she going to say? You're so stupid? You're so pathetic? You're so dead? I was so preoccupied, I didn't notice Mr. Teller call my name.

Josh, the kid to my left, punched my shoulder, and I heard someone in the back say, "Hey, munchkin, wake up, he's calling your name."

"Knock it off, Mr. Dolores," Mr. Teller said. He tried again, "Paul Adams?"

"Here," I managed to say without sounding like a mouse this time.

When Mr. Teller got to Lily's name, I made certain to keep my head down and not make any noise at all.

Just as Mr. Teller finished calling roll, a bright-red, XXXL Hawaiian shirt filled the doorway. It was the enormous guy who'd knocked me over earlier. He still had that big, spaced-out smile across his face. I couldn't help but smile as well when I saw him filling the entryway. I looked around and noticed nearly every other person in the room was smiling, too. It was like we couldn't help it. Simply the sight of the guy made us feel happy for no apparent reason.

He glanced at a paper that probably listed his class schedule. Then, still with that huge smile on his face, he said, "Hello, Mr. Teller, I'm Kamakanamakamaemaikalani Pohaku, but you can just call me Big, yeah? Sorry I'm late. This is my first day, and I don't get around too fast, if you know what I mean."

Even Mr. Teller smiled. He looked back down at his tablet and said, "Let's see, Cammie transferred, so you can have her desk, Kamakana . . . or, uh, Big. It's the one right there on the front row."

Big must have noticed how uncomfortable Mr. Teller was with the nickname, because he said, "It's okay to call me Big, Mr. Teller. Everybody does. It's because of my big"—he paused, pointed to his mouth, and grinned—"smile."

Everyone laughed, including Mr. Teller.

"Okay, Big it is, then," Mr. Teller said.

The empty desk was on the front row next to Josh. Big had to go past me to get to it. As he lurched by, he looked at me. Recognition spread across his face, and his already huge smile got even bigger. He said with what sounded like genuine excitement, "Hey, little dude. We have a class together."

Everyone chuckled, but for once I didn't care. I was too shocked to have someone notice me and actually seem glad I was there. I didn't know how to respond, so I ended up not saying anything.

Big stopped at his desk and eyed it for a few seconds. His smile started to fade. "Mr. Teller, there's no way I'm going to fit in this desk." His smile came back, and he added, "Or if I did, it would take the Jaws of Life to get me out again, yeah?"

Mr. Teller stood there with his mouth open while the class laughed.

Big finally helped him out by saying, "It's no big deal, I'm used to it. Most teachers just give me a regular chair to sit in. Just make sure it's a sturdy one."

Mr. Teller chuckled, shook his head, and went and found Big a sturdy chair.

I couldn't believe it. I loved this guy. Big was huge, and he just owned it. His bright Hawaiian shirt, his jokes, his contagious smile. He seemed totally comfortable with himself. I wished I could be more like him.

Class went fine until the very end of the period. I was starting to plot my strategy for escaping the room unscathed when Mr. Teller told us we would be reading *Of Mice and Men*. That was fine with me. I'd seen the movie not long ago, so I figured I could breeze along this term and focus on more important things like rock climbing and survival. But then Mr. Teller said he was assigning us a partner and we'd present certain "information essential to an in-depth understanding of the text" in front of the class.

I hated getting up in front of the class. I hated it so much that if someone said, "Hey, Paul, you can either cut off your own pinky finger with a pair of rusty pruning shears or present in front of the class. Which do you prefer?" I would have gone with the pinky removal. Mr. Teller might as well tie me to a post and hang a big T-bone steak around my neck as bait for all the hyenas.

Mr. Teller started pairing up students and assigning them topics. I was terrified I'd end up with Lily or the Dolores guy, who kept making comments about me from the back of the class.

I heard Dolores get paired up with someone else, so that was one down. Now I just needed to dodge Lily. Then I realized Mr. Teller was assigning partners based on who was sitting next to each other. I let out a whimper, and a few people in my immediate area turned and looked at me funny. There was still hope, though. I might be paired with Josh Richmond, and then Lily would be paired with the person on the other side of her.

"Sandra Peterson and Josh Richmond," Mr. Teller said, "you will be presenting on the Great Depression."

No. This couldn't be happening.

"Paul Adams and Lily Small," he went on, "you will be presenting on mental illness in the early 1900s."

I felt an anxiety attack coming on. I thought I was going to hyperventilate. I was captured. A helpless rabbit trapped in the claws of a Bengal tiger. I put my head down on the desk and closed my eyes, willing myself to disappear.

"Looks like you're with me, twerp," Lily whispered, sounding amused.

I was too afraid to look at her.

Then Big said, "Mr. Teller, what about me?"

"Oh, that's right," Mr. Teller said. "We have an odd number of students, so I guess you can be in whatever group you want. Do you have a preference?"

I thought fast and called out, "He can, uh, be in our group, Mr. Teller." My hope was that Big could protect me from Lily. Or, at the very least, stop her before she did any permanent physical or emotional damage.

"That's kind of you, Paul. Does that sound okay to you, Big?" Mr. Teller asked.

"Oh, yeah. Paul, Big, and Small," Big said. "We're going to rock this presentation."

# Chapter 4

Once again, I skated home as quickly as possible after school got out. I ditched my books and board, grabbed my climbing stuff, and hopped the bus to Ogden. The climbing class only met on Monday, Wednesday, and Friday, which meant I didn't have to worry about Lily being there, thank goodness. I already had enough stress with my botched apology, being partnered with Lily, and having to give a presentation in front of the class in a few days. I needed to climb more than ever just to blow off some steam.

When I got to OCC, I headed for the bouldering area as usual. On my way, I saw Andy dangling from a rope, bolting holds onto what everyone called "the prow"—the biggest wall in the whole gym. It was in the center of the roped climbing area where the peaked roof of the building was at its highest. It was about eighty feet tall and overhanging all the way up, growing steeper the higher it went. The prow was the focal point of the gym.

It was also for "real climbers," because there were no topropes. Instead, you had to lead climb it. With a toprope, the rope ran from the ground, up to the top of the climb, and back down to you, so if you fell, you wouldn't go anywhere. You'd just sort of sit on the rope and dangle. Not very scary.

Lead climbing, on the other hand, meant that you started with the rope on the ground. It hung below you as you climbed, and you clipped it into quickdraws as you went up. The higher you climbed above your last quickdraw, the bigger the fall you took before it caught you. Lead climbing was scary.

"What are you doing, Andy?" I asked.

Andy finished bolting a big hold to the wall and turned to look down at me. "Hey, Paul. I had this idea last night. Tell me what you think. I want to set a route that gets progressively harder as it gets closer to the top. Each of the holds will be numbered. Climbers will get as far as they can, and then post their name and the number of the hold they reached on the website and on a board up front where everyone can see it. It'll be an ongoing competition throughout the fall to keep everyone motivated. Maybe I can even get the owners to cough up a prize for whoever makes it to the top first. How does that sound?"

I liked that Andy wanted my opinion. Nobody else cared about what I thought about anything. Except my dad, of course. But he was my dad, so he didn't count.

"Sounds good, I guess," I said. I would have liked the idea a lot more but I didn't want to post my name on the internet for the whole world to see. I didn't want to be the loser at the bottom of the list. Plus, lead climbing was out of the question for a wimp like me.

Andy must have read my mind because he said, "You don't have to post your name, of course. You can just try it without anyone having to know."

"In that case, I like it a lot."

"You might be surprised to see where you stack up. You're getting pretty good, you know."

I'm not going to lie, it felt good to hear that. Made me feel all warm and fuzzy, but I knew I was nowhere near as good as some of the other regulars.

"Speaking of which," he went on, "great job in the climbing class yesterday. I knew you'd do fine, and that's why I picked on you, but I didn't expect you to make it all the way to the top. That was pretty amazing."

"Oh, uh, thanks, I guess." I started to walk away. "Well, good luck with your route."

"Hey, wait," Andy said. "One more thing. The annual high school coed climbing competition is coming up. You should get a team together and enter. There are some flyers up at the front desk."

"Oh, um, okay." Yeah, right.

# Chapter 5

he hyenas of Fairfield High School had some lovely traditions. One was to start every new school year by forcing the sophomores to "push pennies" down the hall. Not all the sophomores, of course, just the weak and pathetic ones like myself. Pushing pennies might not sound that bad, but they make you push them with your nose.

The hyenas' favorite method for this torture was to corner a pair of weaklings and make them race. Whoever won was allowed to leave with whatever dignity they had left, and the hyenas would grab another defenseless kid to race. The loser had to keep racing until he finally managed to win or an adult showed up, whichever came first.

Which was how, first thing in the morning on the third day of my high school career, I found myself with my nose to the ground, a dirty copper Abe Lincoln only inches from my eyes, waiting for the race to begin. The alpha male running the show was none other than Hunter from the climbing class.

Hunter had tossed a penny onto the ground for one of his victims to push, but it rolled into the middle of the hallway, where a passing student accidentally kicked it, and, out of pure bad luck, it stopped right at my feet where I was hiding behind a vending machine. When one of Hunter's clan came sniffing around for it, he found me.

He laughed and said, "Why are you hiding? Come out and play with us." Then he dragged me by the back of my collar to join the fun.

"Hey, Hunter," he called. "I found Frodo here hiding behind the candy machine. I think he wants to compete."

"Oh, good, I was hoping to . . ." Hunter's high-pitched voice trailed off when he saw me. I don't know why he hesitated, but he looked from me to some of the other hyenas gathered around before finishing, "To make this a race. It's boring with just one sophomore."

Hunter took me from the other guy, and, before he shoved me to the ground, he leaned down so close to my face I smelled bacon on his breath. He whispered, "Sorry about this. No hard feelings, I hope." He gave me a gap-toothed smile and chuckled like we were buddies sharing a joke before placing a penny on the floor in front of me.

Two races later, Hunter and the other hyenas tried to get some of the spectators gathered around to place bets on who would win, but no one would bet on me. I couldn't blame them.

I looked over at my newest opponent. He wasn't the typical victim. Usually, the hyenas cut the small and sickly ones out of the herd to devour. This guy looked pretty average in stature, had tightly curled hair, was well-dressed, and would probably have been a good-looking guy if not for the snot dripping out of his nose and the tears on his face. I felt bad for him. Unlike me, he didn't seem to have much experience handling humiliation.

"Think you're pretty tough, don't you, Conor?" Hunter said, clearly enjoying his role as ringmaster of the show. "Strutting around like you're better than us. Well, I got news for you, rich boy, you're not in junior high anymore. You're a pitiful little sophomore around here. Bottom of the food chain. That rich daddy of yours isn't going to come help you push this penny, so quit crying and get ready to go. I have money riding on you." That wasn't true, of course, because Hunter couldn't get anyone to bet on me.

Conor's only reply was to try to suck some of the snot back up his nose. Man, some people have no idea how to endure disgrace properly. You never let them see you cry. Never.

I felt so bad for Conor, I thought about letting him win. Then he turned and looked at me, and the hatred in his eyes was intense. I'd seen some vicious expressions in my day, but Conor's was the most bloodthirsty of all. He looked like he wanted to tear my fingernails out with his teeth.

I was shocked. What was that about? We were both victims, weren't we? Both prey for the hyenas? Why did Conor have the look of a predator? Then it hit me—he hated me because he was being forced down to my level. He hated me because I was powerless and weak, and he was right there on his knees next to me. He couldn't take his anger out on Hunter and the other hyenas, so he was going to take it out on the next person down in the pecking order: me. Maybe he wasn't an apex predator, but he was still dangerous, like a jackal or something.

"What are you looking at?" Conor spat through his tears, his face red and contorted. With him on his hands and knees, he looked like an angry, frothing dog.

I quickly looked back at my penny and got ready.

"That's the spirit," Hunter said.

"Jeez," I heard a spectator say. "Conor's a psycho."

Hunter raised an arm above his head as if he were holding an imaginary starting flag and said, "Whoever kisses my shoe first, wins. On your mark, get set, go!"

I took an early lead. I guess having already practiced a few times helped, but I wasn't sure I wanted to win. Conor was already enraged, and I figured beating him would make it worse. Certainly losing another race was preferable to earning Conor's vengeance for a lifetime. Then I heard the hyenas' mock cheering, "Come on, Dolores. You're losing to *this* kid?"

Dolores? Like the Dolores from my Language Arts class? I looked over at him and replayed his words in my mind: *What are you looking at?* Even through his crying and choking, I managed to finally recognize his voice. Yep, he was the same Dolores. Conor Dolores. I'd never looked to the back of the classroom to see who'd been making all the mean comments.

Suddenly, I ignored all the survival instincts I'd been honing for years and started pushing my penny like crazy. Conor pushed his penny with quick, short nudges, the way a dog noses at a Frisbee. While that technique saved you from losing too much skin off your nose, it was not very fast.

I, having already done this a few times, knew it was faster to pin the penny firmly between my nose and the tile floor and crawl. Using this method, I could go a foot or two before the penny would slip, and I'd have to stop and re-pin it. The sacrifice for my increased speed, however, was scraping away the skin from the tip of my nose.

I pulled ahead of Conor and reached Hunter's shoe with time to spare. I was just about to kiss it when he stepped back. I pushed my penny forward again, only to have him move again right as I puckered up. The whole clan laughed. I kept pushing the penny, feeling the skin of my nose burn more and more from the abrasion. I was definitely going to have a scab.

Hunter stepped away twice more before he'd backed himself into a wall.

I pushed my penny up to his foot and kissed his stinky shoe.

Hunter helped me to my feet and raised my arm in the air like I'd won a boxing match. "Ladies and gentlemen, the new penny-pushing champion of the world!" All the hyenas cheered.

I yanked my hand down and started making my way through all the bodies without looking back. I heard Hunter say, "Whoa, there, Conor. Where do you think you're going? You lost, my friend. You're staying right here. Now, wipe that snot off your cute little button nose and get ready for the next race."

Just as I turned the corner, I heard Conor yell, "You're dead, Adams!"

A few hours later, I headed to Language Arts, my spidey senses on high alert. I'd managed to avoid any hungry predators, but when I was about twenty yards away from class, I ducked into a side hall that led to a janitorial closet and pretended to text someone. But, seriously, who did I have to text?

What I was really doing was watching the time and waiting for the last possible second to go in. Lily was already in the room, but I hadn't seen Conor anywhere. As the halls emptied, I grew more nervous. I didn't want to get caught alone. On the other hand, I didn't want to give Lily any time before class to terrorize me.

I was about to head in when I saw a bright-yellow, XXXL

Hawaiian shirt lumbering down the hall. I didn't have any reason to be afraid of Big, but, just to be safe, I backed into the shadows and waited for him to pass. It was easy to track his slow progress by the sound of his flip-flops slapping against his heels. I was as still as a statue when he came into view.

Big had almost passed me when he stopped. I wondered if he had some weird spidey senses of his own because he cocked his head to the side like he was listening, and then turned and looked straight at me.

"Hey, little dude," he said with a broad smile spreading across his face. "How's it going?"

It was so unexpected, I didn't know how to respond.

When I didn't say anything, Big's smile slipped, and he asked, "Are you okay? What happened to your nose?"

"Nothing," I said, covering it with my hand. "My nose is fine. I'm fine."

Big nudged his way into the hallway as if he could actually hide his huge body in there with me. "Okay, but why are we hiding in this hallway?"

"I'm not . . . I'm not *hiding*." My face burned with embarrassment. "I was just, um, texting someone." I slid past him and poked my head out into the hall. I didn't see any sign of Conor.

"Okay, we're not hiding. Who are we avoiding, then?" He, too, poked his head out into the hall and looked around. It was seriously the most un-camouflaged thing I'd ever seen. The guy didn't have any survival skills. The whole situation was hopeless.

"You ready to go to class or what?" I asked as the late bell rang.

I darted down the hall and into Mr. Teller's room. I hoped I could sneak into my seat without being noticed, but Mr. Teller was already at the front of the class.

"You're late, Mr. Adams."

I thought it was one of those statements teachers make where they don't really expect a reply, so I continued to my seat, careful not to trip over Lily's long legs or make eye contact with her.

"Well? What do you have to say for yourself?" Mr. Teller said. "We've only had three days of school, and you've been late for two of them."

Apparently, I'd been wrong. I tried to speak, but nothing came out.

"Sorry, Mr. Teller," Big said from the doorway. His yellow shirt made it look like the sun was rising right there in our classroom, but it was his smile that filled the room with light. "Little dude was with me, yeah? I made him late. He was nice enough to walk with me to class."

It was the craziest thing. One second, Mr. Teller was looking down at me over the top of his glasses with his brow furrowed in irritation, the next second, he was smiling at Big and saying, "In that case, I guess it's all right. Go ahead and take your seat, Big. It's nice to see you."

Big lumbered over to his chair, nodding at me as he passed. Then it hit me: Big had his own set of survival skills. He was tricky. He couldn't do camouflage, but he had charm, and he could dazzle any predator with his sense of humor and a smile. That was power.

While Mr. Teller finished calling roll and made a few announcements, I overheard two girls whispering behind me.

The first one said, "Did you hear about Conor Dolores?"

The second said, "No, what?"

"Some seniors made him push pennies, and he bawled like a baby the whole time."

"You're kidding."

"No, he went all crazy and ended up calling his dad to take him home."

"No way."

"Yeah, he kind of deserves it, though, don't you think?"

"Yeah, he does. He's a creep. I heard he . . ." The girls lowered their voices even more. Apparently, whatever Conor had done was bad enough to warrant an extra-low whisper. I shuddered.

Later, it was time for us to get in our groups and prepare for our class presentations. Lily and I dragged our desks over to Big's chair next to the window. I kept my head down and waited, which was my usual technique for working in groups. Don't talk, don't show any initiative, and someone else will take charge and do everything for you.

So why wasn't anyone talking? Finally, I glanced up at Big. He stared out the window with a distant smile on his face like he was daydreaming about a tropical vacation.

I didn't dare look at Lily. I felt something boiling in her, sensed pressure building. I pretended to read the list of requirements Mr. Teller had given us for our presentation. Still nothing. I shuffled my papers. Nothing. After what seemed like a very, very long minute, I couldn't take it anymore and cleared my throat.

Big said, "It sure is a beautiful day out there, yeah?" He was still looking out the window. "I wish I was out there right now, feeling the sun on my face." He turned to me. "Don't you?"

His smile was too much for me, and I started to laugh.

Lily, though, snapped. "Are you kidding me? How did I end up in a group with you two? We are going to fail this assignment and look like total idiots." She let out a huff, folded her arms, and stared at the back wall of the room.

Man, her arms were strong. Not like bulging-muscles strong,

but like defined, toned, feminine strong. It wasn't hard to imagine her breaking my neck with those arms.

"Lily," Big said, "you have beautiful eyes. They make me think of chocolate cake."

I'm not kidding. That's what he said. And Lily did have beautiful eyes. I couldn't help but look at them after Big said that, even though it went against my survival instincts.

But then Lily narrowed her eyes and glared at Big. I looked at my lap and prepared for the coming explosion. I imagined it would be like some kind of sci-fi battle where Lily's eyes shot a red death ray at Big, and Big's smile shot out a shining yellow happiness ray at Lily, and they'd meet in the middle with an orange explosion, and it'd become a force of will to see whose power would win.

"I was just making an observation," Big said.

I could hear the smile in his voice without looking up. The yellow happiness ray was winning. It was like slipping into a warm bathtub. It was like playful, fuzzy puppies. It was like getting laughing gas at the dentist. It was irresistible. Lily's death ray never stood a chance.

"I like beautiful things," Big continued. "Look outside. See the sunlight making a rainbow in that sprinkler?"

I couldn't help it; I looked.

"Or the abandoned bird's nest in that tree right there?"

He pointed, and this time we both looked.

"Or the chrome wheels on that Camaro. Mm-mm. Beautiful things, yeah?"

When Lily laughed, it sounded surprised and delighted. Definitely not like a hyena.

We worked through the remainder of class, but we were far from being ready to present. Just as the bell rang, Lily said, "Look, we're not even close to being ready for the presentation tomorrow. Come to my house tonight, and we can finish up. I'll text you my address. What are your numbers?"

Big gave her his number, but I froze, remembering this was the same towering Lily who wanted me dead. I couldn't give a predator like her my cell number. That would be like saying, "Why, yes, I'd love to be bullied by you both in person and over the phone." Plus, there was no way I was going into Lily's lair. I mean, would a defenseless little rabbit go hopping into a tiger's den? I don't think so.

Lily turned to me, and I tried to come up with some kind of excuse, but in my panic, my mind went blank. All that came out was "I, um, I'm not really, uh, supposed to give my number out."

Lily had played nice ever since Big had overpowered her death ray, but now her eyes narrowed again. Her voice turned cold. "Were you dropped on your head? I just want to get this stupid project finished. I'm not asking you out on a date. You got that, Rudolph?"

I raised my hand to cover my sore nose. Unlike Big, I did not have a yellow happiness ray. I was unarmed and helpless with nowhere to hide.

Big tore out a piece of notebook paper and said, "Why don't you write down your address, and Paul will be sure to be there. What time?"

Lily scowled down at me for a full five seconds of silence. I swear even her mole scowled at me as if it remembered how I'd accused it of being cancerous so many years ago. At last, she looked at Big and her expression softened. How did he do that? She wrote down her address and phone number, and told us to be there at seven o'clock. Then, with one last evil glare shot in my direction, she left.

# Chapter 6

After that, I really needed a climbing fix. I went to OCC after school, even though I knew Lily and Hunter would probably be there for the climbing class. I needed to climb, even if it meant risking my life.

I'd only made it a few steps past the front door before I saw a dry-erase board on an easel. In bold, black capital letters along the top it said: "BILDUNGSROMAN." I frowned, wondering what the word meant.

Below that was written:

> *Think you're a real man or woman? Test your climbing skills! Attempt the Bildungsroman route on the prow and see if you measure up. The first to reach the top and ring the bell wins a $100 gift certificate to OCC. Good luck!*

Below that were two columns of numbers from one to fifty. There were already three names written in next to eleven, twelve, and twenty-three. It was only the first day, and someone was almost halfway to the top. Wow.

I headed over to the prow to see Andy's route. I'm not sure what I was expecting, some kind of shaft of light shining down on it from heaven and angels singing, but it looked like how the prow always looked: big, tall, and intimidating. The only difference was a small sign taped to the wall at the bottom that said "Bildungsroman." I also noticed there were fewer holds on the prow, and the ones that were there were numbered from "1" at the bottom to "50" at the very top. Also, a brass bell hung at the top, just like the one on the portable wall at the county fair. The one I hadn't managed to ring two years ago. Overall, Bildungsroman looked like something I should avoid.

Andy walked by, carrying an armload of harnesses for the climbing class. I acted like I was studying the route and figuring out the moves, but then he stopped next to me. His eyes went wide, and he asked, "What happened to your nose?"

I covered it with one hand and said, "Oh, uh, nothing. I just tripped."

He bit his lower lip and studied me like he knew I was lying. I tried to send him a telepathic message to just leave it alone, which must have worked because he said, "Well? What do you think?"

"About my nose?"

"No," Andy laughed. "About Bildungsroman."

"It looks pretty good, I guess."

"'Pretty good'? Are you kidding me? You're standing in front of my masterpiece. It's the indoor-climbing equivalent of Michelangelo's *David*."

"It looks more like a Goliath to me."

Andy laughed. "Well, it's one seriously good-looking Goliath, then."

"It's just that, you know, I haven't been able to try it yet," I said. Of course, I was *never* going to try it because that would mean lead climbing, but Andy didn't have to know that. "I'll go warm up on the bouldering wall and maybe give it a shot later."

Andy looked up at Bildungsroman, then at me, then at Bildungsroman, and then me again. I started to get nervous.

"Alright," he said. "I'll meet you here after my class is over and give you a belay."

"What?" There was no way I could lead that route. I'd never led anything in my life. It meant falling, like, for real. Not just sitting in your harness and hanging like if you fall on a toprope.

"You heard me," Andy said with a smile that told me he knew exactly what I was thinking. "I'll be done in thirty minutes."

"Andy, I, uh, I really don't think, uh . . ." An entire army of insecurities in my head screamed that I had no business climbing that route, and then I heard my mouth say, "Okay, thanks."

Andy nodded and continued to his climbing class.

I spent the next half hour bouldering in the most remote corner of the gym. It was a boring, low-angle area designed for little kids, but it was the only place guaranteed to be safe from Lily and Hunter. I entertained myself by trying to climb the wall using only holds shaped like dinosaurs until I saw Lily, Hunter, and the blonde girl who was always with him leave the gym. Then I grabbed my stuff and went to find Andy.

He was waiting for me at the bottom of the prow. "There you are. You ready to give Bildungsroman a try?"

I looked up at it and resisted the urge to run away. "I guess," I said as I put on my harness. "What's with the weird name, anyway?"

"Bildungsroman?" Andy asked. "It's a German word for a coming-of-age story. You know, like in a book when the main character starts out a kid and goes through all this hard stuff that helps them grow up. Like *Huck Finn* or *David Copperfield*."

I nodded like I knew what he was talking about even though I didn't. I tied into the rope and looked up at the prow again. I swallowed hard; I was standing below the hardest route on the hardest wall in the gym to try my first lead ever. The whole situation was insane. "On belay?" I asked.

"Belay is on," Andy replied. "You're going to love this."

"Climbing," I said, though it came out in a whisper.

"Climb on," Andy said.

I started up the route. My mind went to that quiet place where only the next hold and the next breath existed. I dropped my knee and managed to reach hold number two. I cranked hard on it and hiked my feet up high enough to match my right foot with my right hand. It was a fun move. The next hold was a long way off, but I thought I could lunge for it.

I dipped my right hand in my chalk bag, shook it out, and then eyed the next hold like a sniper sighting a target through his scope. I lunged and somehow hit it, but my right foot popped, and I found myself hanging off my hands with no feet at all for a moment. I swung my right foot back onto its hold and assessed my next move.

Once again, the next handhold was way out of reach. There would be no lunging this time. Instead, I stretched my left arm out as far as it would go and inched my way to a big, yellow sidepull that looked like an ear. I caught the edge of it with the tips of two fingers, regained my balance, pulled a little, and then hopped my fingers the rest of the way onto the hold. I couldn't believe I was still on the wall.

The ear was big enough for me to match my hands on it and

look for the next hold, which was a big, black bucket. I loved buckets; I could hold on to them all day if I wanted. That would have been fantastic, except this bucket might as well have been a mile away. I felt my whole body sag as I registered the distance.

I heard Andy saying something, but I ignored him. There had to be a way. Some hidden foothold, some strange way to position my body, something, anything.

Andy raised his voice, but I blocked him out. Didn't he know I needed to focus, not have him shouting at me? The yellow ear was a good hold, but with every tick of the clock, energy melted from my fingers. I only had about thirty seconds to figure this out before I'd likely fall. I looked and looked, but the wall between the bucket and me was blank. I squirmed into a couple of different positions, turning my foot this way and that, pasting it to the blank wall in hopes of getting some kind of epiphany. Nothing.

My hands were sweating, and it was getting more difficult to hang on. I wanted to dip for chalk, but I doubted I could hang on with one hand long enough to do it. Shoot. There was only one thing to do. Jump for it.

I squatted, readjusted my grip on the yellow ear, stared hard at that black bucket, and then launched. Both hands and both feet came off the wall. For a very short moment, I was flying like Superman. The black bucket got closer and closer as if in slow motion. Then, I was falling. Fast.

I ended up sideways in the air. I squirmed around, trying to get my feet under me, but it was no use. Just as I was about to crash into the ground, Andy pushed hard against my back, forcing me upright, and helping me to land on my feet while also slowing my fall. We both ended up sprawled on the ground.

I did a quick mental checklist of my body, waiting to feel an explosion of pain from somewhere. Nothing. I wasn't hurt at all. Andy was next to me shaking his head, and I realized I was in one piece only thanks to his expert spotting.

"Thanks," I said.

"You okay?"

"Yeah. You?"

"I'm fine," Andy said as he got to his feet. He frowned down at me and folded his arms. "Look, I know you were probably trying to conserve energy, but I don't want you skipping clips. That was bold, but stupid. You'll end up getting hurt."

I wasn't sure what he was talking about, but I wasn't about to admit it. "Sorry, Andy," I said.

He looked at me as if he were deciding if I was sorry enough. He must have thought so because his frown went away, and he said, "That took some guts to dyno off that lieback. Full-on four points off, jumping like a jackrabbit. It's pretty impressive how you can just get into the flow and go for it."

I didn't know what to say, so I just sat there.

"Next time, though, make the first clip from the yellow lieback—hold number four—*before* you dyno. I get it, clipping saps your strength and the next quickdraw is only a few feet above, but seriously, you're going to break your neck if you don't. Especially when jumping for a hold like that." He reached out his hand and helped me up. "I have to get back to work. I'll give you another belay tomorrow. See ya, Rabbit." Andy chuckled, shook his head, and then walked away.

I stood there, dumbfounded. Clip? I knew that meant clipping the rope through the quickdraw, so I wouldn't fall all the way to the ground, but what did he mean by skipping it? I studied the route. There was a quickdraw hanging right next to hold four.

I had forgotten to make the first clip. What an idiot. I was so focused on the next move, I'd climbed right past the first quick-draw.

Even more shocking than forgetting to clip was the fact that Andy was willing to belay me on Bildungsroman the next day. I was both excited and terrified.

# Chapter 7

When I got home, my dad was in the kitchen cooking dinner: mac and cheese with sliced hot dogs. I know it sounds gross, but it's surprisingly good.

"How was school?" he asked without looking up.

"Good, I guess."

He turned from the pot of boiling hot dogs to grab some bowls and froze when he saw my face. "What happened to your nose?" he asked in his usual Zen voice.

I covered it with my hand. "Oh, I crashed on my skateboard on the way home. No big deal."

He eyed me for a few seconds, then he asked, "What really happened?"

I hated that my dad could see right through me like he had some kind of fatherly psychic powers. Since there was no point in lying, I told him the truth . . . mostly. I explained that the sophomores had a tradition of pushing pennies, and I'd gotten a little overzealous and hurt my nose. I didn't say it outright, but I might have implied it was a school-sanctioned thing, and I'd volunteered.

"Are you okay?" he asked.

"Yeah, it doesn't even hurt that bad," I said. That was a lie. It totally hurt. "It just makes me go a little cross-eyed." That was true. The stupid scab on the end of my nose kept drawing my eyes together.

The thing was, I knew he wasn't asking if I was physically okay. He was asking if I was okay in a much broader way. Like, mentally and emotionally. He knew I was being bullied again and was asking if I needed help. I looked him in the eye. "Really, Dad, I'm okay," I said.

He held my gaze for another second, nodded, and turned back to the stove. As he speared the hot dogs with a fork, he asked, "Did you apologize?"

"For pushing pennies?"

"No, did you apologize to Lily Small?"

"Not exactly," I said. "I tried, but it didn't come out very clear, and then we got interrupted, and, well, I think I might have made things even worse."

"How's that?"

"Lily and me got put in a group together in Language Arts class with this other guy, Big."

"It's 'Lily and I'," my dad corrected. "The other guy's name is Big?"

"Yeah, he has some long name—I think it's Hawaiian—but he goes by Big. Anyway, we have to do this presentation tomorrow—"

"Wait, how tall did you say Lily was?"

"I don't know, but she's way over six feet. The top of my head only reaches her armpit."

"So let me get this straight. You're in a group with an unusually tall girl and a guy who goes by the nickname Big?"

"Yep, and he's *really* big, too." I held my arms out as wide as they'd go to show just how big. My dad started laughing. "It's not funny. We're going to look like a circus sideshow up there tomorrow."

My dad struggled to stop and then said, "All right, all right. I'm sorry. Now what happened to make things worse?"

"Lily invited us to her house tonight to prepare for the presentation and asked for my number. I kind of freaked out about giving it to her because, you know, cyberbullying and all that. I think I offended her."

"What time?" my dad asked as he chopped the hot dogs into pieces.

"What time what?"

"What time are you supposed to be there?"

"At Lily's? Seven, but I don't know if I should go. It might not be safe."

My dad frowned at me. "After dinner, cook up some brownies. There's a mix in the cupboard." He dumped the chunks of hot dog into a bowl of mac and cheese and stirred it together. It smelled awesome. "Take the brownies with you as a peace offering. It's hard to stay mad at someone who brings brownies. Go early and, before Big gets there, apologize and clear this mess up." He plopped the steaming bowl in front of me. "Who knows? If Lily is a climber, maybe you two could be friends." Then he added with a wink, "Maybe even *more* than friends."

I rolled my eyes.

I showed up to Lily's house fifteen minutes early holding a plastic container of store-bought brownies since I'd burnt the box mix. Her house was not on the mountainside like I thought it would be. Instead, it was down on the valley floor where there was still some farmland struggling to survive among the housing developments. Her house was made of old red bricks and must have been over a hundred years old. It sat smack-dab in the middle of a hayfield with a couple of huge cottonwood trees shading the yard and a big barn behind it. It had a gravel driveway with three—yes, *three*—pickup trucks and a huge SUV parked in front of it.

There was a big, wraparound porch with a rocking chair and a swing. I half-expected to see some old-timer in overalls sitting there, chewing on a piece of straw and cleaning a shotgun. Instead, toys covered the porch. Inside, I heard a chaotic combination of laughter, deep voices, high voices, heavy footsteps, running footsteps, and kids yelling. It was like the house was a living thing ready to burst open.

I knocked on the screen door, but nobody seemed to hear it. I tried again, harder this time, but still nothing. Inside I heard Lily's voice yell, "Mom, will you get them out of here? I have friends coming over, and they're being annoying." Friends? Was someone else coming, too?

I was just getting my courage up to knock a third time when the front door opened, and I had to jump out of the way. Two white kids, a boy and a girl, both about five or six years old, darted out.

The girl turned around and yelled back into the house, "Fine. But the next time *my* friends come over, *Lily* has to play outside." She turned to follow the other kid off the porch, but then she saw me. Without a word to me, she leaned back through the door and yelled loud enough to hurt my ears, "Lily! Your friend is here!"

The girl strolled over to the edge of the porch and stared at me. I wasn't sure what I was supposed to do. Go in? Make conversation with a six-year-old? Run for my life?

Then she said, nearly all in one breath, "What happened to your nose? Are those brownies? Can I have one?"

Before I could answer, Lily came out and said, "Get out of here, pip-squeak, before I tell Mom you're bugging my friend."

Wait, I was a friend? I looked behind me. Nobody was there. I decided Lily must have used the term as a figure of speech.

The little girl said, "I'm telling Mom you called me pip-squeak."

"Go ahead, *pip-squeak*." Lily stuck out her tongue.

The girl shot Lily a scowl that would have transformed any normal person to stone.

Lily ignored her and turned to me. "Where's Big?"

"I, um, I'm not sure. He should, uh, be here soon, though." I had this sudden fear he might not show up, and I would be trapped alone with Lily.

"You coming in or what?" Lily asked.

I hadn't realized she was holding the door open for me. "Uh, yeah, yeah. Thanks."

Before I could take a step, the little girl started singing, "Lily and . . ." Her song faltered as she realized she didn't know my name, but she quickly recovered. "This boy sitting in a tree. K-I-S-S-I-N-G."

Lily made a grab for her, but the girl leaped down the stairs of the porch and ran across the lawn, continuing the song at the top of her lungs. "First comes love. Then comes marriage. Then comes the baby in the baby carriage!"

"She's such a brat," Lily said, but she said it like she was a little bit proud. "Come on in."

As I walked through the door, Lily pointed at the brownies and said, "What's that?"

"They're sort of, um, brownies. I brought them because I, uh, I wanted to, you know, um . . ." Why? Why couldn't I just talk like a normal human being?

"*Eat* them?" Lily asked, raising her eyebrows.

I chuckled nervously. "Well, yeah, but also I, uh . . ." I took a deep breath. I'd practiced my apology in my head all evening long, so I had it pretty well memorized. I just couldn't get it out.

"Well, hey there," came a deep, booming voice from the hallway.

I looked up to see a giant white man in the doorway and, get this, he really was in overalls. Everything about him was round and huge, including his bald head. He actually had to duck as he came in the room. He walked over to me, and the floor creaked beneath his weight.

He held out his hand, and I shook it. My little hand was lost in a giant knot of muscle and calluses. It was like shaking hands with a grizzly bear.

"You must be Paul," he said with a bit of a country drawl. "I'm Terry Small, Lily's dad. It's good to meet you."

What? Lily's *dad*? He was tall enough, sure, but he was, well, awfully *white*.

He turned to Lily. "When you're done studying, be sure to get the feeding done."

"I know, Dad."

"And don't forget to finish loading the trailer. I have to deliver that hay to Reid first thing in the morning."

"I know, Dad."

"Thanks, hun." Mr. Small gave a little wave with his big bear paw and left through the front door. I could hear the porch stairs groaning beneath his booted feet.

"He's white," I said without thinking.

Lily squinted down at me. "I'm adopted, Sherlock. My whole family is white."

"Oh," I said, feeling my face heat up. "Sorry." Then I realized that might be the wrong thing to say, so I added, "I mean, um, I'm sorry if I was, um, insensitive or something." I risked a glance up at Lily, who was squinting down at me with an unreadable expression. "Not, you know, sorry you were adopted because I, um . . ."

Lily made a huffing sound, and I glanced up again to see her shaking her head. She seemed more amused than angry.

"I'm going to shut up now," I mumbled.

"That's probably a good idea," Lily said. "Come on. We'll study in here."

I followed her into a room just to the right of the front door. It was like walking into a museum display of the 1920s. Everything looked antique. There was a piano in the corner, a fireplace, and a big window overlooking the porch and front yard.

Lily said, "It's the only clean place in the house because my mom won't let anyone in here except when we have company. Don't let her see the brownies, or she'll kill us both."

"Oh, uh, what should I do with them?" I suddenly felt like I was in possession of contraband.

"We'll just set them here beside the coffee table where we

have easy access, and she can't see them. I assume I get to eat them, too?"

"Of course," I blurted. "I brought them for everyone, but especially for you because I, uh . . ." I happened to glance up at Lily's face to gauge her expression and was distracted to see her eyes soften. Just for a split second, she didn't look at me like I was a bug she'd like to squash.

The expression, as short-lived as it was, looked strange on Lily. I wasn't sure what it meant. I lost track of what I was saying and trailed off. Plus, I remembered how Big had pointed out what a beautiful shade of chocolate-cake brown her eyes were. The whole thing was very distracting.

*"Because?"* Lily prompted.

There was a commotion in the hallway, some laughing, and then a whisper. Lily looked at the doorway, and her scowl returned.

"Well," I started again, "because I, uh, wanted to tell you that I was sorry for, um . . ."

"Just a second." She held up a long index finger to stop me.

I looked over at the door and saw the little girl from earlier peeking around the corner. We made eye contact, and she burst into a giggling fit.

"Mom," Lily yelled. "Carol and Jason are bugging us." She jumped up, and I heard more giggling and two sets of little feet go running down the hall. Lily leaned into the hall and said, "Can you make them stay away?"

I heard Lily's mom call back, "What do you want me to do? Hog-tie them?"

"Just make them stay outside or something."

Quieter, but sounding exasperated, Mrs. Small said, "Junior, will you please take the little ones with you to go irrigate?"

There was a dramatic groan, the scrape of a chair across the floor, and then a deep-voiced "Fine." This was followed by loud, stomping footsteps and the same deep voice saying, "Fee-fi-fo-fum, I smell the blood of an Englishman." There was a commotion and feet running and crazy laughter like the kids were being tickled. Finally, there was the slam of a door and then silence.

Lily came back and sat down with a satisfied smile. "You better watch out for Carol," she said.

"What? Why?"

"Didn't you see the way she was looking at you?"

Seriously? Had I made an enemy of Lily's little sister, too? "No, um, not really. What did I do?"

"You didn't do anything." Lily laughed. "She was looking at you all dreamy eyed. I think she has a crush on you."

I let out an involuntary snort somewhere between a laugh and a choke.

Lily went on. "Don't worry. She has a crush on every little boy who comes over here."

A burst of anger ignited in my stomach. Little boy? Apparently, in Lily's mind, I was on the same level as the six-year-old kids who came over to play with her little sister. One thing was for sure, I was *not* going to apologize anymore.

Lily must have noticed my silence because her eyes went wide and she said, "Oh, I didn't mean . . . I wasn't trying to say you're a little boy. I meant the other kids around here."

"Whatever," I mumbled. "Let's just get to work." I started pulling papers out of my backpack and spreading them out on the coffee table.

I felt Lily glaring at me for a few seconds before she said,

"Wait, let me get this straight. You're going to get mad at me for *that*, after you laughed at my—"

There was a knock at the door. We both looked up to see Big's smiling face peer through the glass. Somehow, that was all it took for the tension to clear from the room.

Even though I never said I was sorry, the rest of the evening went much better. Big kept us cheerful, I kept my stupid mouth shut, and Lily told us both what to do for the presentation.

# Chapter 8

My spidey senses were tingling from the moment I woke up. It was as if I had a warning light in my head flashing "Don't go to school" over and over. I wasn't worried about Lily so much as I was worried about Conor. I could still see his tear- and snot-covered face staring at me with hate in his eyes. If he found me at school, I was dead. It was as simple as that.

Also, I had the presentation to do with Big and Lily. I was supposed to stand up and *talk* in front of the whole class. That broke the prime directive of my survival code: Do not get noticed. Not only that, I'd be standing next to an insanely tall girl and a three-hundred-pound guy. I'd look like a scab-nosed garden gnome. I simply couldn't go to school.

Faking sick was out of the question. My dad would use his psychic powers and see right through me. I was going to have to skip class and hope he didn't check the online gradebook and see I was gone.

I got ready for school, ate breakfast, chatted normally with my dad, and left. Then, instead of skating to school, I caught a bus to downtown Ogden. My plan was to climb at OCC all day.

When I got there, some guy I didn't know was working the front counter. He was balding and chunky, and his head reminded me of a big potato. "Can I help you?" he asked.

I dug out my membership card and handed it to him.

He looked at it like I was trying to buy beer with a fake ID. "Aren't you supposed to be in school?"

My mind went blank. I hadn't expected to need an excuse for not being in school. I stood there in stupid silence.

"Well, aren't you?"

I racked my brain for a plausible excuse. Still nothing.

"Look," said Mr. Potato Head, "you can't be here when you're supposed to be in school. I'm going to have to call your parents."

"He's okay," said a girl's voice from behind me. "He's with me."

I turned around and saw a chest. Then I looked up and saw that it belonged to Lily. Did she somehow know I was going to skip class and came to hunt me down? I fought the sudden impulse to run.

"This is my little brother," Lily continued, and I swear she emphasized the *little* part. "I thought it would be fun to get him out of school and go climbing for a day before I had to go back to college. You don't mind, do you? I go to school, like, three states away, and I won't be seeing him again until Christmas break. My parents said it was fine. You can call them if you want. They'll vouch for the *little* guy." Yep, definitely emphasizing *little*. She even ruffled my hair.

Mr. Potato Head stared up at tall, black Lily, then down at tiny, white me, and then gave us both a "how stupid do you think I am" look.

Lily mock-covered my ears and whispered, "He's adopted."

Mr. Potato Head rolled his eyes and let out a dramatic sigh like busting us would take too much effort. "Whatever. Go ahead, but don't cause any trouble."

"Uh, thanks," I mumbled. I wasn't sure which was worse: to be busted for truancy or be left at the mercy of Lily. I tucked my membership card back in my wallet and followed Lily over to the bouldering area, wondering if I should make a run for it.

Lily folded her arms and leaned against the wall. "So," she said with a wry smile, "here I am driving along when, what do I see? One of my presentation partners getting off a bus and skating *away* from school and toward the climbing gym. Looks to me like you decided to ditch me and Big."

"I was still going to, uh, be back in time for Language Arts."

Lily stared at me like I was insulting her intelligence.

"Okay, that's not exactly true."

"Look, I get it. You're embarrassed to get up in front of the class with Big and me."

"What? No, not at all. What are you talking about?"

Lily gave me a stern look, unfolded her arms, and took a step toward me. Man, she could cover a lot of ground in one step.

I knew what I said next mattered to my physical well-being. The problem was, I didn't know what I was supposed to say. "Seriously, why would I be embarrassed by you and Big?"

Lily's hands turned to fists, and she took another step. The whole situation was feeling way too similar to the time she punched me in the face. I panicked.

"No, really, you're tall and athletic and strong and beautiful and tough and nobody messes with you, and Big's got his magical smile and his jokes and everyone likes him, but me . . . I'm just . . ." I suddenly realized I had just told Lily she was beautiful and that, oddly enough, terrified me more than being punched, so I clamped my mouth shut.

Lily stepped back and leaned against the wall again. She unclenched her hands and folded her arms. She narrowed her eyes at me like she was trying to figure out if I was still lying to her or not. I felt my face heat up.

"You're just what?" she asked.

Was this some kind of interrogation trick? Sort of a good cop/bad cop with Lily playing both roles?

"What were you going to say?" she asked when I didn't reply.

I made an incredibly rash decision. I decided to be honest. "I'm a scrawny little twerp, okay? A shrimp, a runt, a munchkin—you name it. So, yeah, maybe, in a way, I'm afraid to present in front of the class with Big and you. It's bad enough looking like a *little boy*"—I made air quotes to remind her what she'd called me—"every day of my life, but if I were to stand up there with you two, I would never live it down. I get bullied enough as it is, thank you very much." It felt good to let everything out in a torrent, so I kept going. "And for your information, as much as I would love to look even scrawnier than I *already* do and stammer like an idiot in front of the whole class like I *always* do, that's not even the reason I didn't go to school today." I realized I wasn't stammering as much as I usually did. Apparently, ranting made me more articulate.

I looked up at Lily, wondering why she wasn't breaking my neck or repeatedly smashing my face into the wall. She seemed unfazed by my outburst. If anything, she appeared more relaxed. When was the bad cop going to show back up?

"So if that's not the reason," she asked, "why are you ditching school today? Because of your nose?"

"No. Not because of my stupid nose." I resisted the urge to cover it with my hand. I was on a roll with the truth, so I said, "Because Conor Dolores wants me dead."

Lily's eyebrows went up. "Why?"

"Why? Have you looked at me? Why does *everyone* want to kick me around? They just do. It's natural selection. You know, punish the weak, cull the herd, tear into the runt of the litter. Make yourself feel tough by picking on someone smaller. Speaking of which, why aren't *you* beating me up right now?" I felt like someone else had taken control of my mouth. Someone who said all the things I always wanted to say, but never did.

"Me? Why would I beat you up?"

"Oh, I don't know, maybe because I ran into you in the hall on the first day of school, and laughed at your name, and then outclimbed you in front of your whole climbing class, and then didn't give you my number when you asked for it, and then failed to apologize with the brownies I brought you, and then I didn't realize you were adopted, and then I tried to ditch out on our presentation, and who knows what else because every time I'm around you I seem to do something stupid even though it's not on purpose like the way I'm talking to you right now, for instance." I paused for a breath before I added, "*And* you've punched me before."

"What do you mean I've punched you before? I've never hit you."

"Yeah, you did. Right after you burped in my face."

"What are you talking about?" Lily looked baffled.

"When we were, like, seven, and we were at the park, and I went to get a drink out of the drinking fountain."

Lily's expression turned from confusion to amusement. She started laughing. "That was you? You made fun of my mole."

"I didn't make fun of it. I was worried about you. I thought you might have cancer."

"What kind of seven-year-old kid is worried about cancer?"

I looked at the ground and mumbled, "I had my reasons."

Lily stopped laughing. "You're just . . ." She shook her head.

"What?"

"Full of surprises, that's all." She paused and then asked, "You brought those brownies to apologize?"

I saw her eyes soften again. "Yes," I said, trying to slow down and pick my words wisely, "but I couldn't manage to do it because . . ." I stopped myself from saying *because your crazy family kept interrupting*, and said instead, "Because I can never say anything to a girl without sounding like I have a speech impediment."

Lily's eyes went hard, and she scowled. "My mom has a speech impediment, you know."

My mouth dropped open, and my stomach turned sick.

"I'm kidding. I'm only kidding." Lily laughed and punched my shoulder. "But, man, you should have seen your face."

"Oh," I said, rubbing my shoulder.

Lily finally stopped laughing. "So what about our presentation?"

"What do you mean?"

"We can't just leave Big to do it alone."

I hadn't thought of that. "I guess at least one of us should show up. You want to rock-paper-scissors for it?"

Lily chuckled as if I'd made a joke, so I decided to let her think I'd meant it that way. "No, we *both* have to be at school for fourth period. But since we're already here, we may as well climb for a bit. What do you say?"

I wasn't happy about going back to school, but what could I do? I was trapped. "Fine," I said.

Two hours later, Lily and I packed up our stuff and headed for the door.

I started for the bus stop, but she called after me, "Do you want a ride?"

"No," I said. "I can take the bus."

"Whatever," she said. "I don't trust you. I'm not letting you out of my sight. You're riding with me."

I couldn't tell if she was joking or not. Was it safe to get in a car with her? I hesitated too long, and her eyes narrowed. I remembered what happened when I hadn't given her my cell number and said, "Yeah, uh, thanks, that would be, um, great."

Lily's eyes didn't quite go back to normal. It was like she'd decided not to shoot her death ray at me, but had left the safety off, just in case. "Come on. My truck's over here." As we walked through the parking lot, she said, "Look, don't be so jumpy, all right? I'm not going to punch you in the face again. Even if you act like a dope sometimes."

Maybe I should have been offended, but I wasn't because, well, it was true. "I know. It's just that, being me, I have to keep my guard up all the time, and I don't know how to relax, you know? And besides, I'm always giving you a new reason to want to kill me."

Lily laughed, and her eyes returned to normal. Phew, safety back on.

Lily's truck was a big, flatbed, diesel-powered Ram that had scraps of hay all over it. The cab was cluttered with leather gloves, dirt, twine, tie-downs, tools, empty pop bottles, and more hay. I waited while Lily cleared me a spot. "Sorry," she said, "I don't often have passengers."

Once we were both in, she started the huge truck, and we pulled out of the parking lot. Before we'd gone half a block, it started raining.

"Thanks for the ride. I would have gotten soaked waiting for the bus."

"No problem." She was quiet for a minute and then asked, "So, what did you do to make Conor want to kill you? I mean, besides being smaller than him."

"Oh, you know, I had the nerve to, um, beat him in a penny-pushing race."

Lily nodded. "So that's how you hurt your nose. I wondered." She said it soft. Not like she pitied me. More like she was sad about how cruel people could be. Which was weird, because I was pretty sure she was one of those cruel people. "At least you beat him, I guess," she added.

"Yeah, which isn't as good as it sounds, because beating him is some kind of unforgivable insult, punishable only by death."

"Sounds like Conor," Lily said. "In elementary school, he used to call me 'Sasquatch.'"

"What? You're kidding." I couldn't fathom anyone having the guts to make fun of Lily.

"Come on, Paul. Look at me. I'm tall *and* black. There were only two other black kids in my whole school and none in my same grade. No matter how much I wished I could blend in, it wasn't possible for me. That made me a natural target for bullies. A lot of kids made fun of me. Conor was the worst, though.

He called me all kinds of names, like 'Stilts' or 'Giraffe Girl.' Sometimes racist things, too."

"But he, uh, doesn't do it anymore?"

"Oh, I'm sure he still does. He is Conor Dolores, after all. He just doesn't say it to my face."

"So what's different? How did you, um, make him stop?"

Lily smiled. "I punched him in the face."

"Really?" I laughed.

"Well, yes and no. I did punch him one day in fifth grade and that helped."

"That's awesome."

"Yeah, well, maybe. What really stopped the teasing were my older brothers. Once I got to junior high, they made it clear to everyone that no one made fun of a Small."

"Junior?" I asked, thinking of the one who'd hauled off her little brother and sister the night before.

"No, Junior's like five years older than me. He was already in high school by the time I got to junior high. I'm talking about Chuck and Colt. You know, the linemen on the football team?"

"I don't know anyone on the football team," I said.

Lily blinked in surprise. "Oh, well, they're pretty good. They're identical twins, and they're huge. Like three-hundred-pounds huge. They're tall like me, but broad like my dad. No one messes with them. I never got the whole story, but apparently they overheard Conor talking about me and put a stop to it in such a way that no one bothered me again for the rest of the year."

"I should get me some older brothers like that."

"They're not all they're cracked up to be. Besides, I'd rather stand up for myself."

"Easy for you to say."

Lily glanced over at me. "Aren't you listening? It's not easy at all. Everything about me makes me an outsider. It's . . . lonely."

"You must play sports, right? What about your teammates? They must love that you're so tall."

Lily's eyes narrowed, and I knew I'd made another mistake.

"You think because I'm tall and black that I must play basketball or volleyball? Is that what you're saying?" she asked, sounding offended.

"I guess I just, um, assumed—"

"Well, you shouldn't have." She gave me a withering look. "I don't assume you're a gymnast just because you're short."

I tried to think of something to say and failed. We drove in silence except for the rattle of the diesel engine, the mechanical swish of the windshield wipers, and the hiss of the tires on the wet road.

As we pulled into the school parking lot, I finally broke the silence. "Sorry, Lily. I wasn't thinking."

"No, you weren't." She sounded more tired than angry. Like my stupid comment had worn her out. "I'm sick of people always thinking they know me just because of how I look on the outside. Did you know I have a 4.0 GPA? Or that I want to study agriculture at USU? I actually prefer books to sports. In fact, the only sport I really like is rock climbing." She let out a long sigh. "Speaking of which, what do you think about entering the comp?"

"The comp?" I was still trying to imagine Lily studying agriculture.

"Yeah, you know, the high school climbing competition at the gym."

"Oh, I, uh, I don't know about that." To be honest, I wanted to enter, but it meant climbing in front of a crowd, singling my-self out, and, well, finding people who might actually want to be on a team with a ninety-pound weakling.

Lily's eyes narrowed like she was getting mad again. "Why not?"

I decided to fall back on the honesty thing again since it'd worked before. "Well, because I don't think anyone would want to be on my team."

"What about me?"

"You want to be on a team with *me*?"

"Well, yeah. You're like the best climber I know, and I want to win."

"Really?" My brain could not make sense of a world where Lily and I were on the same team for *anything*.

"Yes, really. You know how you thought I was mad at you for outclimbing me the other day?"

"Yeah."

"I wasn't mad." She paused. "Okay, I was a little mad, *but* I was also trying to decide if I could get you to be on my climbing team. So what do you say?"

Maybe it was fear of what Lily would do if I said no, or maybe I really did want to enter the competition, but I said, "Well, um, yeah. Yeah, I think I'd like that. But I don't know any other climbers. Who would our third person be?" I was suddenly terrified she might say Hunter.

Lily smiled. "Don't worry. I have the perfect person."

# Chapter 9

Lily and I walked into school just as the bell rang for fourth period. I knew Conor was likely stalking the halls. I felt a powerful need to go into camouflage mode and disappear into the crowds of students.

Except I was walking with Lily. I couldn't ditch her after agreeing to be on her team. There would be no mercy for that. And it was nice to have someone to walk with. I'd never really had that before.

But it was scary, too. Every instinct in me screamed, *Hide! You can't be seen if you want to survive.* I looked up at Lily and tried to read her expression. She was stone-faced. Her shoulders were back, her chin was high, and she looked everyone in the eye as if daring them to say something. It was like walking next to a mythical warrior.

We were almost to class when Lily stopped in the middle of the hall. "What the—"

I tried to see what she was looking at, but there were too many students in the way. "What is it?" I asked.

"Come here." She laughed and grabbed my hand, and it was like being electrocuted . . . only in a good way.

Physical contact with a female was primarily a theoretical, abstract concept for me. I knew it was something that existed, and it probably felt nice, but I had limited experience with the phenomenon. It only lasted for the two seconds it took Lily to drag me through the stampeding students and over to a window, but the feeling lingered long after she let go. Her hand had been warm, kind of sweaty, and rough where she had calluses, and it made me feel wonderfully tingly.

"Look," Lily said and pointed out the window at the small courtyard no one ever used. It was an ugly concrete square with ugly concrete benches surrounded on all sides by two stories of ugly glass windows. It was about as inviting as a Soviet prison yard. I didn't even know students could go out there.

And there was Big, standing in the middle of it, smiling in the rain with his eyes closed.

"What's he doing?" I asked.

"I guess he's . . ." Lily paused, searching for an answer, then shook her head. "Just being Big."

"He's, uh, going to be late for our presentation," I said. "And very wet."

"We better go get him. Otherwise, who knows when he'll make it to class."

We found a door to the courtyard. Lily opened it and yelled, "Big, what are you doing? You're getting soaked."

Big turned and looked at us. It seemed to take a few seconds for him to come back to reality from whatever place he'd been in. Then he smiled even bigger and said, "You have to experience this." His voice was quiet, almost reverent, but it carried across the courtyard.

"Experience what? Rain?" Lily said. "I've felt rain before. Now come on, we have a presentation to do, and we're going to be late."

"No, really, come here. It's beautiful." Big beckoned to us with his hand and closed his eyes again.

"Let's just go to class," I said. "The late bell is going to ring any second now."

Lily looked at me, then down the hall toward our class, back to Big, then at me again. "You can go. I want to see what he's talking about."

"What? Why?"

Lily ran out into the rain. Big whispered something to her, and she closed her eyes. There was a long pause as they both stood there getting drenched, and then Lily laughed the most perfect, beautiful laugh. The laugh fluttered around the concrete courtyard like a living thing, like butterflies, and the next thing I knew, I was running out into the rain to join them.

When I reached Big, I said, "What are you doing? Let's go back inside."

Lily whispered, "Close your eyes and listen."

That was not what I expected. I closed my eyes and tried to listen. At first, I was distracted by how wet I was getting and how cold the rain felt. But I took a deep, slow breath and concentrated.

And I heard it.

Somehow that ugly concrete courtyard had the near-magical ability to magnify the tiniest sounds and make them seem big, significant, and essential. The water pooled on the ground, making the entire place into a shallow pond no more than a quarter of an inch deep. Little drops of rain hit the pooled water, and the sound was amplified. Millions and millions of drops all hitting the water and all being amplified, and it was as if I heard each one of them individually, and each one seemed important, beautiful, and just right. While I heard each of their unique voices, I also heard the chorus they made together. They sang like a mother whispering to her baby, "Hush, hush, hush."

Then the late bell rang. We left the charmed courtyard to reenter the loud and smelly halls of the school. The contrast was staggering, like walking out of a cathedral and into a battlefield. We stopped by the bathrooms to dry off as best we could, so we were pretty late when we got to class.

Mr. Teller gave us one look, with our rain-soaked hair and clothes, and shook his head. His expression said more than a lecture ever could.

The class snickered and whispered as we found our seats. I didn't blame them. We must have been quite a sight: Big, with his huge smile, huge body, and orange Hawaiian shirt sopping wet and dripping on the floor; Lily, tall and powerful and still managing to look proud and defiant despite an uncharacteristic smile; and me, who probably looked like a red-nosed Chihuahua after being dunked in the bath.

We sat down as Mr. Teller finished giving instructions on the presentations. I was relieved when he said we would be last. I hoped to dry out before it was our turn.

The other groups all went, but I hardly heard a word they said. There was too much going on in my mixed-up head. For starters, I was breaking every single survival rule I'd ever made for myself. It's not exactly good camouflage to walk into class late and sopping wet. Then there was the fact that I'd been climbing with Lily the Bengal Tiger only an hour earlier, and for some un-fathomable reason, she'd asked me to be on her team. I hadn't seen that one coming. And to top everything off, I'd heard what was quite possibly the most wonderful sound in the world while standing in a concrete courtyard in the rain. The combination of it all was weirding me out.

I should have been in a panic, but instead I felt good. It was like I'd just eaten a big bowl of warm soup on a cold day, and I could feel it sitting in my belly, radiating heat, making me full and comfortable. Nothing made sense anymore.

Then it was our turn.

Mr. Teller said, "Because one of the main characters in *Of Mice and Men* is mentally challenged, Paul, Big, and Lily will be presenting on mental illness in the early 1900s." By the tone of his voice, it was clear he had not forgiven us for being late.

We made our way to the front, the class snickering and whis-pering all over again. Their laughter wasn't entirely unkind. I mean, they had to be curious as to how we got so wet. And we did look pretty funny together. We were like a human biology diagram illustrating the extremes of body types.

Lily's part was first, and just as she was about to start, there was a cough from the back of the room. Only it wasn't a real cough. It was the word "Freaks" disguised as a cough. I didn't bother looking to see who said it.

Mr. Teller said, "Knock it off, Mr. Dolores." Like that was really going to help anything.

I glanced up at Lily, wondering if she would tear off Conor's arms and legs now or wait until after our presentation. I saw the muscles in her jaw clench and her eyes ignite. It was pretty cool to see the raw power of her death ray when it wasn't aimed at me for a change.

Conor didn't seem to notice at first. He was too busy laughing with his friends, but when he looked up and saw Lily, his smirk disappeared and his eyes went wide. He knew he'd made a big mistake.

Lily started the presentation, but not the way we'd planned. She said, "Yes, Conor, that's right. Freaks." Lily stared straight at him, hardly blinking. "That's what society used to think of people who suffered from mental illness back in the early 1900s. They were different. They didn't always look the same as everyone else, act the same, or think or talk the same. Because they were different, they were misunderstood. Even *feared*." Lily paused to let her words sink in. Her eyes never left Conor.

I decided that since I'd broken every other survival rule, I might as well break another one. I stared hard at Conor, too. I had no idea how to shoot a death ray. My talents were more in the realm of looking docile and nonthreatening, but I did my best to imitate Lily. I probably looked about as threatening as a hissing kitten.

Lily continued, "Can you imagine? Just because someone's a little different than you are, you torture them, beat them, punish them for even trying to be a part of"—Lily made air quotes—"normal society."

The whole class seemed to be holding a collective breath. No one moved. No one made a sound. I could hear the analog clock above the door ticking. Finally, Lily looked away from Conor, and her gaze took in the whole class. She seemed to pause on each person individually. Her tone was dark with irony as she said,

"Isn't it great that we've learned so much since then? That we're not so xenophobic, intolerant, and narrow-minded?"

After that, Lily continued with the presentation as we'd planned it. Her voice returned to normal, and she sounded confident and in control. I had no idea how she managed it. I was in awe.

Next, it was my turn. I stammered my way through my part without ever looking up from my note cards. I could barely read them because my hands shook so bad. My job was to describe the asylums of the nineteen and twentieth centuries. It was pretty depressing stuff, because, for the most part, they were awful.

It wasn't until Big took his turn that I felt the whole class finally relax. He explained the different "cures" for the mentally ill and intellectually disabled that were used in the early 1900s. Crazy stuff that sounded more like torture or something from a horror film. It was pretty depressing, too, but at the end, Big talked about modern advances in medication and therapy and shined his yellow happiness ray down on everyone and soon they were all smiling back at us. Everyone except for Conor.

In the end, our presentation was exactly the horrible and embarrassing experience I expected it to be, but it was also worth it. I wouldn't have missed seeing Lily intimidate Conor for anything. Of course, I knew there would be consequences. Guys like me don't get away with stuff like that. Conor might hesitate to do something to Lily and maybe even Big, but he wouldn't hesitate to destroy me. I was in trouble.

As we walked out of class, Big asked Lily, "Are you feeling okay?"

Lily held her hand to her forehead like she had a headache. "Yeah, I'm fine."

"You don't look fine," Big said.

"My head is pounding, and I'm feeling a bit achy," she said. She offered a weak smile and added, "Maybe I'm getting sick because you dragged me out into the rain."

Big chuckled. "But it was beautiful, yeah?"

"It was," she said, nodding. "It really was."

# Chapter 10

The first thing I did when I walked into OCC was look at the Bildungsroman scoreboard. Someone had made it to hold twenty-five. Two holds higher than yesterday. There were two or three new names scattered around in the mid-teens and, there at the very bottom of the list, was the name "Rabbit" at number four.

After checking out the board, I went looking for Andy. I found him at the base of Bildungsroman, giving pointers to two climbers who were working on it. The climber belaying had over-gelled hair and bulging muscles. Even with his back to me, I knew it was Hunter. He was belaying the blonde girl from the climbing class. She was at my high point, hold four, hanging from the first clip and shaking out her hands.

I was about to head over to the bouldering area when I realized this was my chance to show Hunter that Andy and I were friends. Andy wasn't just the manager of the gym, he was the uncontested best climber in all of Ogden. Everyone respected him. Maybe Hunter would stop harassing me if he thought Andy liked me. It was a gamble to step out of camouflage mode, but I headed over to say hi.

"It's too far, and you don't have the reach," Andy was saying to the blonde girl. "You have to dyno. Number five is huge. Trust me, you can do it."

"That's impossible," she said.

Andy said, "No, it's not. Rabbit did it yesterday, and he's even shorter than you." Then, more to himself, he added, "Where is he anyway? He should be here by now." He turned around to look for me and jumped in surprise when he saw I was right behind him. "Jeez. You scared me."

"Hey, Andy," I said. "I saw on the board someone made it to hold twenty-five." I snuck a glance at Hunter to see how he was reacting. It was hard to tell, but I think he was a little impressed.

"They sure did," Andy said. "We better get you on here so you can catch up. You ready to give it another go?" Without waiting for my answer, he turned and called up to the blonde girl, "Hey, Anne, how about you lower off and let Rabbit here show you the dyno move."

Red warning lights flashed in my head. I'd wanted to impress Hunter, not give him more reasons to bully me. "No, it's alright, Andy," I said. "They were here first. I, um, I can try it later."

The corners of Andy's eyes crinkled up. "You're not getting off that easy," he said. "Anne doesn't care, anyway. Do you, Anne?"

Anne looked down at me. "I really don't. I'm spent." As Hunter lowered her to the ground, she said to me, "You were here the other day, weren't you? You climbed that steep route over where Andy taught us knee-drops. Are you in our class now?"

"Um, yeah. I mean no," I said. "I'm not, uh, in the class, but, yeah, that was me that, uh, Andy made climb it."

"Cool. I'm Anne Bouda. This is my brother, Hunter."

Hunter stared down at me with a condescending, gap-toothed smile. "We've met," he said, and I was surprised all over again at how high his voice was. It didn't seem like it should be coming out of someone who was clearly producing excessive amounts of testosterone.

"You did awesome on that climb," Anne said. "Even Hunter couldn't make it to the top without falling." She stopped and squinted at my nose. "What happened there?"

"Sorry to interrupt," Andy said, saving me from having to make up a lie, "but I don't have much time. Get in a harness, Rabbit, and get on this beast."

Anne untied and stepped aside, but Hunter still looked at me with that condescending smile.

I asked, "Are you guys sure? I'm, uh, fine climbing somewhere else for now."

"It's cool," Hunter said. "Go ahead. We were done anyway." He said it in a way that made it clear they were not done.

I started to put my harness on, but my foot got tangled in the leg loop, and I fell over. I tried to make it look like I'd sat down on purpose, but, judging by Hunter's snicker, I hadn't fooled anyone. Once I got my harness on, I realized one of the leg loops was twisted upside down, and I had to take it off and start the whole process over again.

"Rookie," Hunter whispered to Anne loud enough for me to hear.

I finally got my harness and shoes on, clipped my chalk bag around my waist, and tied in. My heart was pounding. Hunter and Anne made no move to leave. They were going to stay and watch my humiliation. Fantastic.

"On belay?" I asked Andy.

"Belay on."

"Climbing."

"Climb on," Andy said. "But no skipping clips this time."

I chalked up and took a few deep, slow breaths to calm my nerves. It didn't work. My mind buzzed like I'd had way too much caffeine. That's not a good way to be when you're climbing. Especially *lead* climbing. A big part of it was because Hunter the hyena was standing right next to me with his cute sister, but that wasn't all. My nerves were still frazzled from the whole crazy day with Lily, the presentation, and the rain.

"So are you going to climb this thing or just stare at it?" Hunter asked.

"Sorry," I said. I started climbing with the memory of the rain singing "hush, hush, hush" in my mind. Suddenly, I was calm and focused.

I remembered the moves clearly. Or maybe I should say my body remembered. It felt like my mind was a helium balloon tied to my body, just bobbing along for the ride and watching what my body did with mild curiosity. My muscles seemed to know the moves with surprising clarity. I didn't really have to think at all.

I reached the yellow ear, hold number four, before I knew it, and this time I remembered to clip. I reached down for the rope hanging between my legs and pulled it up. After a ridiculous amount of fumbling, I managed to clip it through the quickdraw's carabiner. What a pain. Not only had I wasted a ton of energy clipping the stupid rope, but it had broken my concentration as well.

My mind was firmly back in my body, and it was screaming for me to give up and get off the wall. I had no business being on a lead climb when there was a giant hyena literally twice my size waiting below to tear out my throat. What was I thinking?

I heard Andy say, "Time for the dyno, Rabbit," and Anne say, "Nice work. You got this."

I looked at the black bucket. It was so far away. There was no way my little four-foot, ten-and-a-half-inch body was going to make it.

Andy must have seen me start to panic because he said, "Just breathe, focus, and jump."

So I did. I took two deep, slow breaths—in through the nose, out through the mouth. I stared so hard at that black hold my eyes started to burn. I told myself I could do it, and I almost believed my own lie. I crouched low and sprang with everything I had.

I went exactly nowhere.

My foot popped off, and, instead of launching upward, I fell. I found myself dangling at the end of the rope.

Anne let out a disappointed, "Oh."

Hunter snorted and laughed.

Andy said, "Try it the way you did yesterday."

"Isn't that what I did yesterday?" I asked.

"No, yesterday you had both feet pointing to the left. A dyno like this has *two* parts. First, pull yourself into the wall so your weight is over your feet, then launch upward. You'll get a lot more height that way."

Height was definitely something I needed more of. The toe thing made sense now that he mentioned it. I was pretty sure I hadn't done that yesterday, but I wasn't going to tell Andy that. I shook out my hands, chalked up, got back on the wall, and tried to get a feel for what he was saying. With both toes pointing left, it already felt better. The "two movements" thing was a mystery, though.

"Watch me," I said—climber talk for "Get ready, I'm probably going to fall."

"I got you," Andy said.

I took a few deep breaths, focused on the bucket, and launched. The takeoff was awkward, but I managed to get airborne. Just like yesterday, I had this spectacular moment of slow-motion weightlessness as both feet and both hands came off the wall, and I flew through the air. My fingertips hit the edge of the black hold. Not enough to hang on, but at least I touched it, and felt the real possibility of completing the move, before I fell. Because I'd managed upward progress, I fell farther, and the rope gave me a good yank when it caught.

"Oh, man. I thought you had that," Anne said.

Andy laughed. "I like belaying you, Rabbit. I can hardly feel it when you fall. I have time if you want to give it one more try. Hurry up, and get back on there."

"I think I get what you mean about two parts to the dyno." I repeated the shake-out, chalk-up, breathe-deep, get-back-on, and stare-the-hold-to-death process. Then I did something different—I listened for the rain. It was there in my memory, almost perfectly preserved, calming and focusing my mind. *Hush, hush, hush.*

This time, when I jumped, there were no awkward movements. Instead, everything melded into one fluid leap. It reminded me of a wildlife documentary I'd watched describing the way cats jump. They start by crouching on all fours. Then, they leap, first, with their front legs and, next, with their back legs, where all the power comes from, but it looks like one effortless movement. I don't know how I looked, but I felt fantastically fe-line. This time, I was not Superman; I was a laser-guided, preci-sion missile.

I ran out of upward momentum just as my fingertips curled over the edge of the black hold. My feet swung out into the air and then back, where I quickly pasted them to the wall.

I'd done it. Now what? I had a small moment of panic when I realized how far I'd moved above my last quickdraw. My fall was going to be much bigger now.

I shook my head and refocused. The next hold was an easy move to a pocket to the right. I went for it. For most climbers, it would have been a two-finger pocket, but for me, it was three. Every once in a while being small came in handy. From there, a little hop got me to a baseball-sized knob. My feet swung off again, but I managed to get them back on with my left foot now on the black hold.

"Nice work," Anne said.

"Your next clip is on the left," Andy said.

I had almost forgotten to clip again. It should have been fore-most in my thoughts since those clips would keep me from splat-tering on the ground. I reached down with my left hand, found the rope, and fumbled it into the carabiner.

I looked up. The only thing within reach was a tiny blue edge that didn't even count as one of the numbered holds. The "chip" was probably meant as a miniscule foothold for moves higher up. It looked impossible to hold on to. Above that was hold number eight—another edge nearly as small as the chip. Definitely too small to jump for. High and to the right was a vertical fin; I'd need vise grips for fingers if I was going to hang on to that one. In short, the next few moves looked really hard.

I chalked up and grabbed the chip with my left hand. It was barely bigger than a dime edge. Worthless. I looked again at hold number eight, a foot beyond my reach. Any normal-sized climber could reach up and grab it with ease. Not me.

I was suddenly irritated. I hated being short. If my head had been a helium balloon before, now it was as if someone had untied the knot in the balloon and let all the air out in a long, flatulent sigh. It was the end of the road for me. There was no way someone of my height could make that move. I felt betrayed by Andy.

I decided I might as well jump for hold number eight, fall, and get it over with. I breathed deep, put the tiny orange edge in my sights, and tried to summon the sound of the rain. It was gone.

I jumped anyway. I reached the hold, but, as I suspected, it was way too small. I slid right off and ended up dangling from the end of the rope. My already raw fingertips burned. I tried to grab for it twice more, getting more and more annoyed with each try because I knew it was hopeless. Finally I said, "Ready to lower."

As Andy lowered me back to the ground, I glanced at Hunter and Anne in case they were plotting my demise. Anne's face was lit up with what looked like admiration. That seemed impossible. No one ever looked at me with anything remotely close to admiration.

Hunter had his arms folded and his brow creased. He looked like he was reassessing what he thought of me. Had I earned their respect? It seemed doubtful.

Once my feet hit the ground, Andy took me off belay and said, "Nice job, Rabbit. It may take a while, but you'll get that next section. Don't be discouraged." He slapped me on the back. "I've got to get back to work. See you guys later."

"Okay. Thanks for the belay, Andy," I said, trying hard not to let my frustration show. Andy left, and I turned to Anne. "Do you, uh, want to give it another go? I can give you a belay." I waited for her to laugh or at least look amused.

"No, thanks," Anne said without any sign of laughter. "I'm done with that thing for today."

I didn't want to, but I felt like I had to ask Hunter, too. "What about you? Do you, um, want a belay?"

I got the laugh I was expecting. Hunter snorted and said, "No way. You'd go shooting into the air if I fell."

Despite his remark, I still hoped to leave on good terms with him. It would be nice to have one less person to worry about ambushing me at school. I decided to try flattery. "Have Anne belay you if you don't want me to. I've seen you climb. You're a way better climber than me. You could easily cruise up to hold eight or nine."

"Nah, I don't feel like it right now," he said, waving his hand at the route like it wasn't worth his time.

"Alright, well, um, I guess I'll see you guys around, then," I said.

"Hold up a second," Hunter said. "Are you entering the high school climbing comp?"

My spidey senses tingled. I mumbled, "I, um, I guess."

"Do you already have a team?"

Before I could answer, Anne said, "Yeah, because if you don't, you should totally be on our team."

Hunter gave her an impatient look, and she said, "What? He's good. Maybe not as good as Lily, but if she doesn't want to enter the comp, he's our next-best option."

Hunter rolled his eyes at Anne and then said to me, "What do you think?"

"About what?"

"About being on our team."

"Oh, uh, I'd love to, I really would, but I'm already on a team."

"With who?"

"Um, Lily?" I said her name like a question.

Hunter's eyes narrowed, and his nose crinkled up like he smelled something bad. "Lily isn't entering. I already talked to her about it." He said it like it was an indisputable fact. Apparently, Lily hadn't told him she was getting her own team together for the competition.

"Um, I guess she, uh, changed her mind, maybe?" I had to stop saying everything as if it were a question.

Hunter folded his arms so his muscles bulged out even more. "Look, *Rabbit*, I just told you, Lily's not entering. Do you want to be on our team or not? Otherwise, we'll find someone else. Someone less vertically challenged."

"Knock it off, Hunter," Anne said. "He can be on whatever team he wants."

"No, that's cool," I said. "Um, I'd really like to be on your team. Honestly, you two are some of the best climbers I know. You're totally going to win." I wasn't sure what to do. I couldn't join Hunter's team and ditch Lily. She would kill me. On the other hand, Hunter seemed like he might kill me if I didn't. I had to make a choice, and fast. "Maybe Lily decided to not enter—I don't know. But she asked me first, and, um, I better find out for sure before I go and, uh, join another team or something."

Hunter glared at me, and I got the feeling that if Anne wasn't

91

standing there, he would have started breaking my bones one by one.

"That's okay," Anne said. "Let us know if it doesn't work out with Lily, okay?"

"Sure." I started edging my way toward the door. "I just, you know, need to talk to her about it. I'll see you guys later." Then I turned and walked away, doing my best not to break into a run.

# Chapter 11

I stayed in super-camouflage mode all morning on Friday. I saw Conor a few times, but he never spotted me. I would like to say I was able to evade him using my highly tuned spidey senses, but a blind sloth could have avoided him. It was easy to hear his loud voice and phony laugh over all the other noise and chaos.

Trouble hit just before my third-period art class. I was heading for a back staircase I liked to use because it was out of the way and had a lot less traffic. Just before I reached the edge of the stairs, I heard someone say, "There he is! Grab him!" followed by a scuffling and squeak of shoes on the tile floor. I got an instant adrenaline rush and turned to run. I thought for sure Conor the jackal and his pack were coming after me.

Then I heard a guy say, "No! Let go of me." His voice cracked.

Someone else said, "Now, now, Dolores, don't cry. This will be over soon. You just need to relearn a little lesson."

Against my better judgment, I crept to the edge of the stairwell and peeked down. Four guys convened in a nook created by the base of the stairs. I recognized Hunter the hyena right away.

Two of the other guys were the size of rhinos and strangely familiar, but I couldn't place them. The rhinos each held one of Conor's arms. Conor might have been a predator, but he didn't stand a chance against these guys. Hunter and the rhinos had chosen the spot well. The nook was about the most secluded spot in the school.

"Let go of me," Conor squealed again, and the tears started flowing. He sure had a lot to learn about being bullied. Maybe I needed to slip him a note or something. Rule one: You don't cry in front of predators—ever. I wanted to yell it down the stairs.

One of the rhinos said, "Now, Dolores, we taught you this lesson once before, back in junior high, don't you remember?" He almost sounded sympathetic. Like a reluctant father about to spank his kid.

The second rhino was not as nice. He growled, "In case you forgot, it involved an extremely disgusting toilet. You remember that, don't you?" The rhinos shoved Conor into a corner.

Hunter stood back and watched with a nasty smile on his face. I got the feeling he was supposed to be the lookout, but he wasn't doing his job. He seemed to be having too much fun watching Conor bawl.

I was suddenly very glad I hadn't agreed to be on his team. Nor did I care what he thought of me or my climbing. I wanted to smash Hunter's gap-toothed smile with a baseball bat. I hated guys like him. I'd seen their predatory smiles aimed at me way too many times. Even if it was Conor being bullied, how could anyone find it entertaining? I felt sick to my stomach.

Then something seemed to happen to Conor. He didn't exactly do anything different, but even as far away as I was, I saw something change in his eyes. They turned feral.

"I remember," Conor spat, yanking his arms free from the rhinos. He was still crying, but it was a different kind of crying. A dangerous kind. The rhinos must have noticed it too, because they exchanged a wary look.

The second rhino asked, "Okay, then what were you supposed to remember from your little date with the toilet?"

Conor faced off against the two rhinos. He crouched low, his feet spread and his arms wide, looking like a cornered jackal. "Never mess with a Small," he muttered.

Suddenly I could see the family resemblance. The rhinos were Lily's brothers; they looked just like Lily's dad. Lily must have told them about Conor calling us freaks.

The second rhino continued, "That's right. Now get on your knees."

Conor tried to make a break for it. He faked right and then went left, but he didn't get more than two steps. The second rhino caught him and threw him against the wall. I saw his head bounce off the bricks and cringed, but Conor didn't pause for a second. He darted the other way, and the first rhino caught him just as easily. He threw him against the wall, too, although I noticed it was with much less force.

Hunter laughed.

Conor made a high-pitched squeal and charged right between them. Which, of course, didn't work. There was no escape. The rhinos caught him and threw him to the floor.

Hunter laughed even harder.

I didn't see it happen, but when the second rhino turned, I saw a red streak across his cheek. Conor must have gotten in at least one swipe.

"Get on your knees," the rhino growled at Conor.

Conor dragged himself onto his knees.

"Now, bow to us and say 'Never mess with a Small.'"

Conor bowed and said, "Never mess with a Small."

"Again!" the second rhino demanded.

Conor said it again.

"Louder!"

Conor said it louder.

"Keep saying it until I tell you to stop."

Conor started bawling harder, but he did it. The late bell rang, but no one made a move to leave.

I wanted to be glad Conor was getting what he deserved—he'd been mean to me, so wasn't it right for someone else to be mean to him? Instead, I felt like throwing up.

I considered telling the rhinos to stop, but bravery was for guys who weighed more than one hundred pounds. I couldn't make myself do it. I'd always been prey and always would be. I tiptoed back up the stairs, hearing the echo of Conor's sobs as I went.

After third period, I stopped by the concrete courtyard. I stared out at it, still feeling kind of sick and wishing it were raining. In the reflection of the window, I saw a big smile appear beside me.

"I wish it were raining," Big said as if he'd read my thoughts. He was wearing a bright-blue Hawaiian shirt.

"How many of those shirts do you have?" I asked.

"Five. One for each day of the school week."

"Are you actually from Hawaii?"

"Yeah. I moved here two months ago. I'm from Poipu on the island of Kaua'i."

"Does everyone there wear shirts like that?"

Big laughed. "Nah, mostly just the haoles."

"Haoles?"

"Like, the white tourists, yeah? Most kama'āina—the locals—wouldn't be caught dead wearing a shirt like this."

"But aren't you a kama . . . , uh, a local or whatever?"

"Yep," Big said and laughed again. Then he asked, "Have you seen Lily?"

"No, I haven't," I said. "She had a headache yesterday. Maybe she's sick."

"I wondered the same thing," Big said, and his smile left for just a moment in concern. Then it snapped back. "We should drop by her house and take her a treat, yeah? You know, like a 'get well' kind of thing."

To be honest, I wasn't sure I wanted to see Lily. If she sent her brothers to maul Conor, was she any better than him? I didn't want to try to figure out again how much I was supposed to be afraid of her. Not to mention I would miss out on my after-school climbing time, and I needed a fix now more than ever. I was definitely not going.

"Well, what do you think?" Big asked when I didn't respond right away.

I looked at Big. His big smile came shining down on me like the sun out of the big blue sky of his shirt. He hit me square in the face with that yellow happiness ray of his, and there was nothing I could do. "Um, ok, yeah. Let's do that," I said.

# Chapter 12

We decided, or more accurately, Big decided we should take Lily chocolate chip cookies and vanilla ice cream. The whole thing felt really awkward to me. What kind of teenagers took cookies and ice cream to people they barely knew? Big and his mom acted like they did this sort of thing every day, and maybe they did, but I was a keep-to-myself kind of person. This was *not* my style at all.

I tried to tell myself it was good survival strategy. Allying myself with the biggest and toughest people around made sense, but then I thought of what the rhinos did to Conor, and I felt sick all over again. I mean, taking cookies and ice cream to a mob boss who ordered a hit on someone just didn't feel right.

Big's mom drove us to the store, and Big and I went inside. It took us a while to find the ice cream because, apparently, it had to be vanilla bean ice cream and not French vanilla. I didn't even know there was a difference, but Big assured me it would be sacrilegious to eat French vanilla ice cream with those beautiful chocolate chip cookies.

On our way out, there was a loud crash right by the front

doors, and I looked over to see a skinny woman in her early for-
ties standing over a dropped basket of groceries. A jug of milk had
broken open, spilling all over the floor.

Big started to walk over to help her, but another guy beat him
to it. The guy picked up the few items that had fallen out of the
basket and put them back while the woman stared at the milk in
wide-eyed shock as if it were a murder scene.

I got the feeling something wasn't quite right with her. I don't
know if it was my spidey senses, but I somehow knew she was a
time bomb. I turned to leave, and then I realized the kid helping
her was Conor Dolores.

"It's okay, Mom," Conor said. "It's no big deal. They'll clean
up the milk. Don't worry, it's okay." He said it like he was talking
to a frightened animal.

Conor set the milk jug upright so it wasn't leaking as much,
stood up, and wiped his hands on his pants. He picked up the
basket of groceries and took his mom by the arm. He tried to
guide her away from the scene, but she didn't budge.

She started to cry and mumbled, "They're all looking at me."

"No, they're not, Mom. It's okay. Let's just go." Conor set
the basket on the ground. "We don't need groceries. Let's just
go home." He tried again to guide his mom away, and she still
wouldn't move.

She looked up from the milk and scanned the people in the
store. "They're all looking at me," Mrs. Dolores said. Her face
turned red, tears pouring down her cheeks.

"No, they're not. It'll be okay. We just need to go home."
Conor's voice was calm and quiet, but I heard an edge of panic.
Something bad was coming.

"Maybe we should go," I said to Big.

"Yeah, I think you're right."

We only made it a few steps when Mrs. Dolores screamed, "They're all looking at me!" When that happened, everyone in the store really did look at her. Some customers peeked around corners while others blatantly stared.

Mrs. Dolores yelled over and over, "They're looking at me. They're looking at me. They're *all* looking at me!"

"What should we do?" I asked Big.

"I don't know," he whispered.

"We need to help," I said. I didn't care if it was Conor's mom. She looked so scared. We had to do something.

Conor gave up talking quietly and said in the tone of a parent talking to a misbehaving kid, "Mom, it's okay. We just need to go home. Dad can help. No one will look at you there." He held her elbow with one hand, put his other arm around her waist, but his mom shook him off, then shoved him.

"They're looking at me! Why won't they stop looking at me? They're all looking at me."

Conor started crying and yelling, too. "Mom, please. Let's just go home. Please. It will be okay."

He took a step toward her. Mrs. Dolores tried to dodge away from him, but she slipped in the milk and fell hard to the tile floor. Conor dropped to his knees and scooped her up in his arms like she was a child. At first she tried to fight him off, but he held her tight to his chest and rocked her, and after a few seconds she quit yelling. She sobbed so hard her whole body shook.

Conor rocked her and whispered, "It will be okay. It will be okay. It will be okay." I couldn't help but think he was telling it more to himself than to his mom.

"What should we do?" I asked Big again.

"I think the best thing is to just go," Big said. "Conor wouldn't want us here, and I don't think there's anything we can do to help."

"But they're just sitting there in the milk," I said. Then the stupidest thing happened: I started to cry. Like, *really* cry. I had no idea why. Something was seriously wrong with me. "Will you just take me home?" I sputtered.

Big put his arm around my shoulder, and we walked out of the store.

# Chapter 13

I didn't cry for long. I was done before we reached my house. It was like a flash flood—unexpected, intense, and quickly gone, but leaving the impression that something immense and unstoppable had torn through me.

After Big and his mom dropped me off, I sat on the front porch for a long time. I didn't want my dad to see me with red eyes and a blotchy face. When I finally went in, my dad looked up from his book and said, "Oh, hey. I didn't expect to see you home so soon. I thought you'd still be at the gym."

"I didn't go today." I didn't want to talk about the confusing day, so I added, "I hung out with Big instead." I figured the idea of me hanging out with a new friend would make him happy, and it did.

"That's great," he said with a smile. I could tell he was trying to act natural, like I hung out with friends all the time. "So, how was school? Any more girl trouble?"

He meant Lily. He could be a real comedian when he wanted to be. "No. She was gone today. Sick, I think."

"Do you feel like you have everything patched up with her okay?"

"Oh, yeah, we're good. She even asked me to be on her climbing team." As I said it, I realized I wasn't sure I wanted to be on her team anymore. If Lily was the type of person who asked her brothers to attack people she didn't like, I should probably keep my distance. It had been my experience that everyone I met ended up not liking me sooner or later.

Plus, I didn't want Hunter to see me climb with her. It's not like I wanted to be on Hunter's team either—not after seeing him with the rhinos—but I knew how guys like him thought. When he found out Lily was in the competition but hadn't joined his team, he was going to be angry. That was full-on rejection. Of course, he wouldn't confront Lily about it; that would make far too much sense. Instead, he'd look for someone else to take it out on. Someone who made easy prey. Someone like me.

"What climbing team?" my dad asked.

"The gym is holding a climbing competition for high school kids, and Lily asked me if I wanted to be on her team, but I don't think I'm going to do it. I'd rather do my own thing."

"If she asked you to be on her team, why wouldn't you? That sounds like a great opportunity."

"Well, I'm really not that good, and there's probably going to be a big crowd or something, and I don't want to climb in front of a bunch of people, you know? And Lily wanted to kill me only two days ago, and it seems like I shouldn't climb with people who might still want me dead."

"You don't actually believe that."

"No," I grumbled. Man, I hated his psychic dad powers. "But

I really don't want to climb in front of people. You know what happened the last time."

He looked at me for a long moment. "That was over two years ago, Paul. Besides, this isn't about climbing in front of people, it's about Lily."

"Well, maybe a little," I said. "I'm not sure I want to be her friend. I mean, I thought I did. I don't exactly have a lot of people knocking down my door to be my friend or anything, but I just don't think she's a nice person."

My dad leaned back in his chair and looked up at the ceiling in thought. After what felt like a long time, but wasn't, he looked back at me and smiled. "Let's go to the climbing gym."

I wasn't about to argue with that.

OCC was crowded. It always was on Friday nights. There were all the regulars I'd gotten used to seeing over the last two years, but Fridays also brought in a different crowd. The non-climbers who were there with dates, families who brought their kids for some fun exercise, and groups of teenagers or college students who were looking for an adrenaline rush. It was hardly ideal, but it was still climbing, and I liked it.

The best part was that I had my own personal belay slave: my dad. He didn't come with me often, but the times he did were the best. I was no longer restricted to the bouldering area. I could climb anything I wanted.

"What's this?" my dad asked when we walked in the front door. He was looking at the scoreboard.

"Andy made this super hard route called Bildungsroman right

on the prow, and he made it into a kind of contest. Whoever is able to finish it wins a gift certificate to the climbing shop."

"Bildungsroman," my dad repeated. "What does that mean?"

"It means it's really hard," I said.

"Have you tried it? I don't see your name on it."

"It's right there." I pointed to where it said "Rabbit" next to the number seven.

"Rabbit?"

"Yeah." I wasn't sure if he'd be annoyed by the nickname or find it funny.

"You do climb like a rabbit, I suppose." He chuckled. "Constantly jumping from hold to hold. Who started calling you that? Andy?"

"Yeah. He was belaying me when I first tried the route, and he said I looked like a rabbit. He knew I didn't want my name on the board since it would be the lowest score, so he wrote 'Rabbit' instead."

"Isn't the prow all lead climbing?" my dad asked.

I didn't think he knew that. "Yeah. Is that okay?"

He raised his eyebrows and looked at me as if considering the idea of me lead climbing. "I think so. It's probably about time you started leading, anyway. You're ready. In fact, I think I'd like to see you give this Bildungsroman thing a try."

"What? Oh, no. It's um . . . um . . ." I didn't want to get on the stupid route again. "Dad, there's no way I can do it. I'm too short. I got to this part where it gets kind of reachy, and I'll never be able to do the move, so it's totally pointless."

"Show me," he said.

So much for honesty. We walked over to the prow, where two guys I didn't know were trying to smash their way up

Bildungsroman. The guy leading was probably in his early twenties. He had his shirt off, displaying an array of tattoos that looked like they'd been picked out of a discount bin. He was making upward progress, but it was through brute force, grunts, growls, and outright yelling. No finesse. No technique.

When he arrived at my high point, he clipped the rope in and easily reached up and grabbed hold number eight. It made me angry to see this guy beat me just because he was taller and not because he was a better climber.

"That's where you got to?" my dad asked.

"Yeah, he just passed me. I couldn't reach number eight."

The brute hesitated. He stared up at hold nine—the narrow, vertical fin.

His partner shouted, "Come on! Hit it!" like he'd made a bet on a street fight.

The brute let out a roar and slapped the fin. To my surprise, he held it. He pinched the fin between his thumb and fingers like he was pulling a book from a shelf. Despite everything being wrong with his technique and his awkward body position, he managed to cling to the wall. The guy was strong.

The next move was to a huge, in-cut blue hold, high and left. If he reached that, he could have a nice rest and his next clip. All he had to do was hike up his feet and lean out to the left. That way he wouldn't be pinching the fin so much as leaning off it to the side. The move was obvious even from the ground.

The brute didn't move. Sweat poured down his tattooed back. He had to be melting off those holds. How was he still hanging on? He finally swore and let go, falling four or five feet before the rope caught him.

"You can do that," my dad said.

"No, really, Dad. I think I can do the move he just fell on, but I can't reach the hold before it. It's useless."

"Try."

"Don't you think I have? I can't do it."

"Yet," he said.

"What?"

"You can't do it—*yet*."

I really wanted to believe him. "Okay," I said.

The brute lowered to the ground. We waited while he and his buddy packed up and moved to another climb. They gave my dad and me the up-and-down look before they left, but we ignored them.

I tied in, and, while I waited for my dad to harness up, I closed my eyes and replayed the whole climb up to hold number seven in my mind. As I did, I thought I heard something very faint. Yes, there it was: the rain.

"Belay is on," my dad said.

"Climbing."

I started through the moves. Mind focused, body practically weightless. When I reached hold number seven, I clipped the rope into the quickdraw without fumbling. Nice. I looked up at hold number eight. That stupid, little edge a foot beyond my reach. I didn't waste time thinking about how impossible it was and just jumped for it. I reached it easily, just like before, but it was so small and sloping there was no way to hold it. A second later, I was dangling from the end of the rope.

Frustration started to seep in. I couldn't do it. There are certain things in life short people just can't do: play professional basketball, reach things on the top shelf at the grocery store, and climb Bildungsroman. But my dad was down there. He'd been nice enough to bring me here and belay me, and he wanted to see me try. So I tried. And tried. And tried.

After half a dozen attempts, my fingers were raw and my forearms next to useless. I hung on the rope feeling like I'd swallowed a bowling ball of frustration. I wanted to go home. I turned to tell my dad to lower me and saw Andy standing next to him.

Andy said, "Just skip that move for now."

"What?"

Andy shrugged. "Skip it. You're not quite ready for it. It happens. Work on the rest of the route and come back to that move when you're ready."

"You mean like after I've grown another foot?" Andy didn't deserve my sarcasm, but I couldn't help it. I still felt like he'd betrayed me by making this a height-dependent move.

Andy gave me a patient smile. "Grab the quickdraw and use it to reach hold eight, and then work the rest of the route."

"But even if I get to the top, it won't count because I had to cheat."

My dad cut in. "Andy's right, Paul. If you do what he says, you'll have the whole route dialed in for when you're eventually able to do that move."

"I'll *never* be able to do this move. I'm too short," I snapped. I looked around and saw people looking at me. I felt embarrassed enough to calm down and take another look at the route.

Andy was right. I could easily pull on the quickdraw and reach past this section. Fine. I'd cheat.

Using the quickdraw, I hauled myself up to where I could grab hold number eight. It was truly a terrible sloping edge, but I could at least hold on to it now that I wasn't jumping for it. I stabbed my left foot into the two-finger pocket and put my right hip into the wall. I made a sloppy slap for the fin. Somewhere in the back of my head, I knew I was climbing just as badly as the tattoo guy before me had, but unlike him, I knew the next move.

I switched my left foot back into the pocket, hiked my right foot up to the blue baseball, and leaned off the fin to the left. Now, instead of pinching it, I could hang my weight off it sideways. Pushing with my right foot and using my right arm like a hinge, I reached up for the big, blue, in-cut edge—hold number ten. It was big enough for both hands, and I clipped the rope into the next quickdraw.

My dad smiled up at me. "Well done."

# Chapter 14

Paul?" my dad said, knocking on my bedroom door. "You up?"

"Yeah, come in." I'd been lying in bed, savoring the fact it was Saturday morning and I didn't have to risk my life by going to school.

My dad opened the door. He was dressed like he was ready to go to work even though, as far as I knew, he had nowhere to be. He had a weird look on his face that alarmed me.

"What's going on?" I asked.

"You have some friends here to see you."

"I do?" I tried to remember the last time I had "friends" come over to my house. I couldn't.

"Yes. I believe it's—"

"Hey, Paul." Big's head popped in the doorway above my dad. His smile lit up the room like the morning sun. "Are you decent? Hurry up and get ready. We've got beautiful places to go and beautiful things to see."

"Big and Lily," my dad finished. He turned to Big and said, "Could you give us a second, please?"

Big's smile turned sheepish, and I heard Lily's laugh from the living room. Lily was in my house! The dials, sensors, and warning lights in my head went bonkers. Bengal-tiger-Lily, hit-ordering-Lily, punch-me-in-the-face-for-pointing-out-her-mole-Lily was in my home. Through all the commotion in my head, I also remembered she was pretending-to-be-my-sister-Lily, smiling-in-the-rain-Lily, and a-laugh-like-butterflies-Lily. She was so confusing.

Big said, "Oh, sorry, Mr. Adams. I get a little excited some-times. I'll wait in the front room, yeah?" Big's head disappeared from the doorway.

My dad came in my room, and as he closed the door, I heard Lily say, "I told you we should have called," and Big's reply, "But that would have ruined the surprise."

Once the door was shut, my dad lost his usual Zen compo-sure, and his eyes went wide. "You weren't kidding. I've never met a woman that tall. She actually had to *duck* to come in the front door. And Big is just so . . . *big*. I feel positively tiny next to them." He started to laugh and then stopped. "Sorry. I just . . . wasn't expecting this." He paused, and I could see him struggle to regain his calm demeanor and then fail. "Apparently, they want to take you bouldering or hiking or something for the day. I gather you didn't know they were coming?"

"I . . . I . . . what?" I couldn't wrap my head around what was happening.

"They seem nice enough," my dad said. "I don't mind if you go with them."

"They just showed up?" I asked.

"Just knocked on the door out of the clear blue sky hold-ing a box of freshly baked muffins and saying something about bouldering in the foothills." My dad shook his head. "You really did a class presentation with those two? I wish I could have seen that."

"But . . . what if I don't want to go with them?"

My dad sat on the end of my bed. "I would have thought you'd leap at the chance to go bouldering."

"Bouldering, yeah, but not with *Lily.*"

"Paul," he said, "I think you need to give her a chance. Give yourself a chance to have some friends."

"But, Dad, I'm okay not having any friends. And Lily is scary."

My dad thought for a moment. "Look, you know when you're climbing, and you get to a point where you can't reach the next hold, and you have no idea what it's going to be like, not really, not from below, and you have to jump for it and just hope?"

Zen-dad was definitely back. "But this isn't the climbing gym. What if the hold I'm jumping for has a rattlesnake or something sitting on it?"

My dad frowned at me.

"Okay, fine," I said and crawled out of bed.

Fifteen minutes later, I was sitting between Lily and Big in the cab of Lily's truck, holding a blueberry muffin. I felt like a five-year-old crammed between his parents. Big took up all of his seat and part of mine, pushing me into Lily. It was weird sitting so close to her. She was wearing shorts, and the beautifully sculpted muscles of her right leg kept brushing up against my bony left leg. Every time they touched, I felt a jolt of electricity, but not entirely in a good way this time. She was attractive, for sure, but in a stalking-tiger kind of way.

"What a morning," Big said, his eyes shining. "Look at that

sky. It just goes on forever, not a cloud in it. Oh, wait, there's one—see that little guy way out there? Looks lonely, yeah? Probably wishes he had some other clouds to hang out with."

"So, uh, where are we going, exactly?" I asked.

"Bouldering," Lily said like that explained everything.

"Or maybe he's not lonely," Big continued. "Maybe that little cloud is loving it out there, having the whole sky to himself, just sailing along in the breeze."

"Um, where are we bouldering at?" I asked.

"Just on the hillside above St. Joe's," Lily said. "Haven't you ever been to the boulder field?"

Big said, "I think I'd be lonely if I were that cloud. I'd be like, 'Hey, where did everybody go? Don't you want to be my friend?' You can be surrounded by all the beauty in the world, but with no one to share it with . . ."

"I've never actually climbed outside," I said.

"What?" Lily practically yelled. "You're kidding." She gave me a playful elbow in the side, and I felt another electrical shock like being shot with a mildly pleasant Taser. "What's the matter with you? Ogden has a sweet boulder field ten minutes from your house, and you've never climbed in it?"

"It's just so blue, yeah?" Big said.

I couldn't contain myself any longer. I turned to Big. "Okay, I have to ask. Are you high?"

Lily burst out laughing. Big looked confused and then hurt. His smile disappeared, and I immediately regretted my words.

"*No.* I am *not* high," he said. "I don't know why people are always asking me that."

"Uh," Lily said, "maybe because you're always acting like you're high?" Then she laughed again. I'd never heard her laugh so much. It was nice. Too nice. I had to remind myself she was a vicious predator.

Big did not smile. "Why do people think you have to be on drugs to find the world amazing, yeah? I mean, we're surrounded by all this beauty, all these miniature miracles every second of every day. How could you not be overwhelmed with a sense of wonder?"

I looked around, hoping to see a miniature miracle. The world just looked like the regular old world to me: trees, houses, cars, grass. Big stared at us, waiting for some kind of answer or reaction. It was killing me to see his face without his usual smile, so I did what I always do. I avoided eye contact and looked down. There was my muffin sitting in my lap.

"Like this muffin," I said, holding it up a little. "It's a thing of beauty." I didn't really mean it as a joke, but Lily laughed again and Big's smile came back.

"Indeed," Big said and turned to stare out the window again.

"So, why exactly are you taking me bouldering?" I asked Lily.

"Don't ask me," Lily said. "It was Big's idea. He came over last night with cookies and ice cream for me, and we got talking, and he said we should take you bouldering."

"No, I said I wanted to go out for breakfast," Big said. "It was Lily's idea to go bouldering. I'm not exactly the rock-climbing type, yeah? But Lily said if we really wanted to do something nice for you, we should take you climbing."

"And . . . why are you doing something nice for me?"

"Because we're your friends, brah," Big said, and I felt his warm happiness ray shining down on me without even looking at him.

"What does that mean?"

"What does what mean?" Big asked.

"Brah," I said.

"Brah? You know, it's short for 'brother.'"

"Oh," I said and sat there between the two of them, feeling like a piece of me I hadn't known was missing had been put into place.

A little while later, we were hiking up a trail into the boulder field. I was literally shaking with excitement, like one of those hyperactive dogs that freaks out when their owner grabs the leash and they know it's time for a walk.

I mean, sure, it was weird being with Lily and Big, but it was climbing on *real* rock, which was something I'd never done before. I kept darting up the trail real fast and then having to wait because Big kept stopping to look at the view of the valley.

After what felt like forever, we came to a boulder that Lily said was a good one. She called it "Mother's Womb."

"Why is it called that?" I asked.

Lily shrugged. "It's just the name in the climbing guidebook."

The boulder wasn't very womb-like, just a big rock in the middle of a bunch of scrub oak.

"Mother's Womb," Big said, still huffing from the hike. "I like that. It's poetic. And look at how it's tucked into this little grove of trees. It's cozy, yeah?" He had a collapsible camping chair slung over one shoulder. He made a big production out of setting it up in "just the right spot," whatever that meant. By the time he sat down, I already had my climbing shoes on and my chalk bag clipped around my waist.

I looked at the boulder. It was about the size of a cargo van. It was long and squat and overhung just a little. In the gym, all the routes were marked with colored holds or tape, so you knew exactly where to climb, but this was just a big rock. When I looked closer, I saw leftover chalk on a lot of cracks and edges, so other climbers must have used them, but the whole thing was dotted with them.

"How do I know where to go?" I asked Lily.

She sat on the grass in a patch of sunlight, leaning back on her elbows. She hadn't even opened up her pack yet. She looked tired, and I remembered how she had missed school the day before. Was she still feeling sick?

"Well, gym rat," she said, "you don't. You have to figure it out. Climb whatever looks fun. My favorite, though, is to traverse the entire length of it, starting from the left and ending by climbing up the far right corner there." She pointed to a jagged outside corner at the end of the boulder. It looked dangerous.

"Aren't you going to climb?" I asked.

"I don't think so," Lily said, rubbing her temples. "I thought I was better, but after hiking in, I'm pretty tired and weirdly achy all over. I'll just relax in the sun for a while."

I felt bad. I mean, the only reason she was out here was for me. "We don't have to stay," I said. "Maybe you should, you know, be lying down at home."

Lily gave what looked like a forced smile. "Are you kidding me?" she said. "You saw my family. It's far more restful out here. Climb all you want. I'm in no hurry." She leaned back and used her pack as a pillow. "Besides, you have to practice for the comp. It's only a week away."

I nodded and, still feeling a little guilty, walked to the far-left end of the boulder. I dipped my hands in my chalk bag and stepped up to the rock. *Real* rock. I grabbed an obvious hold at eye level and stepped onto small, but positive footholds. I heard the birds and felt the sunshine on my shoulders. I felt the warm stone under my fingers. I was home.

I closed my eyes for a second and listened for the rain. It wasn't there. For a second, I was worried, but then I realized I was relaxed, calm, and focused. There was no need for the rain.

I started traversing to the right. The moves were difficult, but they came naturally, and I felt fluid as I crossed the wall, like I was performing a delicate, choreographed dance that no one had to teach me.

And then I fell off.

I was only six inches off the ground, so falling consisted of simply stepping down. I didn't mind. The traverse was fun, the moves interesting, and I was on *real* rock.

"Hook your right toe around that corner for balance, and then reach high and right for that crimper," Lily said, pointing.

I got back on from where I had fallen and tried doing what Lily said. It didn't work. Surprise, I was too short. However, I was able to do a slight variation to the move and made it past. Two moves later, I fell again. Lily gave another suggestion, and I worked it out. This went on for several minutes until I had done all the moves in the traverse except the final, serrated corner to the top. Yikes. It was time for a break.

I hopped down and found a good rock to sit on. As I sat, rubbing the tight muscles of my forearms, I noticed Big staring at me like I had two heads. "What?" I asked. "Is my scab falling off?" I reached up to feel my nose.

"No," he said. "It's just that I hardly recognize you."

"Why wouldn't you recognize me?" I asked.

"He's never seen you climb," Lily said.

"What does that have to do with anything?"

Big shook his head. "You're like a different person when you're on there"—he pointed to the boulder—"than you are at school or even right now."

"Yep," Lily said.

"What are you two talking about?" I asked.

"Well, you pretty much rule as a climber, yeah?" Big said. "But that's not it exactly. You're different when you climb—your body language, your expression. It's like you finally let your guard down, and I see the real Paul, but that's not quite it either." Big cocked his head at me. Then he said, "I got it." He leaned forward in his chair and spread his hands out wide. "You look *powerful*, brah."

# Chapter 15

It was all I could do to force myself to roll out of bed on Monday and groggily go through the motions of survival all day. In Language Arts, Lily told me to come to the climbing gym after school, and she would introduce me to the third member of our team.

"You'll like her," was all Lily said.

Her?

All the climbing teams had to be coed, but I was certain most of them would have two guys and one girl. Not the other way around.

When I arrived at the climbing gym, I immediately checked the Bildungsroman scoreboard. "Rabbit" was no longer the lowest score. Anne was below me along with another name I didn't recognize. It felt good not to be the lowest thing in the room for once.

"Hey, Paul," Lily called and waved me over. "Come here."

Lily stood on the edge of Andy's class just as he started the lesson. She leaned down and whispered in my ear, "Sorry, I guess we better wait until after class. Don't leave. I'll come find you." She squeezed my bicep and turned to join the class.

I decided that having a girl whisper in your ear is one of the finer pleasures in life, even if the girl doing it has been known to punch you in the face and order hits on people.

Andy had gathered the class around a vertical section of the bouldering wall where he had half a dozen ropes heaped in piles. Above each pile of rope, a quickdraw was clipped to a bolt in the wall about ten feet up. I desperately needed to learn how to clip the rope through a quickdraw properly when leading, so I lingered, watching. Besides, I wanted to look the class over and see if I could pick out who our other teammate might be.

Andy demonstrated two different techniques for clipping that looked simple enough. Then he had everyone pair up to practice. Here was my chance. Whoever Lily paired up with had to be the new teammate. Unfortunately, there was an odd number of students, so Andy ended up being Lily's partner.

One partner would pretend to be leading and the other would belay. It wasn't a real lead because they were practicing on the short bouldering wall. If anyone missed the clip and fell, they would land on the padded floor and be fine.

Lily tied into the rope while Andy belayed. She climbed up to the quickdraw in three long moves and clipped it smoothly. It looked like she had done it a million times. I was glad to see her master the technique so easily, but I was also a little jealous. My first clips on Bildungsroman had felt like I was wrestling a greasy, writhing snake into the quickdraw.

Hunter and Anne were right next to Lily. After clipping a few times the way Andy showed her, Anne asked, "Why is the thing you clip the rope through called a quickdraw?"

"I'm honestly not sure," Andy said.

"It sounds like something out of a cowboy movie," Hunter said in his high-pitched voice.

Anne held her hand just off her hip like a gunslinger. Then she reached down for the rope and clipped it into the quickdraw as fast as she could. "Did you see that?" she said. "I'm like Billy the Kid."

"That's pretty fast," Hunter said. "Bet you can't do it left-handed."

Anne switched to her left and did it almost as fast.

"Nice," Hunter said. "Let me see that again."

When Anne tried to clip the second time, Hunter intentionally held the rope too tight. Just as Anne got the rope to the quickdraw, it came up short and shot out of her hand.

Anne laughed. "That's cheating."

Hunter replied, "Okay, I'll give you enough slack this time. Go ahead."

Anne tried again, and Hunter did the same thing. They were both laughing pretty hard. Anne said, "Knock it off. I'm going to fall."

I wondered if their game bothered Andy, but he was chuckling and didn't seem to mind.

Hunter said, "Okay, okay, I'll stop. Go ahead, I won't do it again, I promise."

"Whatever. I don't trust you," Anne said.

"Look, here's all the slack you need." Hunter pulled an arm's length of rope through his belay device.

Anne looked down at him suspiciously. Hunter smiled up at her, but clearly he was up to something—Anne knew it; we all did.

"No way," she said. "I'm down-climbing. I'm done. It's your

turn anyway." She acted like she was reaching for a lower hold but instead grabbed for the rope and tried to clip it before Hunter could react.

Hunter was ready and gave the rope a little whip so that it flew out of Anne's hand again. The whip also caused Anne to lose her balance and fall.

It would have been funny except that, on her way down, Anne got tangled in Lily's rope and pulled her off too. Anne landed on her feet and tumbled onto her back, laughing. She didn't realize Lily was about to crash down right on top of her.

"Look out!" Lily yelled. She tried to twist away from Anne in the air, but there was nothing she could do.

Just then, Hunter tackled Lily to the side. It was like in the movies, when someone is about to get hit by a bus or something, and the hero dives into them and knocks them out of the way. Only, I guess in this particular instance, it was more like the hero tackled the bus out of the way. Hunter undoubtedly saved Anne from serious injury.

Hunter and Lily did not fare so well. Hunter clutched at the top of his head as blood started gushing everywhere. Lily did the exact same thing only with her chin.

Even as blood began to pour between her fingers, Lily said through clenched teeth, "Are you okay, Hunter? You're bleeding bad."

"Does it *look* like I'm okay?" Hunter snapped and then groaned. He sat with one hand on his head and the other trying to stop the blood from dripping on the floor.

I felt light-headed. The blood was so red. So very red. As if from far away I heard Andy yell at someone to bring the first-aid kit. Then some girl I didn't know yanked her shirt off, crouched down next to Lily, and held it against Lily's bleeding chin. The girl had a tank top underneath, so it wasn't too weird, but she had the whitest skin I'd ever seen. As if through a fog, I saw the girl's milk-white skin next to Lily's black skin, and the red, red blood everywhere. White and black and red. And then I passed out.

# Chapter 16

You passed out?" Big clarified for the third time at school the next day.

"Well, yeah. I told you, I don't like blood."

Big started laughing again. "Like you actually fell over, unconscious?"

"Yes. I mean, have you seen blood before? It's disgusting. And it was all over the place. There was like a fountain of it bursting out of Hunter's head and from Lily's chin, and it was *so* red. You wouldn't believe how red it was. It was unnatural." Fifteen hours had passed, but I still shuddered at the memory.

"But blood is about as natural as it gets, yeah?" Big laughed even more.

I wanted to be mad at him for getting so much amusement out of my fainting, but he practically hugged me with that huge smile when he looked at me. How could I get mad when I was in the deep, warm embrace of his smile all the time?

"Then what? What happened when you woke up?"

"Well, that's when the only good part of the whole thing happened. So there's this girl, well, woman really—she's pretty old, like in her twenties or something—and she works at the climbing gym. She's really hot. I'm not even kidding. Anyway, when I woke up, she was kind of half-carrying, half-dragging me over to a bench. The only problem was, I couldn't really appreciate it properly because I was feeling all woozy, and I thought maybe it was all just a dream or something. Like, I was dreaming that I was a little kid again and my mom was carrying me, you know?" I hadn't meant to include the part about my mom, so I quickly added, "It was pretty cool being held by someone that hot."

Big laughed so hard he collapsed backward into his locker and slid to the floor.

I waited while he got himself under control. It took a while. Everyone who passed gave us strange looks, but they were smiling too. Some even started laughing and walked on, shaking their heads.

"Weren't you embarrassed?" Big asked while gasping for air.

"I guess, but she's so hot, I didn't care." I shrugged. "It's like getting saved by a sexy lifeguard when you're drowning. I mean, sure, it's embarrassing to have to get saved and all, but if the smoking-hot lifeguard is giving you mouth-to-mouth or whatever, who cares about being embarrassed?"

This got Big laughing again. I was starting to enjoy myself, too. I don't usually make other people laugh on purpose, so this was a nice change. A couple of guys walking by gave me a "what's with him?" look. I shrugged, and they smiled and kept walking. I saw one mime smoking a joint, and they both laughed. This was not helping Big's reputation for being a pothead.

Then my spidey senses kicked in big-time. I looked around and saw a pack of jackals coming down the hall, led by none other than Conor Dolores. They hadn't noticed me yet, and my first instinct was to disappear, which I could have done if I'd been alone, but I was with Big, and Big does not disappear, not even if he wanted to. And definitely not in a bright-orange Hawaiian shirt.

I tried to get Big's attention. "Um, Big?" He had actual tears coming out of the corners of his eyes from laughing so hard. "Um, Big?" I tried again. Still nothing. I grabbed his shoulder and shook him and said louder, "Hey, Big!" When I finally got his attention, I whispered, "Conor's coming." By then it was too late.

I heard Conor come up behind me and say to his friends, "Hey, check these two out." Then he shoved my shoulder and said, "I heard you fainted last night like a pansy at the sight of blood."

What? How did he know that? Did he have friends in the climbing class or something? I turned around and took a step away from him, careful not to make eye contact. "Oh, uh, yeah. I kind of did," I mumbled.

Big stood up next to me and said, "How's it going, Conor? Wow, those are some nice shoes. Are those the new Nike Hyperdunks? Man, I wish I had some of those."

I didn't look up, but I could hear the smile on Big's face. Did he really think his happiness ray could beat Conor's cloud of doom? And when had Big become a shoe connoisseur? All I ever saw him wear were flip-flops. And why was he commenting on a jackal's shoes anyway? Was it some kind of diversion?

I couldn't help it; I looked at Conor's shoes. We all did. Me, Big, Conor, and all of Conor's pack. The shoes were perfectly clean. Not a single scuff. There was this weird pause while we all pretended to admire them. I got the sense Conor was making a decision, and everyone was waiting to see what it was.

Conor sneered at Big. "What do you know about basketball shoes, *fatty*?"

Uh-oh. I snuck a glance up. Conor had stepped right up into Big's face. Classic alpha-dog behavior—showing dominance by stepping into the other guy's personal space. Big should have either stepped back in submission, avoiding eye contact, or asserted *his* dominance by staying put and staring Conor in the eye. But he didn't do either.

Instead, Big ignored Conor's question and poked his head around him to look at the other five jackals, all sophomore jocks.

"Hi, Justin. Hi, Ben," Big said. "How did you guys do on that quiz in science?"

A lanky kid with a buzz cut and a stocky one with braces—I didn't know which one was Justin and which one was Ben—looked at each other, then at Conor, then back at each other. Finally Buzz Cut said, "Okay, I guess. Got a B." He paused, then added, "Thanks to you, Big."

Braces said, "Yeah, Big, you really saved us with that study group."

Big stepped around Conor. "I told you guys you'd do fine. I knew you had it all along." He reached out to bump knuckles with Buzz Cut, who hesitated long enough to steal a glance at Conor, but Big turned on his happiness ray brighter than ever, and Buzz Cut couldn't resist. He bumped Big's fist and so did Braces. They cracked a few jokes about the science class, and, pretty soon, Buzz Cut introduced Big to the other jackals in the pack.

I moved along behind Big, keeping him between me and

Conor, and using his shadow as camouflage. Conor seemed to forget I was there. He just stood there, scowling and silent. He must have been wondering, like me, what just happened.

Somehow, Big had taken a pack of vicious, hungry jackals and made them part of our little herd. It should have ended in our humiliation and possible bodily harm, but Big worked his magic happiness ray and made friends instead. I'd never seen anything like it. The next thing I knew, Big was waving goodbye to all his new friends.

Of course, Conor couldn't leave without a parting shot. As he and his pack walked off, he said loud enough to be sure Big could hear it, "Why do you like him? He looks like a huge Hawaiian pumpkin in that stupid shirt."

Braces said, "He's not so bad."

Just before they turned the corner, Conor looked back over his shoulder and said, "I'd kill myself if I was that fat."

Once they were gone, my fear turned to anger. Where were the rhinos when we needed them? Maybe they weren't so bad after all. Someone needed to keep jackals like Conor in check. I wondered if Lily would put out another hit on Conor for Big and me.

Then I realized that Big had totally saved me. He'd put himself in harm's way for my sake. Conor had attacked me with the whole "fainting like a pansy" thing. Big stood up and drew his attention, so I could escape into his shadow.

My anger turned to gratitude, and I said the only thing I could. "Thanks, Big."

Big didn't say anything.

I looked up at him, expecting to see his face twisted with hurt or anger. But Big just stared down the hall where Conor and his friends had gone. His expression looked . . . sad? Concerned? Thoughtful?

I tried again. "I realize what you did for me, and, well, thanks." Still nothing.

Big was far away in whatever sunshiny beach his thoughts had wandered into. Then his smile broadened, and he nodded to himself like he'd decided something important.

I tried one last time. "That was really cool of you to help me out like that. You know—with Conor. I'm sorry he's such a jerk."

Finally, Big came back down to my world and noticed me standing there. "Who's a jerk?"

Was he joking? Nope. Big really didn't know who I was talking about. "Conor. The biggest jerk in the whole school." I thought about Hunter and added, "Well, one of the biggest."

"Oh, well, his friends are nice, yeah?"

"Okay," I said, trying to make sense of the utter nonsense coming out of Big's mouth. "Well, it was really amazing how you refused to let Conor get to you, and you turned all of Conor's friends to your side. That was an amazing trick."

Big cocked his head in confusion. "What trick?"

I was stunned. "You know, the way you totally refused to let Conor draw you into a fight and diverted everyone's attention by pretending to be their friends and talking about science quizzes and all that. *That* trick."

"I wasn't pretending. Justin and Ben really are my friends." Big paused as if assessing the truth of his last statement. Then he chuckled and said, "They just don't know it yet. You can call that a trick if you want. I just call it being friendly, yeah?"

"But you stopped Conor from picking on me, and somehow

managed not to get beat up in the process. That was on purpose, right?"

"I don't think he wanted to start a fight, not really. He figured you for an easy target and didn't expect me to step in. I just gave him a way out, yeah?" Big's face lit up with that crazy smile of his and he said, "And those really were some cool shoes."

"But he said horrible things about you. Doesn't that bother you?"

Big thought about it. "Yeah, but we both know Conor's dealing with a lot, right now. I feel bad for him. I was thinking maybe we could take him a treat. Maybe some cupcakes, yeah?"

"Are you kidding?" My anger came back in a flash. "I want him to get eaten by a grizzly bear, not take him cupcakes."

Big's excited smile changed to a disappointed grimace. I hated to destroy his happiness ray, but he was crazy, and he needed to know that before he got himself killed.

"Big, if we show up at Conor's house with cupcakes, he's *not* going to say, 'Oh, thank you so much for being understanding that my mom is crazy and I'm having trouble dealing with that.' No, he's going to murder us. Don't you understand? He's going to make you pay for what you just did."

Big let out a long sigh and shook his head. He looked at me with so much disappointment, I couldn't meet his eyes.

"Okay, I shouldn't have said that about Conor's mom," I mumbled. "It's just that he said cruel things about you, and you're talking about taking him a treat. Just because his mom is . . . not well, doesn't mean he gets to be a jerk."

"He acts like a jerk sometimes, but you saw the way he held his mom when she fell in the store. He deserves cupcakes for that at least, yeah?"

No. No, I did not think that. Not. At. All. I really, really wanted to say no.

"Yes," I said.

"Great." Big was all smiles again.

"Big, you're missing the point. You just made a dangerous enemy."

Big waved my comment away. He made his voice low and conspiratorial. "We'll go right after school. We'll leave the cupcakes on the porch with a note, ring the doorbell, and then run. That way he can't murder us."

I tried to picture Big running. Nope, I couldn't.

"Fine," I said. "But only because you helped me out. Who knows what Conor might have done if you hadn't stepped in when you did." I sighed in frustration. If I went with Big, I couldn't go climbing. On the other hand, I wasn't sure I wanted to go to the gym if there were still bloodstains on the floor.

"Now, tell me what happened after you fainted and got carried away by the hottest *woman* on the planet."

I laughed, and most of my anger disappeared. "So I sat on the bench with the lady's arm around me, hoping I would never have to move while Andy, the manager of the gym, and this other guy who was climbing there—he was an ER nurse or something—bandaged up Hunter and Lily. He said they'd both need stitches. Hunter's cut quit bleeding pretty fast. Lily's, on the other hand, never did stop. I could tell the nurse guy was really worried. He kept having to change the bandage because it would get all soaked with blood." I shivered again. "It was still bleeding pretty bad when Lily left."

Big's face turned serious. "Really? It wouldn't stop? That doesn't sound good. Have you seen Lily yet today?"

My chest tightened, like Big's concern was contagious. "No, I looked for her earlier, but I didn't see her."

Then the bell rang for class.

Lily wasn't in Language Arts, so I texted her. I didn't like getting my phone out in class—I didn't want to be called out for breaking the rules—but I managed to sneak a few texts off. Besides, it was cool to have someone to text other than my dad.

Luckily, Mr. Teller had us working in pairs on a worksheet about the symbolism of the rabbits in *Of Mice and Men*. Extra lucky for me, he let us choose our own partners, so I was working with Big. Mr. Teller corrected papers at his desk and never even looked up.

> Me: *Where are you? Hope you are ok.*
> Lily: *I'm fine. 8 stitches. I had to go to the hospital today for a bunch of lame tests. Are you texting in class right now? Or did you skip?*
> Me: *Very funny. Yes, I'm in class. Why are they doing tests?*
> Lily: *Texting in class?! You rebel! Doc is worried because I took forever to stop bleeding. Plus, he didn't like how much I've been sick lately and some other stuff. It's just a precaution.*

I felt my chest get tight again, like an invisible vise was being slowly cranked closed. I hated doctors and hospitals. I never went near them if I could help it. I didn't even like to hear about them. I mean, I knew they were there to help people and all that. It's just that I'd spent an awful lot of time waiting around hospital rooms with beeping machines and nurses and doctors all over the place and weird smells and tubes going everywhere as I watched my mom just sort of slowly disappear into the bed like it was eating her alive.

I felt a hand on my shoulder give me a little shake. "Hey, brah. What's wrong?" Big whispered.

I handed him my phone so he could read Lily's text.

"That doesn't sound so bad. You scared me. You went all pale and were breathing funny. I thought maybe you were going to faint again, yeah?" He smiled to show he was joking.

"It sounds bad to me," I said. "I mean, what are they testing her for? Doctors don't just do a bunch of tests for no reason."

He shrugged and handed my phone back to me. "Ask her if we can come by tonight. We'll take her some cupcakes, too."

*Me: Can Big and I come by tonight?*
*Lily: Only if Big brings a treat!*

"What did she say?" Big asked.

I showed him the text.

Big let out a loud snort, and half the class snickered. "She read my mind, yeah?"

From a few rows away, Conor said, "Who let the pig in?" but no one laughed. A few girls next to him gave him a dirty look, and someone else said, "Shut up, Conor."

Mr. Teller looked up from his desk just long enough to say, "Get back to work," and then went back to correcting papers.

I was pretty shocked that other students had come to our defense. Well, I guess they'd come to Big's defense to be exact, but still, it was pretty cool.

Conor put on a fake expression of innocent confusion, held

his hands out, and mouthed "What?" to the nearby girls. Then he laughed and went back to his assignment.

I whispered to Big, "What time should I tell her?"

Big held up five fingers.

*Me: See you around 5.*
*Lily: Okay.*

# Chapter 17

Despite how much I really didn't want to take a treat to Conor, I found myself standing behind a bush at the edge of his lawn later that afternoon holding a box of cupcakes. I felt like Little Red Riding Hood with her basket of goodies walking up to the den of a hungry wolf in broad daylight.

It didn't help that there was a bronze sculpture of a life-sized, howling coyote standing in the flower garden. Conor's house was surrounded by a perfectly manicured yard that led up to a huge, red-brick house with big white pillars. The place was, of course, perched high on the mountainside overlooking Ogden.

Big's mom parked around a corner a few houses down and waited with the engine running. She seemed to get a kick out of the whole thing and kept referring to herself as the "getaway driver." Big stood beside me, smiling like crazy and sweating in the afternoon sun. "You ready, brah?"

"I guess," I mumbled.

"Okay," he said. "Let's go." He started across what was practically a mile of lawn to the front door.

"Wait," I said and pulled him back behind the bush. "Are

we going to ring the doorbell or just leave the cupcakes on the porch?"

"Ring the bell."

I looked down at Big's flip-flops. "Um, maybe we should just leave them. I don't think we'll get away without them seeing us if we ring the bell."

Big studied the front porch. "We can't just leave them. They'd sit in the sun and get all gross. Or there might be ants or a stray dog or something, yeah? We have to ring the bell, and maybe drive by later to be sure they got them."

This was going to be a disaster. There was only one way we were getting out of the situation unscathed, and I didn't like it one bit. "Look, Big, let's be smart about this. You're in a bright-orange shirt—not exactly good camouflage. Plus, I'm not sure how fast you'll be able to run in those flip-flops."

Big looked down at himself and frowned. "What are you trying to say?"

"Just that maybe you should be the lookout, and I'll go up to the door."

"By yourself?" Even the perpetually optimistic Big seemed to hesitate.

"I can do it. I'm small and fast and pretty sneaky when I need to be. Don't worry." I was very worried.

Big smiled again. "A ninja who delivers cupcakes. I like it."

"Okay, wait here and get ready to run." I still couldn't believe what I was doing. "Maybe even start running early. I'll catch up."

I started across the lawn, feeling exposed, vulnerable, and ridiculous. I kept looking at the windows of the house to be sure no one was watching me. I was glad to see blinds on every window, though it was kind of weird that they were all closed tight. Conor's family must not have liked sunlight too much, I guessed.

I got all the way to the driveway with no problems. Now, to make it to the front door. As I took a step, I heard the sound of a car coming. I turned and glanced out to the street. Big was standing on the sidewalk frantically drawing his hand across his throat. In a total panic, I scampered across the driveway and ducked behind two big garbage cans just as a car pulled in.

I crouched behind the cans with my heart pounding in my chest. Flies buzzed around my sweating forehead, but I didn't dare move even to wave them away.

I heard the garage door open, but for some reason, the car stayed in the driveway. For a full minute, I sat there, freaking out and thinking that at any second Conor was going to jump out of the car and grab me. I could hear muffled voices, but nobody got out. Just when I was ready to ditch the cupcakes and run, a car door opened. I froze.

A woman's voice said, "I don't need any more pills." She sounded angry. "You just want to medicate me into a stupor, so I don't mess up your perfect little life." I couldn't see her, but it was definitely Conor's mom. Her voice was imprinted in my memory forever. She was standing on the other side of the garbage can barely five feet away.

"You know that's not true," said a man I assumed was Conor's dad. He sounded exhausted. "It's for your own safety. I don't like the medication any more than you do, but until we can work something else out, it's for the best."

"Best for *you*, maybe. They make me feel like a zombie. Like I'm not even alive. And they make me fat." She started to cry.

I heard Mr. Dolores walk around to her.

"Don't touch me!" Mrs. Dolores yelled.

"Okay, okay," Mr. Dolores said. "I'm not touching you. There's no need to yell. Please, just go inside. Samantha and Conor should already be here. They'll stay with you until I get back from work. We can talk about this later when I get home, okay?"

"Of course you have to leave. You always leave." Mrs. Dolores switched to a high-pitched, mocking voice and said, "Oh, no, my wife's off her meds again, oops, I guess I'll go to work." She laughed shrill and high.

"Honey, please. I haven't been able to get any work done all day. You know that. Do you think I want to leave you like this? It terrifies me. Please, just go inside."

Mrs. Dolores continued laughing in a way that made me squirm. "Are you even going to your office?" she asked. "Maybe you have a cute little intern somewhere. Is that it? I get all fat and ugly and crazy and you . . . you . . ." Her laughter abruptly turned to tears. "You get a girlfriend."

"Please don't do this, honey. Not right now. Let's go inside."

"Who is she? Is it that new legal assistant? The blonde one who's always wearing the tight skirts? It is, isn't it? I can tell by your face."

"Don't you see what's happening?" The sadness and exhaustion in Mr. Dolores's voice made my chest ache. "You're getting paranoid again. Every time you quit taking your medication, this happens. I love *you*. *Only* you."

"I know exactly what's happening!" Mrs. Dolores screamed.

I heard the sound of a door opening and closing from the direction of the house. Then Conor's voice said, "Mom?" It echoed like he was in the garage.

Mrs. Dolores kept talking. "I know why you want me on those pills. You want me to be so out of it that I won't notice you're sleeping around."

"Mom, are you okay?" Conor's voice was closer now.

"Well, I got news for you," Mrs. Dolores continued. "I'm finished with pills and doctors and—you know what? I'm finished with you." There was a loud smack, and Mr. Dolores groaned.

Conor yelled, "Mom! Stop!"

I heard a bunch of feet shuffling and multiple people crying, I wasn't even sure who. I think it might have been all three of them. The sounds slowly worked their way into the garage, and then I heard the door to the house shut.

It was quiet. It was as if the big, unhappy house had opened its mouth and swallowed them all whole. For a while, all I could hear was the sound of my own heart beating in my ears. Eventually, I noticed the buzzing flies, birds chirping, a lawn mower in the distance. Now what?

Almost like a robot, I got up, walked around the black BMW in the driveway, and made my way to the front porch. I set the basket down in front of the huge wooden door with a big brass knocker. I rang the doorbell and walked off. I didn't try to hide or anything. I didn't even bother running. I felt like I'd torn out a bloody chunk of my heart and left it lying behind the garbage cans for the flies. Big met me halfway across the lawn, and we walked back to his mom's van in silence.

# Chapter 18

For the first time in my life, I was in a teenage girl's bedroom. It should have been momentous for me: the mythical lair of the female. Who knew what secrets it held? What dark mysteries would be revealed?

Lily's room showed me a whole new side of her I didn't know existed. Sure, there were posters of climbers next to posters of country music singers, but there were also about a hundred stuffed cows of all shapes and sizes covering a chair and her bed. And there were big white flowers all over the place. Pictures of them, and fake ones in vases. Even the wallpaper had white flowers on it.

I don't know what I was expecting: a collection of assault rifles? Medieval armor? All I knew was that I wasn't expecting a room full of cows and flowers, that's for sure.

I also wasn't expecting to be sitting at the far end of Lily's room in a little window seat, trying to shake the feeling that a chunk of my heart was missing.

It almost felt like the time I crashed on my skateboard and chipped a tooth, leaving a nerve exposed. Something that should never be exposed *was*, and even the tiniest current of air made it hurt in a very unique way. I did everything I could to keep anything from touching it. That's how my heart felt. So I sat, a safe distance from where Big and Lily were sitting on Lily's bed.

"Tell me about something beautiful, Big."

"I thought you'd never ask. Let's see." Big grinned and rubbed his chin in a theatrical way to show he was thinking deeply. "The most beautiful thing I saw today was—"

"But *why* did they have to do blood tests?" I blurted. Lily had showed us her stitches and told us how the doctor ran some tests, but she didn't say why. Apparently, the idea bothered me more than I thought.

"I told you, Paul, I don't want to talk about it. I want to hear about something beautiful. Now, what was the most beautiful thing you saw today, Big?"

The whole situation was weird. Especially Lily being evasive about the tests the doctor ordered. What was wrong? Why didn't she want to talk about it?

There was one thing in the room that felt exactly right. A big flag hung on the wall. It was bright red with a white, football-shaped shield in the center and crossed spears behind it. On the shield was a design with four long, vertical black lines and a black dot in the middle. A bold, tribal-looking flag of white and black and red—now *that* felt like the Lily I knew. Not flowers and stuffed cows.

"Courage," Big said.

"What do you mean?" Lily asked.

"I mean that I watched a good friend of mine do a courageous act, and it was beautiful."

"Oh, really?" Lily said. "And who might this friend be?"

"He's been known by many names: Little Dude, Brah, Paul, and, most recently, the Fantastic Fainting Rabbit."

I scowled at Big. Who told him about the rabbit thing? Why did all these people know things about me they shouldn't?

Lily laughed, cut it short, groaned, and said, "Don't make me laugh. It hurts my head."

"Where you hit your chin?" Big asked.

"No, it's one of my headaches. They never seem to go away anymore. Tell me more about this beautiful act of courage."

Big cleared his throat as if preparing to do a dramatic voice-over for a movie trailer. "The Fantastic Fainting Rabbit—aka Paul—went on a relief mission to deliver super-tasty supplies to the home base of one of his greatest enemies. I had the opportunity to watch as he courageously overcame his fear of death to complete the mission at all costs." His voice returned to normal, and he said, "Oh, and I also saw a girl at school fold a piece of paper into a crane. It was awesome. She even let me have it."

"Wait, who did you deliver treats to, Paul?"

I looked at Lily. She was propped up on her bed by a giant pile of pillows with a small bandage on her chin. She was smiling at me. It was nice: a little Novocain for my exposed nerve.

"You know what, though?" Big went on, as if he hadn't heard Lily's question. "It wasn't the crane that was beautiful. It was the girl's hands, yeah? Watching them fold the paper . . . It was like her hands were dancing."

"Hold on a second," Lily said. "I want to know where Paul delivered treats."

"A beautiful origami dance of creation." Big fluttered his fingers in the air.

Lily laughed and then held her head. "Paul, will you please

tell me who you took treats to before Big says anything else about some strange girl's hands? It's creeping me out."

I took a deep breath. "Conor Dolores."

"What?" Lily's eyes went wide.

"Yeah, it didn't, uh, go so well," I said.

We told her the whole story, starting with the milk incident. Thankfully, Big left out the part where I bawled like a baby. Lily listened, her dark-brown eyes wide and her mouth partially open. I was reluctant to tell about it at first, but I noticed the exposed nerves of my heart felt better as I talked.

"I knew she was kind of . . . off," Lily said. "I think she has bipolar disorder or something like that, but I didn't know it was that bad."

"You knew Conor's mom had problems?" I said.

"Yeah, I just didn't know any details. That explains a lot."

I got angry. Part of me knew it wasn't a good idea to yell at Lily in her own room. You don't get invited into the tiger's den and then poke it with a stick. Still, I had to say something. "So you knew Conor's mom had, like, serious problems, and you still did what you did to Conor?"

"What are you talking about? When I punched him in elementary school? That was years ago."

"No, I mean siccing your brothers on him last Friday."

"What? I didn't . . ." Lily sat up. She looked angrier than ever, and I nearly turned and ran. "What did they do?" she growled.

"You don't know?"

"No, I don't know. I didn't *tell* them to do anything. I told them what Conor did during our presentation, but I said I handled it. What did those morons do?"

A huge sense of relief washed over me. First, the anger

twisting up Lily's face was not directed at me, and, second, that she wasn't the mafia boss I'd thought she was. She hadn't ordered a hit on Conor after all.

"They cornered him in a stairwell and, um, made him sort of bow to them."

"Are you sure it was my brothers? You said the other day that you didn't even know who they were."

"Yeah, it was them. They made him say 'Never mess with a Small' over and over. It was awful. I mean, Conor's pretty much the biggest jerk on the planet, but he was bawling like crazy."

"I'm going to kill them." Lily started to get up but then fell back onto her bed, holding her head. "After I feel better," she added. "They promised they wouldn't do anything like that. I told them I could handle it." She closed her eyes and rubbed her temples. "Man, I hurt *everywhere*," she mumbled.

"How can I help?" Big asked.

"Tell me about something else that's beautiful, Big. That helps."

"I'll tell you what's beautiful—all these flowers are beautiful. Are they all lilies?"

Lily looked around her room with tired eyes and a half smile. "Yeah, Madonna lilies."

"Is that what you're named after? The Madonna lily?"

"Sort of." Lily turned kind of shy. It was weird to see her that way, but nice, too. And cute. "When my parents were thinking about adoption, my mom was concerned about how they were going to afford it, and my dad quoted her that line from the Bible where Jesus talks about considering the lilies. You know the one? Anyway, right then, they decided to name me Lily."

"Oh," I said. I had no idea what line from the Bible she was talking about. "So is that the flag of Kenya?" I pointed at the red flag on the wall.

"No," Lily said. "That's the flag of the Maasai people. Many of them live in Kenya, though, and Tanzania. My dad calls me his little warrior. He spent some time in Kenya and loved the Maasai people he met there. I don't think I have any Maasai blood, but nobody really knows for sure." She was quiet for a while and then she smiled. "I do kind of *look* Maasai. They're known for being really tall and lean."

"You are absolutely Maasai," Big said. "Lily, the Maasai princess. I can totally see it."

"Warrior," Lily corrected. "Not princess. My parents adopted me when I was a baby, so I don't remember anything about Kenya. I've always lived here, and they've always been my mom and dad. Funny that I ended up tall, just like the rest of my family, though."

It was quiet again. Not awkward quiet, but kind of a nice quiet. We stared at the Maasai flag together. I didn't know anything about the Maasai, or even Kenya really, but Lily was right. She was a warrior. Beautiful and fierce at the same time.

Then Lily said, "The doctor thinks I have cancer."

# Chapter 19

I didn't see Big until I was on my way to Language Arts. I'd been dying to see him so I could tell him all the stuff I'd learned about leukemia. It still wasn't for sure that Lily had it, but the doctor had said he was fairly certain.

I was pretty freaked out, so I looked up a bunch of stuff about it. I didn't understand a lot of what I read, but it's essentially cancer of the bone marrow, and you end up with a bunch of white blood cells that don't work right. More importantly, I found out there was a good chance Lily would be okay. I mean, sure, it was going to be awful, and she would most likely have to go through all the horrible treatments, but the survival rate of teens with leukemia was around eighty percent. That sounded pretty good to me.

I saw Big in the hall ahead of me, wearing his yellow Hawaiian shirt. It was bizarre to see the way everyone's faces lit up as he went by. It was like he was carrying a basket of kittens down the hall. Seriously, how did he do that?

Instead of running up to talk with him, I hung back and watched. Almost everyone who passed him waved and said "Hi,

Big" or "What's up, Big?" There were people from all different cliques, grades, genders, and races. Apparently, Big's friendship knew no bounds. Several were cute girls, one was a teacher, and another was the jackal with the buzz cut from Conor's pack.

As Big passed some of the people, he would engage them in short conversations. To a kid wearing eyeliner and dressed all in black he said, "Markus, my friend, congrats on passing your driving test." To a girl I recognized as a student-body officer, he said, "Wow, I really like your hair, Stacy. That color is perfect for you. Reminds me of cinnamon, yeah?" And to a kid with dreadlocks and a full beard, he said, "Nice shirt, man. I love Cookie Monster. We're like brothers." The kid laughed and slapped Big on the back.

The more people Big talked to, the more nervous I got. He was becoming a school celebrity. Would he still want to hang out with me if he had all these people for friends?

I waited a minute after Big went into class before I followed him in. Lily was already there. She pulled her feet in so I didn't have to walk all the way around her legs. She looked surprisingly cheerful, but Big had probably just gotten done shining his happiness ray down on her.

"Hey, Rabbit," she said with a crooked smile.

"Hey," I mumbled. I wasn't sure if I liked her using my new nickname or not.

Big yelled loud enough for everyone in the room to hear, "Howzit, brah?"

"Good," I replied barely above a whisper.

"You coming to the gym today?" Lily asked as I sat down and got out my books.

"Are you?" I asked. "I thought, um, maybe you wouldn't be feeling up to it."

"I feel a lot better today. I still have a headache, but I'll live."

*Maybe. Maybe you'll live. You have about an eighty percent chance.*

Suddenly those odds didn't sound as optimistic as they did before.

We worked on a bunch of grammar and vocabulary words, and we spent the last half of the class reading aloud from *Of Mice and Men*. We were at the part where Lennie accidentally kills Curley's wife. I'd seen the movie, so I knew it was coming, but a lot of the students didn't. When it got to the part where it said, "And then she was still, for Lennie had broken her neck," there were a bunch of little gasps from around the room. I was surprised anyone was into the book enough to care.

Katie said, "Wait, she's dead?"

Before anyone else could answer, Conor blurted out, "Yeah, she's dead. The retard killed her."

"Conor," Mr. Teller barked. "That is *not* a word we use."

"What? He is," Conor said with a sneer. A couple of students snickered.

Mr. Teller stared at Conor until his sneer faded. Then he turned to Katie and said, "Yes, Curley's wife is dead. Lennie accidentally broke her neck. He didn't mean to."

Conor raised his hand. Mr. Teller let out a sigh. "Yes, Conor?"

The jackal's sneer came back. "It wasn't an accident. He *broke* her neck." It was creepy to see the way Conor smiled as he said this. Like the prospect of a broken neck delighted him. "That would take a lot of force. The retar—I mean, the guy wrapped his big, fat arms around her head and cranked on it so hard he snapped her spine and killed her. That doesn't sound like an accident. That's straight-up murder."

I hadn't thought about it that way. I hated to admit it, but Conor had a point.

Big raised his hand, and Mr. Teller let out another sigh. "Yes, Big?"

Big took a second before he spoke. His characteristic smile was gone. He looked right at Conor and said, "You're right. It wasn't an accident. Lennie killed her. He was scared, and he didn't understand how strong he was. When you think about it, he's not so different from a lot of us, though. We go around, wrapped up in our own little world, scared of things we can't always control, and that fear causes us to do cruel things to other people, yeah?" Big nodded like he was agreeing with himself. "We're all a lot like Lennie. We don't realize the impact we have on those around us. People that are fragile, like Curley's wife—we hurt them, and we don't really understand how much."

"I'm not going around breaking anybody's neck," Conor scoffed.

"Don't you get it?" Lily said. "He's not talking about *literally* breaking someone's neck."

"There are lots of ways to be fragile, yeah?" Big continued in his soft voice. "And there are lots of ways to break a neck. Sometimes it's just a little bit at a time."

# Chapter 20

I went straight to the gym after school. I wanted to arrive early and talk to Lily alone before her class started. I walked in and let out a huge sigh of relief. All the tension of the day slid off me as I took in the usual smells and sounds of the gym.

Andy was at the front desk. As soon as he saw me, he said, "You ready to give Bildungsroman another go?"

"Not right now," I said. "I need to talk to Lily." I couldn't believe I was turning down a chance to climb with Andy. What was the matter with me?

"I haven't seen her yet today." Andy pulled out his phone and looked at it. "Class doesn't start for another fifteen minutes. How about I give you a quick belay?"

"Um, I, uh . . ." I looked around as if Lily might suddenly appear. When she didn't, I said, "Sure, alright."

Andy grinned. "That's what I'm talking about."

I glanced at the Bildungsroman scoreboard. There were at least five new names I didn't recognize on it, and all of them were in the upper twenties. The highest score was now hold number thirty.

"Wow," I said. "Someone made it to thirty? Nice."

"Some guys from Salt Lake heard about it and came up to give it a try earlier today," Andy said as he led me over to Bildungsroman at a fast walk. I had to jog to keep up. Stupid short legs. "They were pretty full of themselves and thought they'd make short work of it." Andy grinned. "They left a lot more humble."

I laughed because it seemed like what Andy expected, but it was fake. If guys were coming from as far as Salt Lake to try Bildungsroman, and they couldn't do it, what business did I have on it?

I got ready to climb and tied in. "Ready?" I asked.

"Go for it," Andy said.

I made it to hold seven without any trouble. Once I clipped the second quickdraw, Andy said, "Right on. You've got this dialed."

I liked that I'd impressed him with my progress, but now I was at the part where I had to cheat. Even though Andy was the one who told me to pull on the quickdraw in the first place, I wanted to give the move one more try. I took a few deep, slow breaths and listened for the rain. There was nothing.

I willed myself to move, but I couldn't focus. Should I jump for hold number eight like I had twenty times before? That was guaranteed failure. What else? There was the worthless blue chip. Could I use that somehow? I felt it with my left hand. No way. What about my feet? I hung off hold number seven, the baseball-like one, with both hands, scrunched my body up into a little ball with my butt sticking out, and poked the toe of my left foot into the pocket. There. Now I was climbing . . . but I had to move fast.

Now what? Could I reach hold number eight? Nope. If I were as tall as Lily, I could have reached straight to hold number nine and not wasted my time on this move. An image of Lily covered in all that red, red blood flashed through my mind. Lily, who probably had cancer.

I shook my head and tried to focus on the next move. I'd have to slap for the orange edge—hold number eight—but how? I couldn't move, and I was about to slip at any second.

Another image of Lily appeared in my mind. I could see her so clearly lying in the sun up at the boulder field. Lily, all long and black. I told myself to knock it off and focus. What now? My hip. That's it. Drop my knee and put my hip into the wall.

Instead, I thought about Lily again—who I suddenly realized I liked a lot more than just as a friend.

And that's when I fell.

"Good effort," Andy said as I swung back and forth on the end of the rope like a pendulum. "I think you might be onto something with that little blue chip. With some work, you should be able to get the orange crimper, no problem."

I thanked Andy for the belay, and he lowered me to the ground.

"I better get to my class," Andy said as I untied. "We'll try again tomorrow."

After Andy left, I found a chair that gave me a good view of the climbing class. Bildungsroman had sucked the desire to climb right out of me. Despite what Andy said, I was never going to make that move. I was too short, too small, too weak, and too unable to focus because I couldn't stop thinking about Lily. If I couldn't get Lily out of my head, then I might as well sit where I could stare at her.

Andy's lesson that day covered techniques for climbing cracks. There was a section of the gym with fake cracks in the walls formed out of some kind of cement similar to real rock. The cracks ranged in size from so skinny I could barely squeeze my fingertips in to so wide my whole fist could fit with room to spare. The cracks reached from the floor to the ceiling.

The cracks were supposed to mimic the fractures that occur in real cliffs, but all I knew was that I hated them. I had tried climbing them once before, and they just plain hurt. It was no fun to try to wedge my fingers and toes in those stupid things. I never made it to the top and only came away with bloody fingers and sore toes to show for my efforts. No thanks.

Andy showed the class several different techniques for climbing the cracks, but I was too busy watching Lily. She stood at the rear of the class, her back to me. Her feet were wide apart, her calves flexing as she rolled up onto her toes and back onto her heels with restless energy. Her thick cornrows fell halfway down her back.

I couldn't imagine a universe where a girl like Lily could have cancer. This girl who looked like a truck couldn't knock her over. This girl who looked like a tall, elegant tree planted right there in the gym. This Massai warrior. No way. It had to be a mistake. I'd never seen anyone so healthy.

After Andy finished his demonstration, the students paired off to try climbing the cracks. When Lily's turn came, she danced up the wall. I'm not kidding. It looked like ballet. I'd never seen her climb so well. She was in a tank top, and her shoulders and arms glistened with sweat. Her long muscles were corded and taut. She looked like a river at night, reflecting the stars, flowing up the wall. Powerful, graceful, a force of nature. She was beautiful.

I was in love.

Or was I? How would I even know? Maybe I just thought she was hot, and the whole thing was nothing more than a bunch of hormones. But I'd seen plenty of hot girls, and I wasn't in love with them. It never even crossed my mind.

But Lily was six-four! The top of my head didn't even come up to her armpit. The whole thing was ridiculous. Even if I was in love, which I wasn't at all sure I was, it was pointless. It's not like I could take her to the homecoming dance or something. The two of us slow dancing would be highly awkward, to say the least. If I said anything about us being more than friends, she would just laugh. Everyone would laugh. Even *I* would laugh. The whole notion of us being together was astronomically absurd.

Lily finished the climb and lowered to the ground. She switched places with a girl who was her polar opposite. The girl was tiny, skinny, and white. So white that if Lily was like a river at night, then this girl was like a stream of milk. A very thin stream of milk. I wondered if she was the same one who had pulled her shirt off to soak up Lily's blood.

Right then, Lily turned and looked around. When she saw me, she waved for me to come over. I hesitated. Lily was belaying only a few yards away from Hunter. It seemed like a bad idea to get between two apex predators, even if I was friends with one of them. When I didn't move, Lily gave me a confused look and waved for me to come over again. In the end, I was more afraid of disappointing Lily than I was of being killed by Hunter. I got up and walked over.

"Have you tried this?" Lily asked, gesturing to the crack climb.

"Yeah," I said.

"It's *so* cool. We have to go crack climbing outside. It's a blast." As Lily spoke, she periodically pulled in rope for the girl she was belaying. "Andy said there's some good crack climbing down by Salt Lake City. But he said the best stuff is down in Canyonlands. A place called Indian Creek. We should road trip down there. Wouldn't that be great?" I had never seen her so animated.

"Um, I guess." I watched out of the corner of my eye as Hunter snuck a glance at us.

Lily looked up and yelled to the girl climbing, "Nice work." Then she turned back to me and asked, "What? You don't like crack climbing?"

"Not really. They just hurt. Plus, I'm, uh, kind of terrible at it."

Lily laughed. I loved hearing her laugh. It wasn't like the one in the courtyard last week that floated around like butterflies, but it was a nice laugh. It made her eyes shine, and her smile made me go all warm inside.

"Did I hear that right?" Lily joked. "There's a type of climbing Paul Adams isn't good at? I didn't think it was possible."

"Oh, it's possible. You should have seen me stink up Bildungsroman a few minutes ago. I was awful."

Hunter was openly watching us now, and my spidey senses tingled.

Lily's climber reached the top and said, "Take." Lily took up all the slack in the rope and pulled it as tight as she could. Her climber said, "Ready to lower." We could barely hear her. She'd need to speak up if she wanted Lily to know what she was saying.

"Lowering," Lily called up to her and let the rope slide through her belay device. To me, Lily said, "I saw on the scoreboard you got to hold seven. That's not too bad."

"Yeah, but that's as far as I'll ever get." I saw Hunter lower Anne to the ground and start to unhook from the rope.

"What are you talking about?" Lily said. "If anyone can do it, you can. We should try it when class is over."

"No, really, I can't. I'm too short."

"I bet you'll figure it out," she said. "Will you at least belay me on it?"

Belaying Lily meant that my whole job would be to do nothing but sit and stare at her. "Okay," I said, warming up to the idea the more I thought about it. "Yeah, that sounds good." It didn't just sound good. It sounded *great*. I'd have Lily all to myself with no one to steal away her attention.

"Cool," Lily said. "Sam's been wanting to try it, too."

"Who?" I asked, distracted because Hunter was walking toward us.

Hunter said, "Hey, Lily."

Lily had her back to him and didn't seem to hear. She finished lowering the skinny girl she'd been belaying to the ground and said, "Oh, yeah, I almost forgot. I haven't introduced you two yet. Paul, this is Sam—the third member of our team for the climbing competition."

Lily was talking about the skinny girl, but that couldn't be right. Sam was a boy's name.

Hunter interrupted, "You asked *Sam* to be on your team?"

Lily turned around. "Oh, hey, Hunter," she said. "Yeah, Sam, me, and Paul are going to enter."

"What about *my* team?" Hunter asked. His voice rose even higher than normal.

"What about your team?" Lily asked.

"You said if you were going to enter, you would be on my team."

"I never said that."

"Yeah, you did. The other night at your house when I came over to work out with Chuck and Colt and you answered the door."

"I didn't say I was going to be on your team. You offered, which was nice of you, but I said I wanted to put together a team of my own."

Hunter looked from Lily to me like this was somehow all my fault. I took a step back and looked at the ground.

"That's not what you said," Hunter said. "But, whatever. If you want to lose, go ahead." He walked back to where Anne was gathering up their stuff and didn't look back.

"That was awkward." Lily gave what sounded like a forced chuckle.

"Aren't you worried he's going to, I don't know, kill us in our sleep or something?" I asked.

"Hunter?" Lily said with a smirk and a wave of her hand. "No. He's been coming over to my house to hang out with Chuck and Colt for a couple of years now." My unease must have been showing on my face because Lily looked at me and then added, "Don't worry." She punched me in the shoulder and said, "I can handle him."

I knew Lily could handle him. It was me I was worried about.

"So, who's this, um, Sam person?" I asked, hoping to change the subject.

"This little rock star standing right in front of you," Lily said.

For the first time I really looked at Lily's climbing partner. Apparently, Sam wasn't just a boy's name. And now that I had a good look at her, she was definitely the same girl who had used her shirt to soak up Lily's blood. She had freckles, blue eyes, and brownish-red, frizzy hair. Her arms looked too skinny for her to be much of a climber.

"You two get to know each other, and I'll go ask Andy if we can try Bildungsroman." Lily walked away, leaving Sam and me to stand there, staring at our feet.

"So," I said, trying to think of anything to say. "How long have you been, um, climbing?"

She said something I couldn't hear above the noise of the gym. I stepped closer and leaned in. "What? You have to talk louder."

She took a deep breath and said barely above a whisper, "I've climbed for years. I mostly climb outside when I can. I've seen you here before, though."

I couldn't remember ever having seen her at the gym other than the time Lily cut her chin open.

"You're really good," she added when I didn't say anything. She was hugging herself in a way that reminded me of a little bird trapped in a cage, wishing it could flutter away. This was one seriously shy and awkward girl. I was still standing there, trying to figure out what to say when Lily came back.

"All right, team," Lily said with a smile. "Andy says we're done with class. Let's get on Bildungsroman."

How could Lily be so cheerful? If I were her, I would have been home in bed, complaining about how unfair life was. I pretty much did that every day anyway, and I didn't have cancer.

As we walked over to the prow, I whispered to Lily, "Should you even be entering the comp? I mean, you know—if you might be sick."

Lily stopped and frowned down at me. The bandage pulled away from her chin, and I could see the blue thread of the stitches. She grabbed me by the arm and said very seriously, "Knock it off, Paul. I'm fine. They don't even know anything yet."

Then her eyes got that crazy, death-ray look, only it wasn't aimed at me. More like she was shooting it out into the world at large.

"And you know what? Even if I do have cancer, I'm not going to let that stop me. Forget cancer. I'm going to do what I love and hang out with my friends and enter climbing comps and climb every crack in the whole Utah desert if I want." For a split second, her lip trembled before she bit down on it. She let go of me and started walking again. "Now, who's climbing first?" she said.

My dad and I had pancakes for dinner that night. We were having one of our silent conversations. They happened quite often in our house.

He looked at me, and waited. He knew something was wrong.

I knew he knew something was wrong.

He raised his eyebrows: *Do you want to talk?*

I focused on drowning a chunk of pancake in syrup: *No, not yet.*

He continued to eat for a while: *Okay, whenever you're ready.*

I let out a big sigh: *I want to talk, but I don't know where to start.*

He gave a little nod: *Start with what's most important.*

"Lily might have cancer," I blurted.

My dad froze with a bite of pancake halfway to his mouth. An amber drop of syrup fell onto the table. "What?"

"She split open her chin at the gym and it wouldn't stop bleeding and she's been pretty sick lately and they did a bunch of tests and they're pretty sure it's leukemia, but they're still waiting for the final official test or whatever it is. She might die. Of cancer." My voice cracked, and my eyes burned. "Like mom."

"Oh," my dad said. He set his fork down, pancake uneaten. He leaned back in his chair and ran his hands through his hair. He looked up at the ceiling. Then he said in his Zen-dad voice, "They don't know for sure yet."

"No."

"She's young and strong and healthy."

"Yes."

"Her odds of beating it will be good."

"Eighty percent," I said. "I looked it up."

There was a long pause. "Just because your mom passed away, it doesn't mean Lily will."

"I know," I said, but I didn't. Not really.

"No, you don't," my dad said.

"I never should have made friends with her. This is *your* fault."

"You really care about her."

"I was doing just fine, and *you* made me apologize to her. I wouldn't even know any of this was going on if it weren't for you. And now I think I might be—" I clamped my mouth shut and put my face in my hands.

"Might be what?" my dad asked.

I raised my face from my hands and stared hard at him: *I think I might be in love.*

"Oh." My dad's eyebrows shot up. "Oh," he said again.

# Chapter 21

ig found me in the courtyard before school the next day. There were low, dark clouds overhead trying but mostly failing to rain. I was sitting, hoping the rain would whisper to me again. It didn't. The wind was blowing little whirlwinds of leaves and garbage around. Dirt kept blowing in my eyes.

It was not beautiful. Not even Big would be able to find beauty here this time. The sky was gray. The concrete courtyard was gray. My mood was gray. Big, however, was red. Bright red. He came in with his XXXL Hawaiian shirt shining like a tropical sunrise.

"Howzit, brah?"

His huge smile almost made me smile, but I was ready for his happiness ray, and looked away before it could have any effect on me.

"Nothing much," I said.

"Wow, look at that." Big pointed at a crack in the concrete a few feet away.

I looked, but all I saw was the crack and a weed growing out of it.

Big walked over to the weed, crouched down, and kind of petted it. "Can you believe this little guy can grow here?"

"It's a weed. They grow everywhere."

"It's a dandelion. Which means some little dandelion seed came parachuting in, probably on a windy day just like this one, and drifted right into this little crack. Then we had that rain last week, and it must have managed to find enough nutrients from what little bit of sand and dirt get jammed into the crack. It's a miracle, yeah?"

"You're weird."

Big continued, "Despite all the odds, it's about to bloom here in this place of all places. In a day or two, there will be a little spot of bright yellow in this gray courtyard." He shook his head like he couldn't imagine anything more amazing. "Beautiful," he said.

"Whatever you say, Big. It just looks like a weed in a crack of an ugly, gray chunk of concrete to me."

"You just wait, brah. You'll see." He stood up and walked over to me. "Are you ready for the climbing comp next weekend? I'm going to come cheer you on. Lily told me you were climbing some crazy-hard building thing last night. You guys are going to dominate."

"Bildungsroman," I said.

"What?"

"Bildungsroman. It's the name of the route we were climbing last night at the gym. A really hard one."

"Huh. Sounds German. Anyway, Lily said you did really well, yeah? She said you and Sam were on fire. I didn't even know Sam climbed—did you?" He sat down next to me and squinted to keep the blowing dirt out of his eyes.

"No, I didn't." It turned out Sam could climb really well. She had made it all the way to hold ten last night, but she had to cheat the same move I did. I couldn't help but be impressed even if she did have toothpick arms. "You know Sam?" I asked.

"She's in my choir class."

"She sings?" There was no way the painfully quiet Sam could possibly sing.

"Like a bird," Big said.

"Wow." Everything I thought I knew about Sam shifted with this new information. "Have you seen Lily? I was looking for her before I ended up here."

Big's smile shrank. His voice got quiet, and I could barely hear it over the wind. "No, she's not coming today."

An alarm went off in my head. "Why? What's going on?"

"She has an appointment with the doctor. They get her test results back today. They find out if she has leukemia for sure."

My stomach was in knots for the rest of the day. I sent Lily a text asking how she was doing, but she never replied.

Worse, I had to stay after school to get some help with geometry. I hated math, but the real problem was that the halls were extra dangerous after most of the people had left. Without a herd to blend in with, I couldn't hide as easily.

After leaving my geometry class, I walked through the halls with my spidey senses on full alert. I'd almost made it to the front doors when I saw a red Hawaiian shirt sitting on the steps.

I was about to walk up to Big when I heard some snickering and shushing. My spidey senses started tingling like crazy. I looked up and saw Conor with two other jackals I didn't recognize on a stair landing fifteen feet above Big's head. They were shooting spit wads through a straw at Big. I saw a few white specks in Big's hair where they had already successfully hit their target.

Big was leaning over, looking at something on the ground near his feet. Of course, knowing Big, it could have been anything from a smear of mud to a squashed piece of gum. Whatever it was, Big was oblivious to Conor and his pack. I really needed to teach him a thing or two about evading predators.

I hesitated. Nobody had seen me yet. I could sneak away, and none of them would ever know I'd been there. A few weeks ago, that's what I would have done without hesitation—but then I'd made friends with Big and Lily. Now things were a lot less black-and-white.

I couldn't sit there and let Big continue to get hit, but what could I do? If I said something, Conor would turn his attention to me. At the very least, I'd take a few direct hits from some spit wads and who knew what else. It occurred to me that I might even escalate the whole situation.

On the other hand, if I stayed quiet, chances were the jackals would grow bored and leave. Big would have to endure nothing worse than finding a few chunks of paper in his hair and wondering where they came from. That wasn't so bad, was it? I decided to sneak away.

Then Conor quit shooting spit wads. Instead, he held a 44-ounce soda cup over the edge of the stairs. The other jackals grinned and nodded encouragement.

"Big! Look out!" I yelled and ran toward him. I didn't know what I was planning to do. Dive in front of him and take the hit? Would that even work with a soda bomb?

I never got a chance to figure it out because I was too late. Before I was halfway there, the cup, which was most definitely full, exploded on Big's head.

Conor's loud and unnerving laugh echoed down to us from above. He looked at me, and we made eye contact for a long, weird second. His eyes were blue, intense and unstable. They reminded me of someone else, but I wasn't sure who. Then Conor yelled, "Freaks," and the three of them ran off, laughing hysterically.

I walked up to Big. He mopped streams of pop off his face. "That kind of hurt," he said and rubbed his head. "And it was a total waste of a perfectly good soda, yeah?" He didn't sound all that upset. "Thanks for the warning," he added.

"Too bad it didn't do any good. Sorry I didn't warn you sooner."

"That's okay, brah."

I could see at least ten spit wads in his hair. "What were you doing?" I asked.

"Oh, no!" Big frantically scanned the step below where he was sitting. "Oh, good," he said with a sigh of relief. "He's okay."

I looked to see what he was talking about. It took me a while, but I finally saw an ant carrying a chunk of what looked like a potato chip. It had narrowly missed being drowned in a flood of soda pop. "You were looking at an ant?" I asked. I don't know why I was shocked. I should have been used to this kind of thing from Big.

Big nodded. "You wouldn't believe it," he said, seeming to

have already forgotten he'd been drenched with a soda bomb. "This little guy has carried that potato chip all the way from over there." He pointed to a crumpled, foil chip bag under a bench twenty feet away. "I've been watching him for the last thirty minutes, just stumbling along beneath the ginormous weight of the chip. It's amazing, yeah?"

"You've been watching an ant carry a potato chip?"

"Sure have. I got worried about him when he started across the stairs, so I sat a few steps above him to make sure no one squashed him. He's probably got, like, a whole ant family waiting for him at home, yeah? Think of his triumphant return when he shows up with that chip. I can imagine all the other ants cheering and waving." Big shook his head like he could hardly believe how amazing it all was.

"Big," I said, exasperated. "Conor shot spit wads at you and hit you with a gallon of soda pop."

"Spit wads?"

"Well, I assume so since you have some in your hair." I cringed at my half lie, but I couldn't bring myself to tell him I'd watched him get hit a few times before I decided to intervene.

"Eww, gross," Big said, feeling around in his hair.

I helped him pick them all out. "Doesn't it make you mad at all? I mean, you took Conor cupcakes, and this is what you get in return."

"I don't think he knows we took him cupcakes, yeah?"

"That's not the point. Maybe we need to get Lily to sic her brothers on him again. Teach him a lesson, you know?"

"That's not cool, brah," Big said like the whole idea was silly. "And you know how Lily feels about that. Speaking of Lily, have you heard from her? I've been worried all day."

"No," I said. "I texted her, but she never texted back." I took out my phone and glanced to see if anything had changed. There was a text. From Lily. "Oh, wait." I sat down next to Big. I didn't even care that I sat in a big pool of soda pop. I opened the text so we could both see.

*Lily: Went to doc. It's official, I have cancer. Yay for me.*

# Chapter 22

Lily wasn't at school again on Friday. This time, I knew she wouldn't be there. She texted me that she wanted another day to "process everything" and wouldn't let Big or me come over. She also texted to say that, just because she had cancer, it didn't mean I was getting out of the climbing competition. She told me to meet her and Sam at OCC on Saturday so we could train as a team.

Big came into Language Arts wearing his bright-blue Hawaiian shirt. He gave me a high five and said, "Howzit, brah?" I nodded in return and acted like it wasn't totally weird for me to give someone a high five.

While we were working on grammar, Mr. Teller got a phone call. After he hung up, he told us he had to step out of the class for a second and that he'd be right back. It's been my experience that when a teacher leaves the room, bad things happen to people like me. I slouched down further into my seat and did my best to turn even more invisible than usual.

It was quiet for a minute while people continued to work on

their assignments, and then I heard Katie whisper to Conor, "I heard you threw a drink at Big yesterday."

Conor, not whispering at all, said, "Yeah, after school, Bryson and Mitch and me dropped a huge one on him from like twenty feet up. It was awesome. Perfect shot. Pop went all over—"

Katie punched him hard in the shoulder.

"Ouch!"

"How would you like it if I chucked a drink at you?" Katie was no longer whispering.

Another girl chimed in, "Yeah, Conor. What did Big ever do to you?"

Then this gangster guy named Blake said, "You hit Big with a drink, bro?" Blake was the guy who had wondered if I'd skipped a few grades on the first day of school.

Conor said, "Yeah, and we hit him with, like, a hundred spit wads, and he didn't even—"

Katie punched him again.

Conor was half-laughing, but he was kind of mad, too. "Stop hitting me. We were just fooling around. The runt was there. He saw. It was funny, right, dude?"

All eyes turned to me, and my mouth dropped open, but no sound came out.

I was saved by Blake, who said, "I'll tell you what, bro. If you do anything to Big again, I'll personally make you regret it." Blake wasn't that big of a guy, but he didn't look like someone you'd want to mess with. Maybe all the gangbanger clothes and silence and broody expressions were just for show, or maybe he liked to sell drugs and do drive-by shootings in his spare time. Who knew?

Conor leaped to his feet. "Oh, yeah, tough guy?" he said, throwing his arms out wide. "I'd like to see you try."

Blake leaned back in his chair like he was getting more comfortable and smiled. His crooked teeth made him look even more like a killer. He gave a little nod and said, "Bring it."

Big said, "Hold on. We can talk about this. There's no reason to get excited."

A girl I didn't really know said, "Yeah, Conor, calm down and quit being such a spaz."

Josh Richmond piped up next to me. "Seriously, Dolores, knock it off. No one wants to see you get your face kicked in today."

"Yeah, chill out," someone else said, and most of the class nodded in agreement.

Conor's blue eyes went all crazy, and he kind of spun in a full circle, taking in the fact that almost everyone in the room was against him. "What? You're taking *their* side? The gangster wannabe and the human blimp?"

I didn't need my spidey senses to know he was about to lose it.

Big stood up. He held his hands out the way people do when they think a dog might bite them. "Conor, no one is taking sides—"

"I am," Blake said. His tone was calm and matter-of-fact.

Conor spun to face him again, but Blake stayed slouched in his desk and smiled like he found Conor's freak-out amusing.

Big gave Blake a pleading look.

Blake shrugged. "I'm just say'n."

Big said in a quiet, almost sad voice, "Conor, why don't you just sit down and—"

Conor turned on him. "Why don't you shut up, you fat

freak!" At the same time, he picked up his grammar book and threw it at Big. The heavy book had a hard cover with sharp corners. It would have done some serious damage to Big's face, but he ducked, and it crashed through the window behind him. Shards of glass rained down on the chair Big had been sitting in.

Every jaw in the room hit the floor, even Conor's.

"Mr. Dolores!" Mr. Teller yelled from the doorway. In one synchronized movement, everyone turned from the broken window to the door. "Go to the office, *now*!"

# Chapter 23

When I arrived at the gym Saturday morning, I spotted Lily right away. Before I could even say hello, she said, "We only have one week before the comp. Do you guys already know how it works?"

It was only then I noticed Sam. She was the first person I'd ever met who seemed to have better camouflaging skills than me.

Sam and I both shook our heads.

"Fine," Lily said like she was exasperated with us not being up to speed, but I could tell she liked being in charge. She explained that the competition would consist of ten routes set up in the bouldering area. Each team would have ten minutes on each route to get as far as they could before a buzzer sounded. Each member of the team would get a point for every hold they were able to reach. That meant we would have to climb fast to accumulate as many points as possible before the buzzer. There wouldn't be time to work out a difficult move. It would just be go, go, go.

So that's what we practiced. We picked a bunch of random routes in the bouldering area and used Lily's phone as a stopwatch. Then we pretended we were in the actual competition. We got some weird looks from other climbers, but I didn't care. I was climbing with Lily, and it was fun to try to cram as much climbing as we could into such a short amount of time.

Despite signs that Lily was not feeling great, she and I climbed fast. Sam, on the other hand, was a slow and controlled climber. She liked to contemplate her next move and know exactly what she was going to do before she did it. She climbed almost as well as Lily and I did, but it took her twice as long. We developed a strategy where Lily and I climbed first and as fast as we could, leaving Sam with as much time as possible. Sam often ran out of time before she finished, but I admired her precision and single-mindedness.

As our practice session wore on, Lily became more and more exhausted. Her muscles trembled, and she fell off holds I knew would never have caused her any trouble before. By the time we rotated to our tenth route, Sam startled me when she spoke for the first time that day. She said in her barely-above-a-whisper voice, "Maybe it's time to stop, Lily."

"I'm fine," Lily said. She still hadn't caught her breath from the last route. She wasn't fine.

I said, "Yeah, Lily. Why don't we quit for now? We got a good system going."

"I said I'm fine," Lily snapped.

"Samantha? Samantha? Where are you?" I heard a woman yell above the noise of the gym. The voice sounded familiar.

A woman I recognized but couldn't quite place came around the corner into the bouldering area. She was probably around forty years old, and dressed like she was on her way to a yoga class. Her tight clothes showed how skinny she was. She was even skinnier than Sam. Her hair and makeup were all done up like she'd spent hours getting ready that morning. And Conor Dolores was walking beside her.

"Oh, there you are," the woman said to Sam. "I texted you ten minutes ago that we were here to pick you up. Don't you ever check your phone? Did you get a chance to practice with your team? I hope you're ready for the contest."

"It's a competition, Mom, not a contest," Conor said.

"Oh, whatever. Competition, contest—tomato, tomahto." Mrs. Dolores let out a shrill, loud laugh that went on long enough that everyone within earshot looked at her.

I don't know how it was possible, but Conor seemed to just then notice Lily towering over him. He looked up at her and then down at me. "You've got to be kidding me, Sam," he grumbled. "Tell me this isn't your team."

Mrs. Dolores gave Lily a nervous glance, like she thought Lily was going to mug her or something. She grabbed Sam by the arm, steered her a few steps away, and said. "Where is your team? I'd like to meet them."

Sam looked from Lily to me with an expression of near panic in her eyes. She seemed unable to speak. I don't know why she bothered looking at me, though. I was too busy trying to process why Conor and his mom were here at all and talking to Sam as if they knew each other.

Lily stepped forward. "Hi, I'm Lily, and this is Paul." She grabbed my arm and dragged me next to her. "We're Sam's teammates."

"Oh," Mrs. Dolores said, looking up at Lily. "Oh," she said again, looking down at me. "I thought this was for high school students?"

Conor snorted.

"We're *both* sophomores at Fairfield High," Lily said. I heard the safety click off on Lily's death ray.

Mrs. Dolores didn't seem to notice. "Well, this is"—she appeared to be searching for the right word—"unusual." Then she laughed that shrill, overly loud laugh again. "It's time to go, Samantha. Are you ready?"

Sam finally found her voice. "I'll be there in just one minute."

Mrs. Dolores gave Lily and me one last look and shook her head. "Okay, but don't take long. We'll be waiting in the car." As she and Conor walked off, I heard her say, "Couldn't Samantha have picked a better team? I mean, that little boy looks like he's ten years old. And that black girl . . ." Mrs. Dolores made a tsk-tsk sound. "She isn't normal either, is she? Samantha's going to look ridiculous climbing with those two."

After they were gone, Sam turned to us and said, "Sorry about that." As she picked up her backpack and stuffed her climbing shoes and chalk bag into it, it finally dawned on me that Sam's real name was Samantha. And she was Conor's sister. "I have to go, but would you guys want to . . ." Sam's voice was so soft, I couldn't hear the rest of what she said.

"Would we want to what?" Lily asked, and we both leaned in so we could hear better.

The close proximity seemed to frighten Sam. She took a nervous step back and said a little louder, "Would you guys want to go climbing tomorrow?"

"I'd really like to, but I can't," Lily said. "We're visiting my grandma tomorrow."

Sam looked at me like she was waiting for something. Was she asking me if I wanted to climb? Like, even if Lily didn't come?

I assumed Sam was really asking Lily, and I just happened to be standing there. When Lily said no, I figured that was that.

Sam looked at the floor and said so quietly I almost didn't hear her, "What about you, Paul?"

"Oh, uh, I, um . . ." It sounded great—but she was Conor's sister. Did I dare climb with the sister of a jackal? Then again, I climbed with Lily, and she was the sister of the rhinos. Besides, how bad could it be if we just climbed together in the gym? "Well, uh, sure, I guess," I finally managed to say.

Sam nodded without looking at me. "Okay, I'll pick you up at nine." Then she threw her pack over her shoulder and left.

Lily said, "I guess we know where Conor gets his winning personality from."

"Did you know Sam was Conor's sister?" I interrupted.

"Well, yeah."

"You *purposely* asked Conor Dolores's sister to be on a team with us?"

"Yeah, I—"

"What were you thinking?"

Lily folded her arms and narrowed her eyes in warning. "She's my friend," she said in a low, even voice. "She has been ever since I met her in the climbing class. Just because she happens to be the older sister of a jerk like Conor doesn't mean she isn't nice."

"But . . ." I choked. I didn't dare say what I really wanted to say for fear of Lily turning her death ray on me. I finally managed to say, "You should have told me."

"I thought you knew," Lily said, seeming to relax. "Besides, Sam's a great climber. She's okay in the gym, but wait and see how well she climbs outside. You'll be glad I introduced you then."

"What do you mean *outside*?"

"When you go climbing with her tomorrow."

"Wasn't she talking about climbing here in the gym?"

Lily smiled her crooked smile at me. "No, Rabbit, she's taking you to do some *real* climbing."

# Chapter 24

"Trust me, I'm not any happier about this than you are," Conor said.

I stood in front of the open passenger door of Sam's Jeep. Conor had gotten out to fold the seat forward, so I could get in the back. What was *he* doing here? How had my spidey senses failed me so completely? Should I run? Make an excuse that I was sick? How was I going to get out of this?

"Get in already," Conor said. "Do you need a boost or what?"

I still couldn't move.

Conor grabbed me by the arm and practically shoved me into the car. He folded the seat back into place, climbed in, and shut the door. I felt like I was being abducted, and I was going to die.

Sam pulled out onto the street. "My dad made me . . ."

"What?" I asked, leaning forward. "I couldn't hear you."

Sam took a deep breath and said a little louder, "My dad made me bring him." I met her eyes in the rearview mirror, and then she added, "My parents left for the day, and they didn't want him home alone."

Conor shot Sam a look that rivaled Lily's death ray. "That's *not* why I had to come," he said. "It's because Dad didn't want you climbing alone with some prepubescent munchkin he'd never met."

"I'll tell Dad if you say anything else mean," Sam said.

"Whatever." Conor waved her off. He let out a big huff of air and stared out the window.

How in the world had I managed to get myself into a very small Jeep with a strange girl I barely knew and her homicidal younger brother?

We reached the road where we should have turned to go to the boulder field, but Sam kept driving straight. Maybe I really was being kidnapped. "Uh, weren't we supposed to turn back there?" I asked, trying hard to sound casual.

Conor looked over his shoulder at me and sneered, "What are you so nervous about, runt?"

"I wanted to take you somewhere special," Sam said.

Conor snorted, but kept his mouth shut after Sam gave him a look.

"Oh," I said.

After I endured a very long and nervous minute, Conor looked back at me again. He laughed, but it didn't sound as malicious as usual. "Sam, you better tell him where we're going. He thinks we're taking him out to the middle of nowhere to kill him and dump his body."

I was surprised at how accurately Conor managed to voice my thoughts. Maybe he was more insightful than I gave him credit for.

Sam looked at me in the rearview mirror again. "It's not far."

That wasn't very reassuring.

Conor laughed again, flipping through a series of obnoxious radio stations.

We turned up a road that wound through one of the older neighborhoods in Ogden. It dead-ended in a small, gravel parking lot at the base of the mountain. Sam turned off the Jeep, hopped out, and went around to the back to get her gear. She had a bounce in her step I'd never seen before.

Conor, on the other hand, seemed to intentionally take his time. He groaned and stretched and eventually got around to getting out of the car. He looked around for a minute and then acted startled to see me. "Oh. I almost forgot you were back there, *brah*," he said. I bristled that he used Big's way of addressing me. Conor was *not* my brother. After a little more stretching, Conor folded his seat forward so I could get out. Jerk.

I looked around. There was not a rock worth climbing anywhere in sight. Just a dry riverbed leading into a parched canyon. "Where are we going?" I asked.

Sam shut the back of the Jeep and came around to the front, wearing a big pack with a coiled rope in her arms.

"Wait, uh, what do you need all that for?" Was she planning to do real rock climbs with ropes and everything? I wasn't ready for that.

Sam gave me a confused look. "What do you mean?"

Conor said, "We're going *rock climbing*, runt. Unless you plan on free-soloing everything, we're going to need some gear."

"I thought we were just, um, bouldering," I said.

"Oh," Sam said. I watched as her excitement visibly leaked out of her. It was like seeing a kid with a brand-new bike get a flat tire before even getting it out of the driveway. She looked at her feet and said, "I thought . . . Do you want to . . ." She took a deep breath. "We can go to the boulder field instead, if that's what you'd rather do."

The only real rock I'd ever climbed was the boulder the week before with Lily. Didn't I need professional training or something to climb with ropes outside? I was pretty sure there was some climbing rule somewhere that said, *Do not go rock climbing for the first time with a vicious jackal and his strange older sister.*

"Well, I, um, I told my dad we were going bouldering," I said. "I don't think he'd like it if I did any, um, big stuff or roped stuff or whatever."

Conor squinted down at me and shook his head. "Seriously, man? Don't be such a loser. For whatever reason, my weird sister wants to show you her favorite crag. It's important to her. So grab your stuff, and let's go." He grabbed the rope out of Sam's hands and started up the trail without looking back.

Sam said, "We don't have to climb here if you don't want to. The cliff is up in the back of that canyon. We call it the 'M and M Wall.' It has some routes I think you'll love, but we can go to the boulder field instead if you want."

"It's okay. I'm sure my dad won't mind. Let's go." I didn't even remember making a conscious decision to speak. The words just sort of fell out of my mouth. The next thing I knew, I had my backpack, and we headed into a secluded part of the mountains.

I followed Sam along a trail that angled into the canyon and then up the dry riverbed, watching lizards skitter out of our way every few minutes. As we worked our way up the canyon, it began to change. The trees grew taller, thicker, and lusher, creating much-appreciated shade. The grass turned from dead, straw-like stuff lying on its side, to tall, soft, green shoots that grew as high as my waist. The canyon got deeper and narrower, and there were hints of good rock peeking through the trees now and again.

A few minutes farther on, the canyon narrowed even more and made a sharp, left-hand turn. Right in the back of the curve, a huge quartzite cliff jutted up from the riverbed. I stopped and gawked. It was even bigger than the prow at the gym. Three jagged cracks that looked like lightning bolts snaked their way up the otherwise blank face. I wasn't a very good judge of height, but they had to be close to a hundred feet at the highest point.

"We're here," Sam said.

"Wow," I whispered.

Sam smiled at me, and her blue eyes sparkled. I could tell she was happy that I was impressed. She dumped her pack at the base of the cliff and started sorting through a mountain of gear.

I couldn't believe my eyes. There had to be well over a thousand dollars' worth of gear—a dozen quickdraws, assorted lengths of webbing, carabiners linked up to form short chains, two dozen of those colorful spring-loaded things you jam into cracks to catch you if you fall—Sam called them "cams"—and some wired aluminum wedges called "nuts."

It quickly became clear that Sam and Conor had done this many times. While Sam sorted through the gear, picking and choosing select pieces and clipping them all onto a single runner, Conor flaked the rope into a pile so it would feed out easily without tangling. When he was done, Conor said, "I get the first lead."

Sam gave him a strange look, but I couldn't tell what it meant. They had a long staring contest, and then Sam said, "Fine."

They both put on their harnesses, and Conor switched to his climbing shoes. After that, he tied into the rope, and Sam handed him the sling with all the gear she had selected on it. He put his head through the sling and hung it over one shoulder so it ran diagonally across his chest with all the gear over his right hip. He looked like a pro climber from a magazine.

Sam clipped the rope through her belay device, and Conor asked, "On belay?"

"Belay is on."

"Climbing."

"Climb on."

Conor started up the left of the three cracks. It was wide enough to slide his whole hand into it. Sometimes it got wide enough that he made a fist inside the crack to lock it off. Unlike at the gym, he used little edges outside of the crack for footholds as often as he was jamming directly into it. He lacked Sam's precision or Lily's grace, but he was strong, and he moved with confidence bordering on arrogance. He climbed like he was angry at the rock.

When he was fifteen feet up, he still hadn't placed any gear. If he fell, he would land right in the rocky riverbed. There was no way he would escape a fall like that without a twisted or broken ankle.

"Put some gear in, Conor," Sam said.

"I know," he said, annoyed. Conor did two more moves—he was nearly twenty feet off the ground—then stopped. He reached down to the gear at his hip, selected one of the cams, stuffed it into the crack, and then clipped the rope to it using a carabiner. "Happy?" he said to Sam.

"No," she said, but I doubted Conor could hear her.

He powered through what looked to be a few hard moves with primal-sounding grunts, but he never seemed to doubt himself in the least. Despite his lack of style and finesse, he knew what he was doing.

I looked at Sam. "He's pretty good."

She didn't answer. She was frowning, watching Conor's every move without looking away. After he'd climbed ten more feet, she said, "Conor, please, place more gear. You're making me nervous."

I was getting nervous, too. If Conor fell now, he would plummet nearly to the ground before the rope caught him—and that was if the single cam he had placed held. This was real climbing, all right. Not like the gym at all.

"I will, just one second," he called down. He sounded like a bratty kid being reminded to do an unpleasant chore. He made one more move, got a wide stance on two big face holds, and placed another cam.

Sam's breath hissed between her gritted teeth. "Quit showing off and start putting gear in more often or I'm telling Dad."

"Seriously? You're threatening to tell on me? Grow up, Sam. And I'm not showing off. If I stop to place gear every two seconds, I'm going to pump out before I ever get to the top. Now, leave me alone and let me climb."

"He's so stupid sometimes," Sam whispered more to herself than to me.

"So, um, how do you know about this place?" I asked.

"My dad was the first to climb these routes," she said. "Him and one of his old climbing buddies. Do you know Hunter and Anne Bouda? They're in the climbing class?"

"Yeah." Unfortunately.

"Their dad and my dad grew up not far from here. They climbed together a lot and put up a lot of the first ascents in the Ogden area." Sam paused as she fed rope through her belay device. "My dad told me they were more like competitors than friends, always trying to one-up each other. Eventually, they had a falling-out and quit climbing together."

"What's the name of the route Conor's on?"

There was another delay before she spoke as she watched Conor climb and fed out more rope. "'The Best-Laid Schemes,'" she said.

"That's a weird name," I said. "What's it mean?"

"Not sure," she said. "My dad said it was a line from a poem or a book or something."

I watched Conor climb for a while. He placed another piece of gear and then made his way above the tops of the trees and into the morning sun. All I could see was his silhouette against the sky, and it was hard to tell what was going on. I hadn't heard the sounds of any carabiners being clipped, so I figured he hadn't placed any gear for a while. Judging by Sam's expression, I was right.

"I never should have let him lead," Sam said.

"So, um, what about the other two cracks?" I asked. "Do they have names, too?"

"Yeah."

When she didn't go on, I said, "And they are . . ."

"The middle one is 'Of Mice and Men,'" she said, feeding out more rope. "That's why we call the place the 'M and M Wall.' It's short for 'Of Mice and Men.' And the last one is—"

"Watch me," Conor yelled. "I'm at the crux." He sounded a little desperate.

Sam quit feeding out rope and quickly locked it off. "Place some gear before you go for it," she yelled. The volume sounded completely unnatural coming from her.

"Can't," Conor said. "I'm too pumped. I'm pushing through."

"No, Conor! Put in some gear—now!"

"Don't worry. I got it."

"He's so stupid," she spat. "It's almost like he *wants* to fall and get hurt."

We both squinted up into the sunlight to try to see what was happening. Judging by the combination of grunting and puffing I could hear, I didn't think it was going very well.

Out of nervousness, I started talking again. "So, um, 'Of Mice and Men.' That's the book we're reading in Language Arts right now. I wonder if that's where your dad got the name for this route? I don't remember the book saying anything about 'best-laid schemes' or whatever, though."

Sam didn't answer. She was too focused on Conor even though there was no way she could see what he was doing. She fed out the rope a few inches at a time as Conor made slow progress.

"What's the last route over there named?" I asked, pointing to the farthest-right crack.

Sam's face was sharp with tension. She had a strange stance for a belayer. Normally, when you're belaying, you stand square with the wall, facing it directly. Sometimes I even put one foot on the wall to brace myself if I think the person is going to fall. Sam, on the other hand, was standing perpendicular to the wall. Her stance was wide and her legs bent like she was getting ready to run a race. The rope stopped moving, and Conor turned quiet. There was a long moment of stillness. I could hear a bird chirping nearby.

Then the silence was torn in half by the sound of Conor swearing, followed by a ferocious growl that grew in intensity. "Falling!" he shouted, and I looked up to see his silhouette detach from the rock face.

Sam took off running away from the cliff and down the river-bed.

I looked after her in confusion. A good belayer was supposed to stand still and be ready for the yank on the rope that meant they'd caught their climber. I'd never seen someone take off at a sprint before. Then I realized Sam was trying to take as much slack out of the rope as she could to keep Conor from hitting the ground.

Conor's foot clipped a small edge and sent him cartwheel-ing through the air. As he spun, his gear fanned out around him like the outstretched wings of an injured, falling bird. He crashed through the highest branches of the trees and sent a shower of leaves and sticks raining down.

Assuming the worst, I closed my eyes, gritted my teeth, and waited for the sound of Conor splattering on the rocks beside me. Instead, I heard Conor grunt not far above my head. Everything became still and quiet.

I opened my eyes and looked up. Conor was five feet away, dangling at the end of the rope. Leaves flickered in and out of the sunlight as they drifted down through the air around him.

"Are you okay?" Sam called. She was twenty feet down the riverbed, flat on her back, clinging to the rope that stretched taut from the belay device clipped to her harness, up to the cam that had caught Conor's fall, and back down to Conor. There was a lot of rope between them, but they were securely connected.

"Yeah," Conor said almost in a whisper. He stared up at the cam that had stopped his fall.

"Are you sure you're okay?" I asked. How could anyone pos-sibly be okay after a fall like that?

"I think so," he said. Then he started laughing. Hard. Like a madman.

I stepped back, tripped on a rock, and fell flat on my butt.

Conor kept laughing, loud and shrill and all wrong.

Through his laughter, I heard Sam say, "Often go awry."

"What?" I asked. I had no idea what she was talking about.

"The name of this last climb," she said. She was sitting underneath the right-hand crack. "It's called 'Often Go Awry.'"

# Chapter 25

I couldn't wait to tell Lily about the crack climbs I'd done with Sam and about Conor's crazy fall. I knew she would love it. She wasn't at her locker Monday morning, so I figured she must be with Big. Big wasn't at his locker either. Where were they? Then I remembered the courtyard.

On the way there, I saw a tsunami of cheerleaders and their entourage coming my way. There must have been some kind of pep rally or something going on later because they were all in their uniforms and full of extra cheer. Too much cheer for me. I stepped into an empty doorway to avoid their excessive excitement and let them pass.

While I waited, I pretended to text like usual. Then I realized I didn't have to pretend. I really did have a friend to text. Cool. I sent Lily a text.

> Me: *Where are you? I went climbing with Sam. It was awesome! I have to tell you about it.*

The cheerleaders were gone, so I put my phone in my pocket and headed for the courtyard. About halfway there, my phone vibrated with an incoming text. I ducked into another doorway and pulled it out.

> *Lily: So jealous!! Wish I could have gone. I can't wait to hear all about it, but I'm not at school today.*
> *Me: Do you have a headache again?*

I waited for a minute, but she didn't respond. Why was she gone again? Was she getting worse? I was under the impression that cancer generally worked slow. She wouldn't be having problems already, right? My stomach turned sick thinking about it.

I turned a corner and found Big, surrounded by a group of kids. At first, I worried they were giving him trouble, but then I recognized Katie from our Language Arts class and, to my surprise, Buzz Cut and Braces from Conor's jackal pack. There were several others I didn't know, but they all hovered around Big like planets orbiting his yellow Hawaiian sun.

I hung back and waited for the bell to ring so I could talk to him alone. I didn't want to draw attention to myself by approaching him in a group. Everyone seemed nice enough, but you never knew.

My phone vibrated again.

> *Lily: No headache. Starting chemo today. Goodbye hair.*

Already? Didn't they ease into it? I didn't remember much about my mom's cancer, but it seemed like a very long, drawn-out process. I wondered if Big knew anything about it, but he was with all his fans, who were practically falling all over themselves to be near him.

I wanted to scream, *Hey, Lily is in the hospital dying of cancer! Don't you even care?* Instead, I turned to leave.

Big must have noticed me because he called out, "Hey, Paul?" I turned back around.

All the planets froze in their orbits and stared at me. Some looked at me with smiles, others with mild curiosity, a few with confusion, like they couldn't figure out who Big was talking to, because it couldn't possibly be the scrawny little kid in front of them.

"How was climbing with Sam yesterday?" he asked.

As usual, I stood there like an idiot with my mouth hanging open. Everyone was waiting for me to talk and, when nothing came out, a few of them started to laugh. I did my best to shoot Big with a Lily-style death ray for putting me on the spot. Then I turned and walked away.

Behind me, I heard Big say, "I'll see you guys later. I'm going to catch up with my buddy, Paul." I knew he was following me, but I kept walking. It was one of those rare times when being small pays off. I could weave through the congested hallway like a moped through a traffic jam. Big was more like a semitruck. He didn't stand a chance of catching me unless he started knocking people to the ground.

I knew I wasn't being rational. There was no reason for me to take out the fear and worry I was feeling for Lily on Big. He hadn't done anything to deserve my anger. Yeah, he'd made me feel dumb in front of his other friends, but I think my anger was more because Big *had* other friends. Friends besides Lily and me.

It had been my experience that if someone had a choice between being friends with me and being friends with virtually any other living thing on the planet, they would *not* choose me. Big obviously had other options, so it was only a matter of time before I'd be kicked out of his growing herd.

I reached the courtyard and went in. I knew Big would eventually find me here, so I guess on some level I wanted him to catch me. Maybe I just needed to feel like I was worth finding.

Sure enough, a moment later, Big came into the courtyard breathing hard. "You gotta slow down, brah. I can't keep up." He held his hand to his chest like he'd just run a race, but he was smiling. His bright yellow shirt reflected in all the windows and lit up the gray concrete around him.

His flip-flops echoed through the courtyard as he walked over to where I was sitting on our usual bench. He looked up at the sky and spun in a slow circle. "It's like being in the bottom of a well, yeah? Like when you look up at the sky from in here?" He cocked his head and added, "A square well, I guess. Is there such thing as a square well? There must be, because here we are, looking up out at the sky from the bottom of a square well."

I caught myself looking up at the sky, imagining I was at the bottom of a well. Why would I do that? It was infuriating how Big could get me to do stuff. His power of suggestion was impossible to resist. It was like he was a hypnotist and could get you to do whatever he wanted. I forced myself to remember I was mad at him and said, "You know, there's a good reason why people always think you're on drugs."

I saw Big flinch, and his smile drooped. He looked away from the sky and down at me. I felt like a jerk, and, for some reason, that made me more determined to stay angry. I was about to say something snarky like, *Why don't you go hang out with all your new friends?* but before I could, Big said, "How's our dandelion doing?"

I looked to where the weed was growing out of the crack in the concrete.

"It bloomed," Big said as he walked around the bench. Its bright-yellow face seemed to be looking up into the sky, like Big had done, hoping for a glimpse of the sun. He squatted next to it and patted its yellow head.

When you're as short as I am, people are always patting your head or ruffling your hair like you're a little kid or a dog or something. It's degrading, and it made me mad.

"Leave it alone, Big," I snapped. "It doesn't want to be patted like that."

Big looked at me. I felt stupid. I leaned forward, rested my elbows on my knees, and looked at the ground. Why was I being like this?

"What's wrong, Paul?"

"Lily's in the hospital," I blurted out.

"What? Why?" Big asked. "What happened?"

"Well, not the hospital necessarily. Or maybe the hospital, I don't know. Wherever you go to get chemo. She's starting chemo today. That's why she's not here."

"Oh . . ."

We stared at the dandelion for a while.

I said, "You probably knew that already, but Lily didn't tell me until this morning." Big started to answer, but I interrupted him. "And then I find you hanging out and laughing and joking with practically the whole school. Don't you even care?" My voice broke, and I clamped my mouth shut.

Big sat down on the bench beside me. "I didn't know she was starting chemo." His voice was low. His smile gone. "And I do care. I care very much. You know that, right?"

"Yes," I said, and I did.

"She doesn't tell me much, either. She's not really the type to open up, yeah?" He let out a big sigh and shook his head. "Does this mean it's bad? What will the chemo do to her?"

"I don't know for sure," I said. "It will be pretty bad, though. The chemo will make her really weak and tired. That's what I mostly remember about my mom. She slept all the time. I remember getting mad because she wouldn't play with me. She didn't have the energy, I guess. My dad said the chemo made my mom really nauseated."

I was quiet for a while. I'd never said so much about my mom to anyone other than my dad. It was hard, but it felt good, too.

I thought about one of the last memories I had of my mom. I remembered her coming home from the hospital after being there for what felt like a long time, but it was like they brought the hospital with her. They set up this special bed with rails on the sides in the living room because it wouldn't fit in my parents' bedroom. There was this machine hooked up to her arm and medicine bottles on a table next to her. I knew it was my living room, but it looked like a hospital room.

Even worse, my mom didn't really look like my mom anymore. She hardly had any hair, and her face was all swollen up and puffy. And there was something wrong with her eyes. I wasn't sure what exactly, but they didn't seem like my mom's eyes anymore. Like, when I looked into them, she wasn't in there. Or more like she was there, but she'd retreated so far inside I couldn't see her.

I'd been a little kid, so none of it made much sense to me. All I knew was that my mom was really sick, so I made her a "get well soon" card. I don't remember what I drew on it, but I do remember I was really proud of it and very excited to give it to her. I brought it up to the bed where the woman that was supposed to be my mom lay. She was moaning softly to herself with every breath. Like even breathing hurt.

I said, "I drew you a picture." She didn't answer, so I said it again. Her eyes fluttered open, but she still didn't answer. It was like she was looking right through me, like I was invisible. It made me mad, so I said it louder and kind of shoved the picture toward her face.

Her head jerked back, and her eyes opened wide. Finally she seemed to focus on me. There she was. I saw her. My mom. My real mom, the one who was hiding deep inside this other person's body. I saw her just for a moment. Just a glimpse. Like she was peeking out through a mask. Then she moaned and closed her eyes. She lived a little while longer, but that was the last time I really saw her.

"Your mom had cancer?" Big asked.

"Yes. She died." It felt strange to say it aloud. Scary. But it also felt like I took a bit of a burden off myself, one that I didn't even know I was carrying, and handed it to Big. Just a small piece, but I felt lighter. "It was back when I was a little kid. I don't really remember much." Another little piece was lifted off me. Had I been carrying this weight my whole life without knowing it?

"Cancer stinks," said Big.

"It really does," I said.

Big nodded right as the bell rang. He put his hand on my shoulder and started to say something, but the door to the courtyard opened, and we both turned to look. Conor strolled in with a smirk on his face.

"Hey, runt. Have you seen my weird sister?" Conor said.

I sat there with my mouth open, saying nothing. I thought

maybe after climbing with me yesterday, he would be nicer. So much for that. Unless this was the nicer version of Conor.

When I didn't respond, Big smiled and shot his best sunshine ray right at Conor. "We haven't seen Sam this morning. How are you doing today?" You would have thought they were best friends by the way Big said it.

Big's sunshine ray was no match for Conor's dark cloud. His face twisted into a sneer, and he said, "I wasn't talking to you, Tubby." Conor walked over to us with his hands in his pockets, looking around the courtyard. "This place is a total hole." He stopped right in front of us. He stared at us for a second and then said, "So are you two gay or what?"

That caught me off guard. Was he serious? Then I realized Big's hand was still on my shoulder. I shrugged it off.

Big shook his head and said, "No, Conor, we're just good friends."

"You could have fooled me," Conor said. He turned to leave and looked down at the dandelion in his path. He squinted at it, cocked back his leg, and kicked. The yellow head of the dandelion popped right off and went flying through the air. Conor strolled out of the courtyard, laughing.

# Chapter 26

I spent the rest of the morning sick to my stomach. I was tired of feeling that way, but I couldn't stop thinking about Lily getting chemo. I knew she'd have to take a bunch of drugs and that they were supposed to kill the cancer, but I also knew she'd feel like the drugs were killing her instead.

I was glad when it was time for Language Arts. I needed to see Big and have his happiness ray shine down on me and get rid of the awful chemo thoughts. I found Big in the hall on the way to class. I knew he was nearby because everyone I passed had a smile that meant they had recently been in Big's presence. Sure enough, right around the next corner, I saw Big's huge yellow shirt lighting up the whole hallway.

I caught up to him and said, "Hey, Big."

Big somehow heard my squeaky voice over the noise of slamming lockers and yelling teenagers. "Howzit, brah?" he said and smiled down at me.

It felt good to have someone not only notice me, but seem excited to see me. That hadn't happened to me until I met Big. It felt like he lit a candle inside me that glowed soft and warm.

"I'm okay. Still worried about Lily," I said.

"What's wrong with Lily?" someone on the other side of Big asked.

I peeked around the yellow dome of Big's belly to see Katie next to him. How long had she been there?

Big said, "She's . . . been real sick lately. She couldn't come to school today because she had to go to the doctor."

"Oh, that's too bad," Katie said. "I hope she feels better soon."

I was relieved she didn't ask more questions. Lily hadn't expressly forbidden it, but I was pretty sure if we told everybody about her cancer, she'd hunt us down and break our kneecaps.

As we walked the rest of the way to class, more and more people would say "Hi" to Big and Katie and then join our little procession. After the fourth or fifth person fell into step with Big at the center, I began to feel uncomfortable. My spidey senses weren't tingling, but I decided it would be safest to slip back into camouflage mode and disappear.

I slowed and veered off to one side, expecting no one to notice. Before I could get even one step away from Big, I felt his huge arm drape over my shoulder. "Oh, no, you don't." I could tell by the amusement in his eyes he knew exactly what I was trying to do.

By the time we reached Language Arts, there were probably ten people walking with us. For the first time in my life, I was a part of one of the human tsunamis that rolled down the halls of the school. I felt like a surfer riding a wave right up to the door of our class. Then the group broke up as if the wave had crashed onto the beach, and all the people went their separate ways.

As we walked into class, I saw a piece of plywood nailed where the window had been. Big's chair was right next to it. I wondered if he would feel like he was being punished because the board meant he couldn't stare out the window anymore.

I glanced to the back of the class and saw Conor chatting with his friends. What had been his punishment for trying to hit Big with a book? Neither he nor Sam mentioned anything about it yesterday, and I'd been too afraid to ask. I thought he would at least be suspended, but maybe they didn't do that when your dad was a rich lawyer.

After grammar and vocabulary review, we finished reading *Of Mice and Men*. Well, *almost*. We got to the second-to-the-last page but never quite got to the end.

We were taking turns reading aloud, which I absolutely hated. It was almost my turn, so I was busy fighting off a panic attack. Josh, the kid sitting next to me, was reading the part where—spoiler alert—George shoots his best friend, Lennie, in the back of the head and kills him.

Katie blurted, "He shot him?"

Mr. Teller said, "Yes, he felt he had to—"

"He *killed* Lennie?" Katie asked.

I turned around to see her eyes brimming with tears.

"Yes. As I was saying, he felt he had to because—"

"I hate this book," Katie said and slammed it shut.

Conor laughed, but a sharp look from Mr. Teller shut him up. I thought Mr. Teller would get mad at Katie, too, but he didn't. Instead, he walked up to Lily's empty desk and sat on it, facing the class. In a calm and quiet voice he said, "George was faced with a terrible choice. Lennie had killed Curley's wife, and Curley was out for revenge. Someone tell me what Curley said he wanted to do to Lennie. Anyone?"

"Shoot him in the gut," Conor said, smiling.

"Why in the gut?" Mr. Teller asked.

"Because it wouldn't kill him right away," Josh said. "Curley wanted Lennie to suffer."

"George could have stopped him," Katie said. "Someone could have stopped him."

"True," Mr. Teller said. "But then what would have happened to Lennie? They certainly wouldn't let him go free after what he did."

"They would have thrown him in an insane asylum," Conor said.

"Yes," said Mr. Teller, "and we learned how horrible the asylums were back then. You remember how Crooks said they would chain Lennie up like a dog? It would have been a nightmare for Lennie. George knew that. He knew either Curley was going to kill Lennie and make him suffer, or Lennie was going to spend the rest of his life chained up like an animal in an asylum. He made the only choice he felt he could. The one that would cause Lennie the least amount of suffering possible. If you were Lennie, isn't that what you would have wanted George to do?"

There was a long, silent minute. Then, in a firm, low voice, Conor said, "I would have."

# Chapter 27

The next day, Lily was gone again. I went to the courtyard and sat on the bench to text Lily.

*Me: Are you coming to school today?*
*Lily: No. I have to stay in the hospital for ten days for my first stage of chemo. I'll have to miss the climbing comp, too. I hate cancer.*

The door to the courtyard opened, and Big walked in wearing his bright-red shirt. "Howzit, brah?" His smile vanished after he looked at me. "Uh-oh. What's wrong?" He sat down next to me.

I handed him my phone and he read Lily's text.

"I wondered. I talked to Lily's brother Chuck after school yesterday. He wouldn't say much. Probably under threat of his life from Lily. But it sounded like she wouldn't be in school for a while. We should go visit her tonight, yeah?"

I started to say that I would love to, but then this wave of anxiety hit me. "I, uh, I don't know, Big." I was shocked at how much I suddenly did *not* want to go to the hospital. Was Lily in a cancer ward? Would she be hooked up to a bunch of beeping machines with tubes going in and out of her? Would there be sad people all over the place? Would she be bald like my mom had been? "She, um, might not want visitors," I said. "You know how she is."

Big cocked his head and studied me for a few seconds. "Let's at least ask, yeah?" He texted Lily asking if we could visit. There was a long minute of silence while we waited for her to reply.

> *Lily: Only if Paul promises to tell me about climbing with Sam. And you have to tell me about something beautiful.*

"Will you come?" Big asked me.

The thought of going to the hospital made me feel like I couldn't breathe. "I, um, I want to, but I don't think I can."

"I understand, brah," Big said. "It's okay."

At lunchtime, I got ambushed outside the cafeteria. One second I was walking along, minding my own business, and the next second, I was lifted into the air and dropped into a garbage can. I should have seen it coming, but my spidey senses weren't functioning at full capacity. I think it was because I was mad at myself for not having the nerve to visit Lily in the hospital.

I looked over the rim of the garbage can to see Hunter and a few other hyenas strolling down the hall. They didn't bother to look back or even slow their stride. To them, I was nothing more than a piece of trash to be thrown away. At least I'd been stuffed into the garbage can right-side up this time.

As I was crawling out, I saw Sam and Conor coming toward me.

"Hey, runt," Conor said, smirking.

"Knock it off, Conor." Then Sam said to me, "Are you okay?" At least I think that's what she said. I could barely hear her over the noise of the hallway.

"Oh, um, yeah. I'm fine," I said, trying my best to sound casual. "Just another day at the office."

Conor laughed and shook his head. "I can't believe you hang out with this loser, Sam. He's so . . ."

Sam glared at him, and he shut up. Then she turned and said something.

I leaned in closer to her. "What?"

Sam fidgeted and stared at her feet. Then she said just loud enough for me to hear, "Can we talk to you for a second?"

"Sure, uh, what's up?" I asked, keeping a wary eye on Conor. Was this some kind of trap?

Sam bit her lip and then said, with what seemed like a huge effort, "I talked to Lily. She told me what was going on with—"

Conor interrupted. "Look, Sam told me Lily's sick or something and can't be in the climbing competition this Saturday. That means you guys need someone to take her place if you still want to enter." Conor paused like he was waiting for me to say something.

But I didn't know what I was supposed to say, so I just stood there.

Conor huffed and said, "Sam asked me to climb in Lily's place."

"Why would you do that? You don't even like us."

Conor got a strange look on his face, like I'd hurt his feelings, but I knew that couldn't be possible. Then he sneered at me and said, "Correction: I don't like *you*. Sam's my sister, so I have to like her even if she is weird. Besides, my dad said if I helped Sam out, he'd unground me."

"Can we even switch teammates?" I asked. "So close to the competition, I mean?" I was terrified to climb with Conor. I was even more terrified to tell him I didn't want him on our team. My only hope was that Andy would say we'd passed some kind of deadline.

Sam said, "I told Andy what was going on, and he said it would be fine under the circumstances."

What was I going to do? I couldn't be on a team with a jackal. Then I thought of another way to weasel out of this. "What about Lily?" I asked. "Won't she be mad if we just replace her?"

"She's the one who told me to get a new teammate," Sam said.

"Well, I doubt she meant"—I was about to say "Conor," but I managed to stop quickly enough to save my life—"right away. I mean, what if she gets feeling better or something?"

That strange, hurt look snuck back onto Conor's face again. I didn't know what to make of it. Then his expression turned hard, and he said, "Look, if Sasquatch feels better, I'll let her have her spot back. It's not like I *want* to climb with you."

He glared at me until I heard myself mumble, "Okay, sounds good."

"Great. I'm glad you approve," Conor said with a heavy dose of sarcasm. As he turned to leave, he added, "By the way, runt, you stink like garbage."

After school, I found Big at his locker. He was surrounded with other friends, so I tucked myself into a nearby window nook to wait until everyone left. After a few minutes, the crowd slowly started to disperse.

Katie and two other girls were the last to leave. Katie said,

"Hey, we're going to that new Italian soda place. You want to come?"

One of the other girls, a really pretty one with hair down to her waist, chimed in, "Yeah, you should come, Big."

"Oh, I love that place," Big said. "They have a drink there that's got like Coke and cream and coconut flavoring and I don't know what else in it, but it's absolutely beautiful—like carbonated poetry. Mm-mmm."

Katie laughed. "We're heading over there right now."

I knew what was coming. Now that Big had new friends, it was time to cull the herd. He didn't need a runt like me hanging around anymore.

"That sounds good, but I've already got plans. My buddy Paul is supposed to meet me here any second now. Thanks, though. Maybe another time, yeah?"

I couldn't believe it. Big was choosing me over hanging out with three good-looking girls? What was wrong with him?

Then I heard someone down the hall yell, "Where you going, Conor?"

I looked to see Conor coming down the hall, with Blake and three more of his gangster friends following him.

"Back off," Conor shouted over his shoulder. His face was bright red, and he had a basketball on one hip, like he was heading for the gym.

When Blake and his friends saw Big and the girls, they stopped following Conor. Blake leaned against the wall and smiled his crooked-toothed smile and said with fake pleasantness, "Okay, Conor. I'll see you soon."

Yeah, Blake was definitely a future member of Utah's Most Wanted.

I shivered and shrank as far back into the corner of the window nook as I could, breathing a huge sigh of relief when Conor passed me without noticing.

"Are you okay, Conor?" Big asked.

Conor glared at him. "Shut up, doughboy." He opened the door to the gym and disappeared inside.

"I can't believe he just said that," the long-haired girl said.

"I can," said Katie.

The third girl said, "I wish he'd do the world a favor and kill himself already."

The door to the gym opened back up. Conor came out followed by four other basketball players. There was no doubt what they had in mind. They marched straight past Big, Katie, her friends, and me without a word.

Blake saw them coming, folded his arms, and said, "Oh, good, you decided you want to play after all." He was the only person I'd ever seen that seemed to become more relaxed as things got more intense.

Big called out, "Conor, you don't want to do this." He jogged past me and caught Conor by the shoulder. "Hey, brah, why don't you go back in the gym and play basketball, and I'll have a talk with Blake."

Conor turned and shoved Big hard with both hands. "Mind your own business," he growled.

Big didn't budge. He grabbed at Conor's arm again. "Really, Conor, you don't want to do this. Just go back—"

Conor stuck a finger in Big's face. "Touch me again, and I'll kill you. Do you understand me?" I saw spit fly from his mouth as he spoke.

"Okay, Conor, I won't touch you," Big said in a calm and quiet voice, "but why don't you just go back in the gym and—"

"Don't tell me what to do, fatty. You think I'm afraid of you? I'll take you on any time you want. Let's go right now!" Conor shoved Big again, and then everything went crazy.

The girls all started yelling for Conor to leave Big alone, Blake and his friends ran forward, and Conor's friends stepped up to meet them. Big stood in the middle of all the chaos with his arms out, trying to calm everyone down.

And what did I do? I hopped out of the window nook, walked across the hall, and pulled the fire alarm. Then I left and went to the climbing gym.

# Chapter 28

Big visited Lily in the hospital on both Wednesday and Thursday. He tried to get me to join him, but I couldn't make myself do it. Every time I even thought about Lily in a hospital bed, I'd get all sweaty and it would be hard to breathe. I hated myself for being such a wimp and chastised myself constantly, but it didn't seem to matter. I still couldn't make myself go.

I skipped the gym on Friday because Lily had forbidden it. In a text she told me I needed to save my strength for the competition on Saturday. She said if our team didn't win, she would hunt down each of us individually and break our fingers so we could never climb again. I knew she was kidding, but I really did want to win for her. If I couldn't do anything else to help her—not even visit her in the hospital—then at least I could try to win the competition.

Big said Lily was "doing pretty well, all things considered." I wasn't sure what that meant, exactly, and I didn't ask. I think Big could tell I wasn't ready to hear more because he changed the subject to Lily's stuffed cows.

Apparently everyone who came to visit her brought a new

cow, and her whole room was covered in them. He said it looked like a stuffed animal stampede, and all the other kids in the unit loved them. When I asked what kids he was talking about, he told me that even though Lily was sixteen years old and six feet, four inches tall, they still put her on the pediatric floor with the little kids.

"The best part, though," Big said, "is that Lily got all the kids to moo when they go by her room. She told them that's how cows say hi. So all day long, kids are going by her room, being pushed in a wheelchair or a bed or just walking by, and every time they pass, they start mooing, and Lily and her brothers or whoever is there will moo back, and it makes the kids laugh every time." Big's eyes got kind of watery, and his smile turned soft. "It's beautiful," he whispered.

I thought about Lily surrounded by a herd of stuffed cows and mooing at kids. Somehow, it helped me feel calmer about visiting her. So after school on Friday, I caught a couple of buses to the hospital. I told myself that I didn't have to go inside the building. I could just go there and see how it went.

I stood outside the front doors for a long time. I didn't have a panic attack or anything, but I couldn't get myself to move. I just stood there, getting in people's way for ten or fifteen minutes before I decided to walk around the entire building. When I came back to the front doors, I still couldn't do it.

"Hi, Paul," I heard a quiet voice say from behind me.

I turned around and saw Sam standing there in a hoody. She held what looked like a coloring book and a set of colored pencils to her chest.

"Oh, uh, hey, Sam," I said. "What are you doing here?"

"I wanted to . . ." Her eyes darted around the parking lot like someone might attack her at any moment. Then she took a deep breath and said, "I wanted to visit Lily because she's always been so nice to me."

That sounded so strange; I guess I was still getting used to the idea that Lily could be nice. "Is that for her?" I asked, pointing to the coloring book and colored pencils. They were tied together with a red ribbon.

Sam looked at her shoes and hid her face behind a curtain of frizzy hair. "Yes," she said eventually. From what little I could see of her face, I saw her blush. Was she embarrassed? "I thought . . . I know that . . . I wondered if she might be bored and . . ."

Definitely embarrassed.

When Sam's voice trailed off, I said, "I think she'll really like it."

She glanced up briefly, relief in her eyes, before hiding behind her hair again. "Are you on your way in? We could visit her together."

"I, um, I . . . ." I started having trouble breathing. "Oh. I was just, um, leaving, actually." I turned to go, but Sam grabbed my arm. The shock of physical contact from a girl was enough to make me forget I was in the process of freaking out.

Sam cleared her throat and said quietly, "A lot of people are afraid of hospitals, you know."

That wasn't at all what I was expecting. "I'm not afraid, exactly. I just, um, can't seem to go inside. Or even think about going inside."

"But you want to visit Lily."

"Well, yeah, she's my friend."

"There's a gift shop right inside the front doors. What if you just went in there? You could pick something out for Lily, and I could take it up to her. I'll let her know it was from you. She'll understand."

My chest tightened up right away. It was ridiculous how the mere thought of going in the hospital scared me, but knowing it was ridiculous did nothing to make the claustrophobic, suffocating feeling go away.

After I didn't say anything, Sam said, "Do you want to try?"

"I don't know."

"It will be okay."

"Maybe you could just, um, pick something out for me."

"The gift shop is right there," Sam said, pointing at a window next to the big glass front doors. The shop was full of stuffed animals, figurines, vases, and balloons. "You only have to go in the front doors and turn right. You're hardly even in the hospital at all."

"I, um, I . . . don't think so." I turned and practically ran away before Sam could stop me again.

# Chapter 29

**W**e're here to make sure you win," Chuck said. Or maybe it was Colt. I had no idea. All I knew was that twin rhinos were standing next to the front door of the climbing gym like two huge bouncers. I was glad my dad was with me, even though he wasn't much bigger than I was.

"Yeah," said the other one. "Lily said that if you don't win, we're supposed to break your fingers and maybe your arms, too—for good measure."

My dad looked from the rhinos to me with wide eyes that said, *Are these guys for real?*

I looked back at my dad with what were probably equally wide eyes that said, *I'm not sure. Maybe we should run.*

The rhinos started laughing. The second rhino said, "Just kidding, man. You should see your face." He punched me in the shoulder.

"Lily really did send us, though. She said she wants a play-by-play of everything that happens," said the first rhino.

"And you know Lily," said the second one. "What Lily wants . . ."

"Lily gets," finished the first one.

When I didn't say anything, the first rhino hit me in the shoulder again. "Man, lighten up."

They opened both the doors for us, like we were making some kind of grand entrance.

Once inside, I spotted Big right away. He was in a bright-red T-shirt with a chocolate-chip cookie holding hands with a carton of milk on it. When I got closer, I could see that the cookie was saying "I love you" to the milk, and the milk was smiling and blushing.

Big's mom was with him. Both of them smiled at me as I walked up. I felt like I'd just walked out from under a shadow and into warm sunshine.

"Howzit, brah? You ready to win this thing?" Big said. He introduced my dad to his mom. While they made small talk, he turned to Lily's brothers. "Hey, Chuck. Colt." He shook hands with each of them as he greeted them and then drew them into a hug. I tried to note which one was Chuck and which one was Colt. How did Big tell the difference?

"How's Lily?" Big asked them.

"She's doing alright," said Chuck.

"Mostly she's bored," said Colt.

"And moody."

"Yeah, those nurses better watch out," said Colt. "She's dangerous."

"She threw one of her stuffed cows at Colt yesterday. It was awesome," said Chuck.

"That's our Lily, yeah?" Big said, shaking his head like he was talking about his own sister. The rhinos laughed. Just that fast, Big was one of them, now. It made me both jealous and sad. If I'd been able to visit Lily in the hospital, would I have been accepted into their family, too?

Chuck turned to me. "Hey, Paul, I almost forgot. Thanks for sending the flowers. Lily loved them."

Flowers? What flowers?

"Yeah, she didn't say how much she liked them, because that's how Lily is," said Colt, "but we know she did."

"Yeah," said Chuck. "She moved her favorite stuffed cow out of its place of honor to make room for them."

"And giving her lilies," said Colt. "That was good. Wish I would have thought of that. Maybe she wouldn't have thrown a cow at me."

"I, um, I didn't . . ." I started to say, but then Colt's eyes focused on something behind me, and his face lit up with a wicked grin.

"Conor, buddy," Colt said. "Fancy seeing you here. How you doing, pal?"

I turned around as Conor and Sam walked over to us. When I saw Sam, I realized exactly what had happened. After I'd run away from the hospital like a coward, she'd gotten flowers from the gift shop and told Lily they were from me. I owed her one.

Conor glared at Chuck and Colt. He looked tired, stressed-out, and unhappy to see them.

"Look, I'm here for my sister, so you guys can back off," Conor said.

"Hey, relax," Colt said. "You don't make any trouble, and we won't either."

"Yeah, that's always been the rule, Conor. You know that," Chuck said.

"Sam!" Big gave her a bear hug like he hadn't seen her in twenty years.

Her blue eyes were wide and terrified, and her freckled cheeks turned red. I was pretty sure Sam was not used to getting hugs.

I almost started laughing.

Conor rolled his eyes and said, "You've got to be kidding me. *You're* here?"

"Now, Conor, I thought we were all going to play nice," said Chuck.

Big released Sam and said, "You guys are going to rock this competition. I can't wait to watch you climb." He turned to Conor and smiled. "Hey, good to see you. It's awesome that you're filling in for Lily."

Conor seemed shocked by Big's greeting. It took him a second to remember to be a jerk because then he said, "Yeah, well, don't get too excited. I'm doing it for my sister—not you."

Just then, Andy announced over the intercom that all teams should report to the prow for final instructions.

"Let's get this over with," Conor said and shoved his way between Chuck and Colt on his way to the prow. The guy totally had a death wish.

I fell in beside Sam. "Hi," she said, darting a glance at me.

"Hi," I said. "I heard about the flowers, and I just wanted to say, uh, thanks."

"You're welcome."

"Where's your mom?" I asked. I felt bad, but I was really hoping she wouldn't show up.

"Oh, uh, she wasn't able to make it."

"That's too bad," I said, doing my best not to sound relieved.

As we listened to Andy explain the rules, I felt my spidey

senses tingling. I looked around and saw Hunter staring at me. We made eye contact for a second, and then I looked at my feet. He snickered in amusement. When I dared to glance up again a minute later, he was focused on Andy. I decided I should probably do the same thing.

Andy was right in the middle of explaining how we earned points, when a shrill voice echoed through the gym. "Samantha? Conor? Where are you?"

They both looked at each other, faces pale.

"No," Sam whispered. "Please, no."

"She's here," Conor said.

"How?" Sam asked.

"I don't know. I hid her keys in the freezer. She couldn't have found them."

"Samantha? Conor? For heaven's sake, where are you? Don't make me wander all over this dreadful place to find you."

"Should I call Dad?" Sam asked.

Conor frowned. "No, not yet," he said. "That might make her worse. Let me talk to her first." He slipped into the crowd.

As Andy continued to explain the rules of the competition, I heard Mrs. Dolores working her way toward us through the crowd.

"Conor, there you are. Where's Samantha? . . . No, I will *not* wait in the back. Why should I? . . . Maybe I would like to hear the rules, too. Did you think of that?"

As Mrs. Dolores got closer, Sam looked more and more like she wanted to sink into the floor and disappear.

"Are you okay?" I whispered.

Sam shook her head just as Mrs. Dolores said, "Excuse me," to a surprised climber standing behind us. She pushed her way past him and appeared next to us. Conor was right behind her, apologizing to all the people in her wake. "There you are, Samantha," Mrs. Dolores said with a huff. She looked Sam up and down. "Would it have killed you to put on some makeup and do your hair? People are going to be looking at you in the contest."

Conor whispered, "Mom, it's a climbing *competition*, not a beauty contest. Now, will you please be quiet? You're embarrassing yourself."

Mrs. Dolores turned on him with a crazy gleam in her eyes that reminded me of Conor right before he threw the book at Big. "Oh, I'm embarrassing myself, am I?" She looked around at all the people nearby as if to ask, "Can you believe my son is talking to me this way?"

Everyone looked away and tried to pretend they didn't notice her.

"Should I be embarrassed for wanting my daughter to look nice in public? She's the one who should be embarrassed. Coming out here with no makeup and her hair a mess and her team made up of"—she looked at me—"I don't even know what."

Mrs. Dolores was so loud, Andy faltered for a moment in giving his instructions. He was only able to finish when she stopped talking.

"I guess that's about it," Andy said. "If you still have any questions, come see me. The first round will start in five minutes."

Mrs. Pohaku, who was standing nearby, stepped over to Sam and said, "Don't worry. You'll do fine, dear. I think you look beautiful." She gave her a sideways hug and a kiss on the cheek.

"Excuse me," Mrs. Dolores said. "And you are?"

"I'm Big's mom," Mrs. Pohaku said.

Mrs. Dolores looked confused. "Who?"

DAVID GLEN ROBB

"Me," Big said with his shining smile. He stuck out his hand for Mrs. Dolores to shake. "I'm a friend of Sam's from school. It's nice to meet you."

Mrs. Dolores stepped back like the thought of shaking Big's hand disgusted her. "Who are you?"

"I'm Big," he said, still smiling.

"You most certainly are," Mrs. Dolores said with a shrill little laugh.

"Alright," my dad interrupted. "We better let the team warm up. The competition is about to start."

As we walked over to an open section of the bouldering wall to warm up, I heard Conor whisper to Sam, "Call Dad. Tell him to get here quick."

# Chapter 30

The competition was starting, and our first route was a face climb with thin, painful-looking holds. As we got ready to climb, Conor turned all business. "Okay, we have ten minutes for each route. That means just over three minutes each unless someone makes it to the top before their time is up. Sam said she thought we should do it the way you practiced with Lily last week, so I'll go first, then Paul, and Sam will go last."

Sam and I both nodded.

"You guys ready?"

We both nodded again.

Conor swung his arms around to loosen them up and hopped up and down a few times with excess energy. His eyes were bright with excitement.

The buzzer sounded, and Conor started powering his way up the first route. Everyone cheered him on, even the rhinos. He fell twice, shook out his hands, chalked up, and got right back on. He made it to the top right as his three minutes were up. He jumped down, and for a moment, he almost looked happy. I'd never seen

Conor like that before. He always seemed so predatory. He was almost . . . likable.

I was next. It was a hard route for me because I couldn't get away with jumping for holds. It was all about balance and delicate climbing, but I eventually made it with only one fall. After I hopped to the ground, Big leaned over to his mom and said, "See, I told you."

Then it was Sam's turn. Her eyes became intense and focused as she approached the wall. Every move she made during her climb was deliberate and precise. It was like watching a slow-motion dance. We all sort of forgot to cheer because it was so beautiful to watch. She reached the top without falling and with time to spare.

After she was back down, everyone congratulated her. Conor even gave her a high five. She seemed surprised, but I noticed her smile lingered for several minutes.

I was relieved to see all the teams were so busy working on their own routes, they didn't have time to watch anyone else. Including Hunter's team. For the first few routes, I kept a wary eye on him, but he was too busy with his own climbing to give me any trouble. After that, I mostly forgot about him.

I think we all would have enjoyed ourselves more if not for Mrs. Dolores. While Conor and I climbed, she spent her time pestering Sam. She fretted over what the climbing was doing to Sam's fingernails. She told Sam that her skin was the color of chicken fat, and she really needed to use the tanning bed. She complained about the "ratty old sweats" Sam was wearing. And on and on and on.

Sam endured it all in silence. Conor, on the other hand, would occasionally say things like, "Please, Mom, just let her concentrate on the climbing," or "I think her hair looks just fine, leave her alone."

The rest of us tried to help, too. Mrs. Pohaku reached over to squeeze Sam's hand or pat her shoulder every once in a while. Big and my dad did their best to distract Mrs. Dolores by engaging her in conversation. All of us cheered extra loud for Sam when she climbed. But nothing seemed to stop Mrs. Dolores.

I had the distinct feeling when I looked at Mrs. Dolores that there was something building. It was like watching weight being added to an already strained cable. I think everyone else must have felt the same thing by the looks they kept exchanging. Conor, in particular, watched his mom with a growing anxiety that filled the air around him.

Despite the tension, my team was climbing really well. After finishing the seventh route with time to spare, my dad said, "I've been watching the other teams, and most of them aren't finishing the routes. I think there's a good chance you guys could win."

"Really?" Conor asked. His eyes lit up with hope.

"As long as you do moderately well on these last two routes," my dad said, "you've got it in the bag."

Conor, Sam, and I looked at each other in awe. We were really going to do this. We were going to win.

The buzzer sounded, and we moved to the next route.

It was a crack. I felt all my excitement drain away. I was worthless on cracks. I was going to mess up our chance of winning. I was going to mess this up for Lily.

Conor attacked the crack with his usual ferocity and finished in only two minutes.

"Sam, can you go next?" I secretly hoped she would take so long there wouldn't be time for me.

Sam gave me a questioning look.

"Please," I said, gesturing to the route. "I stink at cracks."

"Oh, sure, now you let her go before you," Mrs. Dolores said and rolled her eyes at me. "Now that the contest is almost over."

But Sam was very good at crack climbing, which meant she climbed faster than she had all night. She moved with her trademark precision, tiny fingers slotting deep into the crack, skinny white arms cranking hard, toes stabbed into the wider spots. She reached the top in just over two minutes and hopped back down.

"Come on, Paul," Conor said and slapped me on the back. "You got this." He said it like he really meant it. Like I was a friend.

I had no choice but to step up and take my turn. Just looking at the crack made my fingers and toes hurt. Why would anyone purposely climb this? It was like slotting your fingers and toes into a vise with jagged edges and cranking it down until they were locked in place. Not my idea of fun.

I slotted my fingers in anyway. Actually, I slotted my entire hand in. Where Conor could barely fit his fingers, I could sink my hand in up to the wrist. You'd think all that room would help, but instead my hand sort of rattled around in there.

"Try it thumbs down," I heard a soft voice say right beside me. I turned to see Sam holding her hand out into the air like she had jammed it into an imaginary crack. I mimicked her move and, sure enough, my left hand locked in place. Huh, weird. I put my right hand in above it, but there was no way I could do it thumbs down, not without breaking my wrist, anyway.

"Put your right hand in like this," Sam said. She showed me how to cup my hand with my thumb tucked into my palm to make it wider. I tried it. Though my hand was still a little loose in the space, I had a much better grip. I pulled myself up and stabbed my toes into the crack, but they barely got any purchase at all. I felt my hands start to slip.

"No, not like that," Sam said. "Slot your foot in sideways, and then crank it back upright to lock it off." I looked to see her standing on one foot like she was doing some kind of Tai Chi meditation. I tried it, and my foot was suddenly solid.

"Good," Sam said.

"Don't help him," Mrs. Dolores said.

"Mom," Conor said with a sigh, "we're on the same team."

"So? She should make him do it by himself. He never helped her."

"He's been helping her the whole time," Conor groaned.

I stood up on my now-solid foot and repeated the same move again: reach up with my left hand, thumb down, reach with my right thumb tucked into my palm, slot my foot in sideways, crank it straight and lock it off. Start over again. Wow. I was climbing a crack.

I made my way up several more feet without too much trouble. I had to change things up a little as I went, but by following Sam's advice, I was able to make significant progress.

Somewhere in the middle of the climb, I realized I wasn't jumping from hold to hold like usual. Crack climbing wasn't height dependent. There was just a big, long crack stretching from floor to ceiling, and it didn't matter how tall I was or how far apart the holds were because there were no holds. Suddenly, I liked cracks a lot more. In fact, they became my favorite type of climb right then and there.

I looked over my shoulder to tell Sam thanks, and I could tell right away something was wrong. Sam was there, spotting me, but her eyes were wide and watery like she was trying not to cry. I noticed everyone staring at Conor and Mrs. Dolores in alarm. I didn't know what was going on, but Conor appeared to be trying to calm down his mom. I looked at Sam to see what I should do. She nodded for me to keep climbing, so I did. I turned back to the wall, breathed deep, and went for it.

"I will not be ordered around by my youngest child," I heard Mrs. Dolores say in her shrill voice.

I slotted my left hand into the crack, thumb down, and locked it off.

"I'm fine," Mrs. Dolores said. "You don't know what you're talking about. I feel fine."

I turned my right foot sideways, stabbed it in, and locked it off.

"I can do what I want with my own hair. It's Samantha you should be worried about. Honestly, she looks like a transient."

Pushing with my right foot and pulling with my left hand, I moved up and started the process over.

"I'm not tugging at my hair. Stop telling me what to do. Don't touch me."

The crack was getting progressively wider the higher I climbed, and I was able to stick my whole hand in and make a fist like I'd seen Conor do up at the M and M Wall. It locked off perfectly.

"What do I care if you call your dad? Go ahead."

Now the crack was getting too wide. When I moved up, my fist rattled around in the crack uselessly.

"I don't care what your dad says. I came to see my daughter climb and that's exactly what I'm going to do."

I couldn't move up. The crack was too wide to get any

purchase. As a last resort, I tried to lean off to the side and "lie back" the edge of the crack. It wasn't working. I heard someone's phone ring, the tone playing a pop song.

Then I fell.

I landed in a heap on the padded floor. I heard Mrs. Dolores shout, "What do you mean, why am I here? I'm here to support my children." I stood and turned to see her shrieking into her cell phone and throwing her free hand in the air like she was waving away hornets. "Oh, you bet he tried to stop me. Went so far as to hide the keys from me. He says I lost them, but I know what he was trying to do."

"Mom, please, lower your voice," Conor said.

Mrs. Dolores looked at him and then said, even louder, "I called a cab, that's what I did. Had to take a cab to my own daughter's climbing contest because you don't think I'm fit to be in public. Well, if you think I'm bad, you should see what your daughter looks like. You'd think she was an orphan girl the way she's dressed. And her teammate. Don't even get me started on her outlandish teammate."

My dad stepped up to Mrs. Dolores and said in his Zen voice. "Maybe this is a call you should take outside?"

"Mind your own business, pip-squeak." She looked down at my dad like he was something rotten she'd found in the refrigerator.

"Mom, please, don't do this," Conor said. "Think of Sam."

"I am thinking of Samantha. That's why I'm here, remember?"

Sam sat down cross-legged on the floor and stared at her toes. She stayed silent.

Mrs. Pohaku sat down next to her and put her arm around

her. I heard her whisper, "Would you like to go for a walk with me? We don't have to stay here."

Sam shook her head, and I saw one tear and then another fall from her eyes.

Mrs. Dolores started shrieking into her phone again. "What are you talking about? I feel great. Never felt better. Taking my pills and everything just like you wanted me to, and now I'm a new woman. Can't you tell?"

My dad tried again. "Why don't you let me walk you outside, okay? This seems like the kind of call where you need a little privacy."

He took her by the elbow, but Mrs. Dolores slapped him away. "Get away from me. I'll have you arrested if you touch me again. My husband is a lawyer, you know." Then she said into the phone, "You wouldn't believe all the freaks of nature that are here. There are identical twins here the size of André the Giant, and the fattest boy I have ever seen, and then there's a little man who looks like a child. It's like a circus sideshow. And *our* daughter is hanging out with them. Do you really think I should have let her come down here alone?"

"Mom, Sam and I would like to go now," Conor said. "We don't really want to be in this competition anyway. Sam can drive us all home."

Mrs. Dolores ignored him, listening on the phone. In her silence, the buzzer sounded for us to move to the next route. We all tried to get out of the way of the next team coming in, but Mrs. Dolores wouldn't move. She had wandered to stand directly below the route, and the next team couldn't climb until she got out of the way. They gave us nervous looks, unsure of what to do.

Andy must have noticed the situation, because he suddenly

appeared out of the crowd. He said to Mrs. Dolores, "Can I be of assistance?"

She gave him an irritated frown and lifted her index finger at him as if to say, "Just one second."

"Look, ma'am, you can't stand here. There's a climbing comp going on and you're in the way. I'm going to have to ask you to—"

Right then, Mrs. Dolores screamed into the phone, "The real question is, why aren't *you* here?"

Conor said to Andy, "Please, she's not well. If you try to make her move it will only get worse."

Andy nodded and waved the other team around us. They moved to the route we should have been starting while Mrs. Dolores continued, "Work, my foot. You're with *her*, aren't you? Your cute little legal assistant. I don't know why you worry so much about what I'm doing. I'm the one who should be worried about what *you're* doing!"

Mrs. Dolores threw her phone at the wall. It ricocheted off and landed between Big and me. She screamed at us, "What are you staring at? Aren't you supposed to be climbing?" Then she uttered the most mournful wail I'd ever heard and collapsed onto the floor. She started pulling at the hair on the sides of her head and bawling. Her hair had been stacked up on the top of her head in a fancy way, but once she started pulling on it, she uncovered two scabby bald spots just above her ears. They were right where she was pulling now.

Big moved forward to help, but Conor waved him back.

He crouched down beside his mom and took her hands in his. "Mom, stop, you're going to hurt yourself again." He was trying hard not to cry. "Mom, please, stop, you don't want to mess up your nice hair, do you?"

She wailed again through her tears and tried to break free of Conor's grip. He held on tight and wouldn't let go.

I'd never heard anyone who sounded like they were in so much pain. It was all I could do not to start crying, too. I looked at Sam where she was still sitting cross-legged with tears streaming down her cheeks. Big's mom sat with her arm around her shoulders. I sat down on the other side of Sam and took her hand.

Mrs. Dolores's phone rang. Somehow it was still working even after its impact with the wall.

Big picked it up. "Hello, is this Mr. Dolores?" He paused and listened. "No, he's right here, but your wife's not doing very well." Another pause. "Yes, she's here, too. Is there anything we can do to help?" Pause. "Okay, we'll see you in a minute." He hung up and said, "Conor, Sam—your dad is almost here. Just hang tight."

# Chapter 31

The next day, I went to the hospital. I stood in front of the doors for a long time, trying to make myself enter. I told myself to walk in. I didn't move. I told my legs, *Just take one step.* I might have even said it aloud, because I got a strange look from a passing nurse. My legs ignored me. Why couldn't I do this? I wanted to visit Lily. I wanted to see her, talk to her, show her that I was her friend. I wanted to explain why we hadn't won the competition for her. I wanted her to know it wasn't my fault.

I gave up and sat on the curb. I watched big black clouds closing in from the west. Rain was coming. I didn't want to be waiting at the bus stop in the rain, but it was too late now. The clouds were practically on top of me.

My phone vibrated. I had a text. Thankful for the distraction, I pulled it out.

*Sam: Are you busy? I need your help.*

That was weird. Nobody ever needed my help. I couldn't think of anything she might need, but it gave me an excuse to ignore the hospital for a while.

*Me: No, not busy. What do you need?*
*Sam: Conor is missing. I'm worried. Will you help me look*
*for him? Please.*

The "please" is what got me. I mean, I wasn't too worried about Conor. He seemed like the type of guy who did whatever he wanted whenever he wanted. He was probably just at one of his jackal friend's houses playing video games or torturing puppies or something. But Sam's little "please" made me realize how worried she must be. And how desperate she was if she was asking someone like me for help.

*Me: Ok, no problem. But I'm at the hospital. Can you pick*
*me up?*
*Sam: Be there in 10. Thanks.*

Eight minutes later, Sam pulled up in her Jeep. I climbed in, and she took off before I had even shut the door.

"Where do you want to start looking?" I asked as I fastened my seat belt.

"The boulder field. Then the M and M Wall." There was something strange in her voice.

"I'm sure he's fine," I said. I barely managed not to say "uh" or "um" through sheer force of will. I wanted to sound confident and reassuring. "Are you sure he's not at a friend's house?"

"He doesn't have many friends outside of school." What was it about her voice?

"Really? Seems like he's always surrounded by people when I see him."

"He's good at attracting a . . ." She seemed to struggle for the right word. "An audience—but not real friends."

All at once, I realized what was weird about her voice. I mean, sure it was strained because she was worried and scared, but that wasn't what was different. She was talking at a normal volume. That made me nervous.

"You think he went climbing?" I asked.

"Yeah. He took his climbing shoes and chalk bag with him when he left."

"Oh, okay." I tried to think through the possibilities. "I guess you tried his cell?"

"It goes straight to voice mail."

"What about the gym?"

"I called. Andy hasn't seen him."

That didn't leave much else. Conor had to be at the boulder field if all he took were his climbing shoes and chalk bag. He would have needed ropes and other gear if he'd gone to the M and M Wall.

As we got closer to the boulder field trailhead, I asked, "What kind of car does he drive?"

"He took my dad's BMW. He doesn't even have his license yet. Just a learner's permit." She bit her lip. It looked like she was fighting back tears. "My dad's going to kill him if he finds out."

"Your parents don't know he left?"

"No. They've been gone all day. My dad had to take my mom to the, um, doctor. Conor left right after they did."

"When was that?"

"Around nine this morning. I thought he was just going bouldering to blow off some steam. Then he—" Sam's voice caught and she sniffed. "He didn't come back."

"It's all right. We'll find him."

We pulled into the trailhead parking lot. It was almost empty.

I think everyone was smart enough to see the ominous dark clouds and stay off the mountain. There was a rusty old Subaru and a pickup truck. No BMW. My stomach sank.

"It doesn't make sense that he'd be at the M and M Wall. He doesn't have any gear. Where else might he be? He must have *some* friends."

"I've called them." She sat for a moment, thinking. Her expression changed. Instead of looking frightened and nervous, her eyes turned dark and focused like when she was climbing. She quit crying. She took a deep breath and said in a quiet, calm voice, "He's there. I know he is."

"Where? Up at the M and M Wall? He can't be."

She pulled out of the parking lot. This calm Sam scared me more than the nervous, crying one had. I didn't like it one bit.

"I have to at least check," she said. "It's just that he's been really unhappy lately. He's struggling with some stuff at school, and then with everything going on with our mom . . ." Her voice turned tight and trailed off. I could tell she was trying not to cry again.

I didn't know what to say, so I just nodded.

As we drove, the clouds started to open up. Just a sprinkle at first, then a bit more. Then it started to dump. Big drops of rain came down hard and angry. The windshield wipers on the Jeep couldn't keep up, and Sam slowed down, struggling to see where she was going.

As we neared the last corner, she said, "Thanks for coming with me."

"Of course," I said. "You're my friend." I looked at her as she concentrated on the road and, for the first time, I saw past the awkwardness, the frizzy hair, the jittery blue eyes, the freckles, and I caught a glimpse of a hidden part of Sam just below the surface.

It reminded me of my mom, back when she was fighting cancer and didn't have any hair and was tired all the time. It was the kind of beauty that you sometimes see in people who are suffering, if there is such a thing. There had to be beauty in that, right? Is it beautiful when someone is still fighting even though it could be futile? That's what I sensed, just for a second, in Sam's face. And I must have been learning a thing or two from Big, because I thought it was beautiful.

I was still trying to make sense of all of this when I heard Sam gasp. I followed her eyes to the black BMW parked at the trailhead for the M and M Wall. We pulled up next to it. No one was inside.

Sam turned off the Jeep, jumped out, and started running up the trail.

I jumped out after her and yelled through the rain, "What are you doing?"

"I'm going after him," she called back.

I slammed the door to the Jeep. "Wait up."

Sam didn't even look back to see if I was coming. She was half running and half stumbling up the trail, slipping in the mud and on the rocks. I ran after her, hoping to catch up. In seconds, I was soaked to the skin from the rain.

Pretty soon, my lungs burned, and my heart banged against my rib cage. The trail angled into the canyon and then disappeared into the riverbed. I was slipping all over the place and had to slow down or risk breaking my neck. The once-dry riverbed now held a rushing brown stream filled with rainwater and mud.

When I looked up, Sam was nowhere in sight. How could she move so fast when I could barely stay upright?

I continued up the riverbed, often walking right through the middle of the chocolate-milk-colored water. It wasn't like it was going to sweep me away or anything—there wasn't *that* much water—but it still made it hard to walk.

"Sam?" I called. No answer. "Sam?" Still nothing. There was a flash of white and, a second later, thunder shook the whole canyon. This was crazy. What were we doing out here? We were going to drown, get struck by lightning, or fall off a cliff—maybe all three at once.

I turned a corner of the canyon and the M and M Wall came into view. I tried to spot Sam and Conor through the downpour. It was getting dark, and it was hard to see, but I thought I could make out Sam crouched over something. She struggled to lift it, or roll it over, and then she let out a scream. It was by far the single loudest noise I'd ever heard her make. She stumbled up and away from the thing and curled up in a ball against the cliff.

I tried to see what had made her scream. It was Conor. He lay on his back, halfway in the stream. What was he doing? Why didn't he get out of the water? As I got closer, I realized something about the way he was lying didn't look right. One arm was sticking out in the air at an odd angle.

My confusion was replaced by a growing fear.

"Conor!" I shouted. "What are you doing? Are you stupid?"

He didn't move. His arm stayed fixed at the same weird angle. I stumbled closer and saw Conor's skin was a pale gray-blue color. Sand and leaves were stuck to the side of his face where it seemed strangely misshapen. "Hey, get out of the water."

I could still hear Sam screaming and crying over the sound of the rain and the stream. I reached Conor just as lightning flashed, and I saw his eyes.

Wide open. Staring. Not blinking.

No.

The thunder was deafening.

I kneeled down in the water next to him and checked his pulse even though I knew it was pointless. His skin was waxy, the same temperature as the cool air. There was no pulse.

"Sam!" I yelled. "Do you have your phone? Call 911!"

She pulled out her phone and started dialing.

I looked back at Conor, unsure what to do next. Was I supposed to do CPR? For some reason, his arm was really bothering me. It jutted into the air like he was waiting to be called on by a teacher, waiting to say something, answer some unasked question. I tried to push it down. It wouldn't move. His whole body was stiff and cold. He'd been dead awhile. There was no point in CPR.

Stunned, I fell backward onto my butt in the stream. How had this happened? I looked up at Sam to see if she had any answers. She was trying to talk into her phone, but she couldn't get any words out.

It was too late to help Conor, but I could help Sam. I climbed out of the stream and went to her. I sat down, put my arm around her, and grabbed the phone out of her hand.

"Hello? Is this the police?" I asked.

We huddled together, shivering, for what seemed like years while I talked to the dispatcher on the phone. Sam cried the entire time, sometimes loud sobs that wracked her whole body and sometimes quiet tears. I cried, too. The rain eventually stopped.

Conor lay there, unmoving, eyes open, hand still in the air.

Had he fallen while free-soloing Of Mice and Men or one of the other routes? I didn't remember seeing any broken bones. I wasn't an expert in stuff like that, but I was pretty sure it would have been obvious if he'd taken a fall. Then I remembered the way his head didn't look quite right, like part of it had caved in. Did he fall while closer to the ground and hit his head on a rock?

Just before it grew too dark, I finally saw it: the gun. It lay in the rocks halfway between Conor and me. He hadn't fallen. He'd shot himself.

# Chapter 32

**M**y dad and I finally left the police station around 2:00 a.m. We drove the whole way home in silence. When we pulled into the driveway, my dad said, "Paul, you did a very brave thing tonight. I'm proud of you."

I wanted to say that I hadn't done anything. Conor was dead. Where was the bravery in sitting in the rain until the police showed up? But I was too tired to argue, so I just nodded and said, "I'm going to bed."

I stumbled into the house and went to my room. I tore off my mud-covered clothes, put on the sweats I used for pajamas, and collapsed into my bed without bothering to shower. I was certain I'd pass out the moment my head hit the pillow. I didn't. I lay there with my head pounding and feeling strangely numb and hollowed out. It was useless.

After about an hour, I climbed out of bed and went into the living room. My dad was sitting in his chair, reading. He looked up from his book and said, "Can't sleep?"

"No. Care if I watch something?"

"Go right ahead." While I put on a wildlife documentary I'd seen a thousand times, he said, "How are you feeling?"

"Tired. And I have a headache." I knew that's not what he meant, but I didn't know what else to say. Honestly, I had no idea how I was feeling except numb. Thankfully, my dad simply got me a couple of aspirin and a glass of water and sat beside me on the couch.

We watched the TV in silence. Every once in a while, my dad would look over at me and ask in his silent, telepathic dad way, *Do you want to talk?* I'd shake my head, and we'd keep watching crocodiles ambushing zebras at a water hole or whatever was on at the time.

We'd already talked about it all anyway. I mean, he'd been at the police station with me the whole time, given me a big, rib-breaking hug, let me cry and get snot all over his shoulder, and all that. He'd waited while I wrote it all down for the police and listened as I told the whole story. He knew everything that had happened. What else was there to talk about?

I woke up, confused. Why was I on the couch? I looked at the time—12:33. At night? No, daylight leaked in around the closed curtains. Wasn't I supposed to be at school? Then the memories crashed down on me. Sam. The rain. The muddy river. Conor, stiff with rigor mortis. Dead. It couldn't be true.

I searched through the fog of my still-sleepy brain, looking for evidence it had all been a dream. No. It was real, even if it felt unreal, like maybe I'd watched it in a movie or read about it in a book and hadn't actually experienced it myself.

I waited to feel something. I wondered if something was wrong with me because I was so numb and hollow. I mean, I had found Conor Dolores dead. Wasn't I supposed to be freaking out? I knew I should feel something, but it was like someone flipped a switch in my head and shut off all my emotions. I didn't feel anything.

My dad stayed home from work. He hovered around like I had the flu. He even stayed in his pajamas all day. I'd never seen him do that before. It was nice. I wasn't at school, and my dad wasn't at work, and we just hung out and watched movies.

The only problem was, every once in a while, I would kind of forget why I was home. I would start to enjoy myself a little, and then I'd remember Conor with his arm stuck up in the air, and this sick feeling like tar would pool in my stomach. How could I enjoy anything when Conor was dead and Sam and her parents were suffering? That made me think of Lily and her family and how they were suffering. Then I felt even worse. At least I was finally feeling something.

"Dad?"

"Yes?"

"What do I do?"

He thought for a while and then said, "To be honest, there's not much you can do. People have to grieve. It's going to be hard for the Dolores family for a long time. All you can really do is be a good friend to Sam. Make sure you listen if she wants to talk. Be there for her even if she doesn't ask you to. Be patient and encouraging. That kind of thing."

"I don't really know how to do that. I'm not used to having friends."

"You can start by calling her," my dad suggested.

I thought about that. What would I say? Talking to her seemed overwhelming. "What if I text her instead?"

"It's a good start."

"Okay," I said. My dad waited while I sent Sam a generic-sounding text saying how sorry I was for what had happened and asking if I could help.

"I'm a terrible friend," I groaned. "I can't even make myself visit Lily in the hospital."

"You haven't visited Lily? You said you went to the hospital just yesterday."

"I went to the hospital, but I couldn't go in. I kind of froze up at the entrance."

My dad was about to reply when there was loud knock at the door. We looked at each other. Who was at our door? We didn't really get visitors.

I was still in my pajamas, so I peeked out the window. It was Big in a bright-yellow Hawaiian shirt, looking worried. I wasn't sure if I wanted to see anyone. I didn't know how I was supposed to act. Did I just pretend like it was a normal day? Did I try to show I was all sad? It was strange. I felt like I was in a movie, but I didn't know what role I was supposed to be playing. I opened the door.

"Paul, my brother," Big said. He yanked open the screen door and wrapped me in a huge, soft hug. It was awesome. I'm pretty sure God designed Big specifically for giving hugs. Completely enveloped in his warm, sunshiny embrace, it felt like Big took some of the weight off me again. Some of the weight I didn't even know I was carrying. Like when I'd told him about my mom.

After a minute, he let me go and held me by the shoulders. He looked straight into my eyes and said, "You're a good person,

Paul. A good friend. Sam said she didn't know what she would have done without you."

"You talked to Sam?"

Big nodded. "Yeah. I just came from there. My mom and I took her some flowers. She's in pretty bad shape, but if you hadn't helped her, it would have been a lot worse."

"How did you know?"

"Word got out around lunchtime at school. It was terrible, yeah? Everyone had these dazed looks, and they were gathered in these groups whispering, and people in the halls were crying, and that would make other people cry. I saw Katie crying and asked her what was going on, and she said—" Big's deep voice cracked, and he stopped talking.

It took me a second to realize he was trying not to cry. Big, the guy with the perpetual smile, was fighting back tears. I couldn't begin to process it.

He cleared his throat and went on. "Anyway, she told me about Conor. I didn't know you were there until I talked to Sam, and that's when I came over here." He wrapped me in another hug and asked real serious, "Are you okay, brah?"

I was stunned. I didn't realize the news would get around school so fast. I thought it would take a day or two before anyone else knew. I thought I would have more time to let it all sink in. Did other people know I'd been there? Would they ask me about it? How was I supposed to stay invisible if everyone knew about this? When I didn't say anything, Big let go of me and held me by the shoulders again.

"Paul?" my dad said from behind me. "Why don't you invite Big in?"

That snapped me out of the daze I was in, and I said, "Oh, yeah. Come on in, Big. Sorry."

"I don't want to intrude, yeah?" Big looked at me when he said this. Kind of like he was asking my permission.

"You're fine," my dad said with a smile. "I think you're just what we need right now." And he was right.

# Chapter 33

I wasn't sure what I expected to see when I walked into my school the next day. People still crying and hugging? Half the student body absent? Quiet, reflective expressions on the students as they walked the halls? Everyone wearing black and talking about their memories of Conor?

It wasn't any of those things. Not even close. Instead, it was business as usual. Apparently, it took less than twenty-four hours for the school to get over Conor's suicide.

I had planned to find Big first thing. Instead, I wandered the halls before the first bell rang, looking around at everyone in shock. With only a few exceptions, they talked, laughed, shouted, kissed, texted, slammed lockers, and knocked me around like a human ping-pong ball like it was any other day. Like nothing had happened at all. The more I looked around, the more my shock turned to anger. By the time the bell rang to go to first period, I felt ready to explode.

I mean, I knew there were a lot of people that went to my school, and I knew not everyone knew Conor, but still, a kid had died. I personally knew what a jerk and a bully he could be, but still, this was a guy who had hurt so much inside he'd taken his own life. Then his sister had found him dead and cried for hours in the rain, sitting in the dark by his cold body.

The only thing different than any other day was the announcement my history teacher made at the beginning of first period.

"In case some of you don't yet know, a student at our school"—he looked down at the paper in his hand—"Conor Dolores, died on Sunday."

I waited to hear gasps. There were none. I hoped it was because everyone had already heard and not because they didn't care enough to be surprised.

"If at any time today or throughout the next few days you feel the need to talk, there are crisis counselors available at the front office. Are there any questions?"

Someone on the front row said, "I heard he killed himself."

The guy next to me nodded. "He did. He shot himself up in the mountains somewhere."

The teacher said sternly, "That is not a discussion we will be having in class. If you need to talk about it, please go to the office and ask for a counselor. Understood?"

"That's so sad," the girl on the other side of me said to no one in particular. "I remember him from elementary school. He had this big, curly hair. We made fun of it all the time until he finally shaved it off one day."

And that was it. The teacher started class, and no one I knew of went to see any counselor.

Second and third period were the same. I caught a few snatches of conversation in the halls where people were talking about Conor, but they didn't seem like they were upset about it. Most of them talked about it like it was the latest gossip.

On the way to fourth period, I started to see lingering smiles on the people passing me. That meant Big was up ahead. I sped up and, sure enough, there he was in a bright-red Hawaiian shirt. He had his entourage around him, and he was listening to some girl I didn't know rattle on about something that had happened in debate class.

Annoyance burned in me. I snaked my way through everyone and stepped in front of Big. The group stumbled to a stop around him.

Big's smile grew even larger when he saw me. He started to say, "Howzit, brah?" but he never got a chance because I blurted out, "Nobody cares, Big!"

His smile fell. The eyes of everyone around him went huge. A few jaws dropped. I don't think most people in that group had ever heard me talk, much less yell. I was almost as surprised as they were.

Big turned to everyone around him and said, "Why don't you guys go on ahead, yeah?" They hesitated and then wandered off, whispering to each other. Big waited until we were alone and then said, "What do you mean? Who doesn't care?"

"Everybody." I threw my hands out, indicating everybody in the halls, the whole school, the whole world.

A couple of people looked at me curiously, but I met each of their eyes, practically daring them to say something. No one did.

"Everyone is just going on like nothing happened. They don't care about Conor or Sam or anyone. They don't care about anything." I waved my arm again and hit the chest of a random guy in a letterman's jacket. What was the matter with me? I was going to get myself killed if I didn't calm down.

Big pulled me to the side of the hallway where I was less likely to incur the wrath of a passing alpha male. "I think they care, Paul. I really do."

"No, they don't. They're walking around like it's any other day."

Big cocked his head to the side. "I think they just didn't know him like we did."

"What do you mean? We hardly knew him. We only knew he threw drinks at us and threatened us and made fun of us. But we still care." It was weird to admit out loud that I cared about Conor. But did I? I'd hated him when he was alive. Why would I care about him now?

"Sure, but we know Sam. We know how much this is hurting her. Even though we didn't know Conor very well, we know someone who loved him. That's a connection we have that most of these people don't, yeah?"

"But he was still a human being. He was still a student here. Someone just like them, and he *killed* himself. Why don't they . . . I don't know, react somehow?"

"I don't know, brah," Big said. "Maybe they are in their own way. The world has to go on, yeah? We still have classes and homework and the friends who are still with us. It can't just all stop." Big didn't sound all that sure of himself.

The tardy bell rang. We were late.

"Do you want to talk to a counselor?" Big asked.

"No, I don't want to talk to a counselor." I felt almost insulted, although I wasn't sure why. "Let's just go." I started for class and then stopped just outside the door. I didn't want to go in. I couldn't go in.

"You okay?" Big asked.

"You know," I said, "maybe I will go see a counselor." I turned and walked away before Big could reply.

I didn't go to a counselor. Instead, I went to the concrete courtyard and sat on the bench. I stayed there for the entire class period just staring at the dandelion Conor had kicked. It had a tight little green ball at the top of a new stem.

I didn't even like Conor. Why did it matter to me if anyone acted like they cared?

My thoughts settled on the only other person I'd known who had died: my mom. Did anyone besides my dad and me remember her? Did anyone besides us care when she took her last shuddering breath in that ridiculous hospital bed in our living room? Did anyone besides us care she was gone and never coming back and there was nothing anyone could do about it?

Conor was never coming back, and there was nothing anyone could do about that either. I felt like crying, but turned my sob into a growl. I leaped to my feet and paced back and forth. I had to do *something*. But what? I wasn't sure. All I knew was that I was done crying, I was done being invisible, I was done letting people push me around and stuff me in garbage cans, I was done pushing pennies, I was done being prey, and I was done standing by while people like the rhinos made others bow to them.

The rhinos. The whole thing was *their* fault.

I grabbed my pack and headed for the door. The bell rang, marking the end of fourth period and the start of first lunch, just as I entered the hallway. Lunchtime? I knew where the rhinos would be. I marched straight down the middle of the hall. I stared down everyone who got in my way. I didn't move for anyone. I got knocked around plenty, but a lot of people saw me coming and got out of *my* way.

Once I was in the cafeteria, it wasn't hard to spot the rhinos. They were waiting in the lunch line, holding their trays, dwarfing everyone around them.

As I approached, one of them saw me and said, "Hey, Paul." He held out his huge fist for a fist bump. He seemed glad to see me, but I didn't let that deter me from my purpose.

I smacked his fist away and knocked the tray from his other hand onto the floor. The usual roar of the cafeteria turned silent, and I felt five hundred pairs of eyes focus on the back of my head.

"Whoa," the rhino said.

"Calm down, little guy, before you get yourself hurt," said the other rhino through clenched teeth.

"Why?" I yelled up at him. "What are you going to do? Make me bow to you and say 'Never mess with a Small'?" I saw both of them flinch.

The first rhino said, "Easy, Paul. What's going on?"

"You two are murderers. You are nothing but a couple of vicious predators, and you killed Conor."

"You need to shut up, Paul," the second rhino said, low and quiet. Normally that tone would have sent me running with my tail between my legs. Not today.

"No! I'm done sitting back and saying nothing while people like you and Hunter torture others into killing themselves. I don't care what you do to me. I'm never staying silent again."

I saw movement out of the corner of my eye. Teachers were coming at me from two different directions. Fine, let them come.

Let them take me to the office. Let them expel me from this stupid school. I didn't care.

The first rhino said, "That's not how it was." He sounded like he was pleading with me to understand. "He was bullying Lily. We just wanted him to stop. That's all."

"Oh, he stopped all right." I shoved him as hard as I could. "He stopped by putting a bullet in his head. Is that what you wanted?"

The teachers arrived. One grabbed me by the bicep, and the other got between the rhinos and me. "That's enough," the teacher between us barked.

The teacher holding my arm started hauling me away and said, "You're going to the office, young man."

"It wasn't our fault, Paul," the first rhino said.

"We never thought anything like that would happen," said the second rhino. Now he sounded like he was pleading, too.

Even as I was being dragged away, I kept at it. "Oh, sure, I bet you didn't think about how his sister would be the one to find him either. I bet you didn't think about how she would cry for hours in the rain and in the dark with her dead brother lying in a muddy ditch at her feet."

The teacher nearly had me out of the cafeteria door, so I turned my attention to everyone in the cafeteria and screamed, "None of you think! None of you ever think about anyone but yourselves! None of you even care!"

With my last outburst, I felt something crack deep inside me. I swear, I physically felt it crack, and it felt *good*. Like I was free. Which was weird, because I was literally being hauled away in the iron grip of an old, but surprisingly strong teacher.

Halfway to the front office, the teacher let go of my arm and stopped. What was going on? Was I supposed to just keep going on my own? I looked up at him. His skin looked like crepe paper. He had a polished bald head and sagging eyes.

He sighed. "Was all that back there about Conor Dolores?"

"Yes."

"Was he a friend of yours?"

"No. Not really . . . but I cared about him."

The teacher nodded. "Conor wasn't always a nice kid. But none of us wanted this to happen." He let out a long breath. "Do you think the Small boys really drove him to do what he did?"

I started to say yes, but then I thought about it. Was it true? I had thought so two minutes before, but I was no longer so sure. "No, probably not," I said. "They were jerks to him, but a lot of people were. Conor had other problems. I don't really think it was their fault."

"Then why were you yelling at them?"

"Because it doesn't seem like anyone really cares."

The teacher folded his arms and looked down at me.

I stared up at his saggy eyes and waited.

Finally he said, "People care. More than you think, I bet. I don't know if you know this, but when there's a suicide, the school's policy says we aren't allowed to make a big deal about it. They worry about copycat suicides. It's a real problem. So it might seem like everyone is callous and uncaring, but really we're just doing what has to be done to keep other students safe. Does that make sense? There are people, students and faculty alike, who would like to do something—have a vigil, make a memorial, something like that—but we can't. Do you understand?"

I didn't. Not really. Copycat suicides? Was that a real thing?

"So, if it wasn't a suicide, if he'd died in a car accident or of cancer or something like that, it would be different?" I asked.

"Yes, definitely. We've had memorials, fund-raisers, and all kinds of things over the years to honor students or faculty members who have passed." He shook his head. "It's too bad we didn't do more to show we cared when they were still alive."

"I understand," I said. And I really did. It felt like I was thinking clearly for the first time since we'd found Conor. I was angry about Conor's death, no doubt about that, but it was more than that. I was upset because I was worried nobody would care if Lily were to die.

I clenched my eyes shut to fight back tears. Lily was *not* going to die. No way. And if she did? Then I would find a way to make sure she knew I cared long *before* she died. And I was going to start by visiting her in the hospital.

"I'm not going to take you to the principal," the teacher said. "I can see you're not a troublemaker. How about you see one of the counselors instead, okay? I think that's what you really need right now."

"Okay," I said.

He walked back toward the cafeteria.

I started for the office, and then I walked right past it. I walked out the front doors of the school and out into the sunshine. I walked the two blocks to the bus stop, thinking all the while. How was I going to show Lily I cared? Just visiting wasn't enough. Anyone could do that. I had to do more.

# Chapter 34

The bus arrived, and I sat down, thinking. What could I do for Lily? I didn't want to buy her a stuffed cow like everyone else or get her a card. I wanted to stand out. I wanted this to be *big*. Something Lily would never forget. A declaration of my love, even. A grand statement so there was no way Lily would ever doubt I cared. But what could I do?

Then I saw it. It had been there all along, practically waving its hands at me to get my attention. Above the seat across the aisle from me was a bank advertisement. There were ads all over the bus, but that wasn't what caught my attention. This one showed a rock climber on one of those tall, skinny, red sandstone towers. She was climbing a thin, sinuous crack. It was beautiful.

That's when I knew what I was going to do. I was going to take Lily to Southern Utah to go crack climbing. It's what she'd dreamed of doing. She'd said so herself only a few days before in the gym. She'd be out of the hospital soon, and I'd convince Andy or my dad to take us down to Canyonlands or Indian Creek or wherever that place was Lily said she wanted to go. Sam could come, too, if she was feeling up to it. It would be perfect. I was actually going to do something right for once. Something a real friend would do.

Twenty minutes later, I arrived at the hospital only to learn Lily had been sent home that morning. Just my luck. I finally got up the nerve to visit Lily in the hospital, and she wasn't there. I'd just go to her house, explain everything, and hope she understood. Then I had a terrible realization: I would have to visit her at home—where the rhinos lived.

While I waited for the next bus, I texted Lily to make sure it was okay for me to come over. A part of me secretly hoped she'd say no. She didn't. She said I could come over any time. I paced in front of the bus stop. What was I going to do? The rhinos were going to kill me. When Lily found out what I said to them in front of the whole cafeteria, she might encourage them. Especially after she'd spent a week and a half in the hospital with no visits from me.

I thought of Sam, crying in the rain. I thought of Conor, dead in the muddy water. Then I thought, *So what if the rhinos are there?* I'd tell them the same thing all over again. They could do whatever they wanted to me. It could never be as bad as what I'd already gone through. It could never be as bad as what Conor had gone through. It could never be as bad as what Sam and Lily were going through. So forget them. I was *not* afraid of guys like that anymore. Okay, that wasn't exactly true. I was afraid of them, very afraid, but I wasn't going to let that stop me.

The bus dropped me off about two miles from Lily's house. As I walked, I alternated between excitement at the thought of telling Lily about my road trip idea and dread at the thought of a painful death at the hands of the rhinos.

When a flatbed pickup truck pulled up next to me, I knew exactly who was inside, but I kept walking without looking up.

"Paul?" the rhino in the passenger seat said. "You need a ride?"

"Not from you," I said. I glanced around, looking for an escape route. Lily lived pretty far outside of town, so it was just hay and cornfields with a house every quarter mile or so. Wide ditches lined the road full of dark, muddy water. They were deep enough to swallow a car. I had nowhere to run.

"Are you coming to see Lily?"

"Yes."

"You've got over a mile still to go. Let us give you a ride."

I stopped walking and glared at him. "Why? So you can torture me into committing suicide, too?"

I heard the driver swear. "He won't need to commit suicide because I'm going to kill him right now."

The other rhino turned to the driver and yelled, "Shut up, Colt. Paul's right. It was *our* fault. Conor might be alive right now if it wasn't for us."

"It's not our fault," Colt yelled back. "Conor was picking on Lily, and he deserved what he got. We didn't hold that gun to his head. He didn't have to shoot himself. He did that all on his own."

"We may as well have." Chuck's voice broke. "I told you we should have let Lily handle it like she wanted."

Chuck threw himself across the cab at Colt, and the whole truck shook. The driver's side door flew open, and they tumbled onto the ground, wrestling right in the middle of the road like two huge bulls. After some intense scuffling, Chuck got Colt in a headlock, and his face turned purple. I was worried Chuck was going to choke him until he passed out.

"Stop!" I shouted.

They both looked at me, but they didn't stop, though Chuck appeared to loosen his grip a little.

"It's not your fault, okay? Conor had other problems. You two were just one of many."

Chuck let go of his brother. They stood up and dusted themselves off.

"What do you mean?" Colt asked.

I sighed. "Give me a ride, and I'll tell you what I know."

We climbed into the truck. I sat in the middle because that's where tall people always expect short people to sit for some reason. As we drove, I told them about Conor's mom. They had seen her break down at the climbing gym, so they knew she had issues, but they didn't know to what extent. I also told them about how reckless Conor had been climbing at the M and M Wall and about the penny-pushing incident.

"It's not like I really knew him that well," I said, "but you guys were just a small part of a lot of other big things. I think he was deeply unhappy. He wasn't very . . . stable, you know? Sam said he didn't really have any friends, and there were other people that harassed him at school. It wasn't just you guys."

"But we didn't help, that's for sure," Chuck said. "I feel like throwing up when I think about it."

"We didn't want him to kill himself," Colt said.

"No, we didn't."

When we got to the house, Chuck and Colt went straight to the kitchen and started rummaging around for food.

"You want something?" Chuck asked me with his head in the refrigerator.

"No, thanks," I said. "Where's Lily? In her room?"

In answer, Colt shouted, "Lily! Paul's here!"

"Stop your bellowing," Mrs. Small said from behind me as she entered the kitchen. She scowled at Colt. "She *was* sleeping, but I'll bet she's not now."

As if on cue, I heard Lily holler, "I'm up here."

Mrs. Small gave Colt a withering look and then smiled at me. "Hi, Paul. Lily's upstairs. Go on up. She'll be excited to see you."

"Okay, thanks," I said and hurried out of the kitchen. Even though the rhinos didn't appear to want to kill me, I was glad to get away from them.

I found Lily lying on her bed, propped up by a pile of pillows. Her room wasn't how I remembered it. A flat-screen TV had been mounted to one wall, and the card table next to her bed was covered in snacks and medicine bottles. One side of the room was completely covered in a herd of stuffed cows of all shapes and sizes. A glass vase with lilies in it sat by the window. The lilies Sam had said were from me, I realized. I was happy to see they were still alive. I was also happy to see the Maasai flag hanging in its place on the wall.

"Hi," I said.

"Hi," she said.

"I like your cows."

Lily gave me a weak smile. "You should have visited me."

"I know. I'm sorry. I tried. Three times."

"Sam told me. It's okay."

"No, it's not okay. I should have made myself. That's what friends do. And I'm going to be a good friend from now on no matter what because I care about you, I really do, and I want you to know that."

"I don't think you do."

"What?"

"I don't think you care," she said with an unreadable expression.

"What do you mean?"

"You didn't win the climbing competition for me after I gave you explicit instructions to do nothing short of dominate." She let the corner of her mouth twist up into a smirk, and then I knew she was kidding.

I laughed. "I tried, I really did. And I'm here now to show you I care and to tell you about my master plan."

Lily raised an eyebrow. "Oh, really? What master plan?"

I told her all about my plan to take her to Indian Creek. I explained that ideally we could get Sam to go with us, if we gave her a little time after the funeral, and that I'd try to get Andy to be our guide since we didn't really know where we were going. I told her even if no one else could go, I'd find a way to make it work.

Lily listened with a patient smile. When I was finished, she said, "Paul, I can barely make it up the stairs."

"Well, yeah, now, but you're all done with your chemo, right? You'll be feeling better again soon, and we'll go then. I mean, look, you didn't even lose your hair." I gestured to her cornrows that were still just as long and thick as ever.

Lily sighed. "I wish that were true, but I'm only done with the first phase. I'm going to be on chemo for at least *two years*. I take four drugs in the morning and four at night. They put a port in my chest to take my blood and give me medicine and stuff. My head is so cloudy, I can hardly think, and I'm going to lose my hair sooner or later. Walking to the bathroom is exhausting. I can't go climbing."

I don't know why I was stunned. Of course she wouldn't be able to go on a road trip to Indian Creek. What was I thinking? I knew leukemia was going to be a long, hard battle for her. I guess I didn't realize just *how* long and hard. I was so stupid. So much for my grand gesture of love.

"But, Paul?"

I looked up at her.

"I *will* take you up on that offer. It's just going to be a little later. In the meantime, you can keep getting better at climbing cracks and start collecting the gear and stuff, so we'll be ready when I'm feeling up to it. Okay?"

"Okay." I sat down on the bed next to her. "I just . . . I just wanted to do something nice for you."

"You are doing something nice for me. You're here, aren't you?"

"I am *now*," I said with a groan.

We were quiet, just staring at our own reflections in the dark TV screen.

"You seem different," Lily said.

"I am. I really am different."

"Because of what happened with Conor?"

"Yes . . . no . . . maybe. I don't know. I went a little crazy today and yelled at Chuck and Colt in the cafeteria."

Lily squawked with laughter. "You *didn't*."

"I did. I even knocked Chuck's lunch out of his hand. Or was it Colt's? I forget which."

Lily laughed more. "Are you serious?"

"Yep. A teacher had to drag me away, kicking and screaming."

"No way. That's the best story I've heard all week. I wish I could have seen that. Then what happened?"

"The teacher told me to see a counselor, but I went to the

hospital to see you instead. Of course, you weren't there anymore. I'm sorry I was never able to go in the hospital. I was scared, I guess, and I still am, but I don't care about being scared anymore. I just want to show you how much I care because . . . because . . ." I turned to face her directly. "I think I might love you."

Lily's eyebrows went way up, and her mouth fell open. "You mean you love me like a friend, right?"

"No," I said, and, in what was quite possibly the bravest moment of my entire life, I reached out and took her hand. "I mean, I really might love you." I felt my face heat up with what was certainly the biggest blush in the history of the world. But I didn't care. I didn't care if I made a total fool out of myself. If I couldn't take her on her dream climbing trip, then I could at least tell her how I felt. There was no way I was going to watch Lily fight cancer without her knowing I was pretty sure I loved her.

"Oh," she said. She looked nervous.

"I know it's weird with me being so short and scrawny and all, and you being so tall and tough and beautiful. I want you to know, and I don't care what anyone else thinks anymore. I'm not going to hide from people and, well, my own feelings, I guess, or even you because, like I said, I might love you."

"Might?" she asked.

I shrugged. "Well, yeah. I don't exactly know what it's like to be in love with someone. This feels pretty much like how I imagined it, but it's hard to be sure."

"Yes," she said. "I guess it is." Then she laughed.

"What's so funny?" I asked.

Lily took a second to catch her breath and said, "I've missed you, Paul."

"I've missed you, too," I said.

She cocked her head and looked at me for a long time.

"What?" I asked.

Lily said in what was the gentlest voice I'd ever heard her use, "I don't think you're in love with me. Not in a romantic way, anyway. I think the very fact that you're not sure if you love me means that you probably don't. And that's for the best."

"Yeah, well, we'll see about that," I said and settled back against the pillows beside her so our shoulders were touching. I didn't let go of her hand, and she didn't let go of mine. I looked at our reflection in the TV again. We were a pretty hilarious pair.

Lily smiled. "I guess we will," she said.

# Chapter 35

After my outburst on Tuesday, I was nervous about going back to school. All day Wednesday I kept worrying I might freak out again. Thankfully, I didn't blow up on anyone, but I *was* different.

I walked down the middle of the hall like anyone else. I didn't hide or dart around, dodging people. I met people's eyes, and I even said hello to Katie and some of her friends when they passed me in the hall. That sounds like no big deal, I know, but it was huge for me. Talking to a group of cute girls in the hall was not something I'd ever done before. *And* they said hi back.

At lunchtime, I wanted to prove to myself and everyone else I wasn't afraid. I thought I'd end up sitting alone in the cafeteria, but Chuck and Colt saw me and insisted I sit with them. They introduced me to their friends, and everyone was nice enough, but I felt totally out of place. What did I have in common with a table full of jocks and their girlfriends?

Then Chuck and Colt told them about how well I'd done in the climbing competition. They called me a "rock-climbing prodigy," and everyone at the table seemed to reevaluate me. I wasn't sure if I was going to make a habit of sitting there, but it was nice to make an impression.

People were still jerks, of course. That never changed. But for every comment I heard making fun of my size, someone else complimented me for standing up to Chuck and Colt. For every time I got hip checked in the hall, someone else waved or nodded a greeting.

Once, when I got knocked down, some guy I didn't know reached out and helped me up. He walked with me for a while and said he'd seen me confront Chuck and Colt. He said it was one of the coolest things he'd ever seen and called me a "beast."

The way the guy said it made it sound like it was supposed to be good, so I took it as a compliment. He bumped fists with me before he headed in another direction. I wondered if these people had been there all along. People willing to be friendly and helpful. Why had I never noticed them before?

On Wednesday night, Big's mom made dinner for the whole Small family. It was like a Thanksgiving feast. It took Big and me three trips from the van to the house to take all the food inside. I'd never seen anything so beautiful in my life. I thought family parties like that only existed on TV. The Smalls invited Big and me to join them, and Lily even came down from her room for the occasion, but I could see how much it tired her out.

Thursday night, I helped Big and his mom deliver an equally beautiful dinner to the Dolores family. I was hoping to see Sam, but she didn't come to the door, and her dad didn't invite us in. He was polite, but he seemed like he was anxious for us to leave as soon as possible. Before I could ask about Sam, he said thanks and shut the door. I ended up texting her, telling her that we missed her, and we hoped she was doing okay, but she didn't respond.

After Big and I left the Dolores' house, we went to Lily's again. We took her all the homework her teachers had collected for her and hung out in her room. Lily seemed to enjoy our company, so we came back on Friday. The three of us talked, studied, and watched TV. I loved every minute of it.

All three nights that week, my dad picked up Big and me from Lily's when he got off work. Then he dropped Big off at home and took me to the climbing gym, where he belayed me on Bildungsroman. I don't know if he was doing it to help me get my mind off what had happened with Conor or what, but I took advantage of the opportunity. I climbed until my arms and hands felt like soggy noodles. I made progress every day, and it felt fantastic. Of course, none of the high points I made officially counted because I still had to cheat past the height-dependent move, but I was okay with that.

On Saturday, I went to Conor's funeral with my dad. The only other funeral I'd been to was my mom's, and while I really, really didn't want to go to another one ever again, there was no way I was going to miss it. I had friends now, and I needed to be there for them.

The funeral was held at a church near the Dolores' house. Conor's casket sat at the front of the chapel. We waited in a line to go up to the casket, where people were taking turns saying their goodbyes. When it was my turn, I put my hand on the dark, polished wood. My dad came up beside me and put his arm around my shoulders.

"Am I supposed to say something?" I asked.

"Not necessarily," my dad said.

"Do I just tell him goodbye?"

"If you want. Tell him whatever you like. You don't have to do it aloud. You can just do it in your thoughts."

I took a deep breath and thought about what I should say.

*Me: You know what, Conor? You're a real jerk. You were a jerk while you were alive, and you're a jerk for all the pain you're causing with your death.*

*Conor: Whatever, runt. Call me a jerk if you want. You don't know how much I was hurting. I didn't know what else to do. The thought of living another day was unbearable.*

*Me: Yeah, well, I feel that way all the time, and you don't see me lying in a stupid casket making people cry. You're a selfish jerk.*

*Conor: You think you feel like I did? I don't think so. You may be scrawny and get pushed around a lot at school, but you don't know what it's like to live in my house.*

*Me: Your family loved you.*

*Conor: Well, I know that now. It wasn't so obvious while I was still alive.*

*Me: I'm sorry, Conor. I wish I would have done more. I wish I could have helped. I'm sorry. I really am.*

*Conor: You don't need to be sorry. You couldn't have fixed me or my family. Goodbye, brother.*

*Me: Brother?*

*Conor: Yeah, you heard me. Don't make a big deal out of it.*

*Me: Okay. Goodbye, brother.*

I felt my eyes start to get a little leaky, so I left the chapel and went into the hall. My dad followed me.

"I should have been nicer to him," I said. "I should have helped."

"You didn't know. You did your best. You couldn't have known."

"I did, though. I knew he was having a hard time. Everyone did. I should have helped."

"You didn't know how," he said. "You'll know a little more for the next time you meet someone like Conor." He grabbed me and made me look right in his eyes. "I think that's the best thing you can do for Conor and for yourself. Next time, when you see someone who needs a friend, be there for them."

I nodded and wiped my eyes and nose with my hands. My dad handed me a handkerchief. An actual fabric handkerchief.

"Are you serious?" I asked.

"I know, right?" he said. "Who carries a hanky anymore?" That made me laugh and stop crying. "You ready to go back into the chapel?" my dad asked. "They're going to start the service soon."

"I guess," I said.

We stood in the doorway, trying to find a place to sit. The place was packed, and the only open spot was the area up front that had been roped off for Conor's family.

Eventually, I saw Big stand up and wave us over. Instead of his normal Hawaiian shirt, he was wearing a black suit with a white shirt and black tie. He didn't look like himself until he smiled a huge smile. Even at a funeral he had a smile, and somehow it didn't feel out of place. Just seeing him made me feel better. I grabbed my dad, and we crossed the chapel to where he sat on a pew with his mom.

"We saved you a spot," Big said when we got closer. "And Lily, too, if she makes it."

While I waited for the funeral to begin, I looked at the faces of the people around me. One man was clenching and unclenching his jaw, his lips pressed tight together. I watched a woman swallow hard and look up like she was trying to fight off tears. I saw a guy my age staring at the pew in front of him like he was trying to burrow a hole through it. An old man near the front kept shaking his head like he couldn't understand what had happened. They all seemed to be wishing right along with me that they had somehow found a way to help Conor.

I made a promise to myself that I would never again sit in a funeral and wish that I had done more.

Someone behind me said, "Hey, twerp."

I turned around to see Lily towering over me. "Lily," I said a little louder than was probably appropriate for a funeral. "Oh, sorry," I whispered to the people around us as I stood up to greet her.

Lily was holding on to Chuck's arm for support. She looked exhausted, dazed, and very beautiful. She was wearing a dress. Lily in a dress. That was something I *never* thought I'd see. It was long and black with white flowers printed on it, and she had a black scarf around her neck. She looked . . . elegant. I resisted the urge to hug her and instead offered her my seat.

"We can all fit," Big said and scooted down the row. By the time we were all done, I was shoehorned firmly between Lily and Chuck. I felt absolutely tiny, but I also felt pretty good, too. I liked being squished up against Lily. It was nice to be that close to someone you care about—and might even be in love with—even if it was at a funeral.

I liked it so much, I wanted to hold Lily's hand. I kept thinking about it and fighting with myself. Her hand was just sitting

266

there on her thigh. I wanted to hold it so badly. So, a few minutes after the funeral started, I just reached over and took Lily's hand and held it between both of mine.

I hoped no one would notice we were holding hands, but then I heard Chuck kind of choke back a snicker next to me. Lily reached across me with her free hand and punched Chuck hard in the thigh. Like, definitely-going-to-leave-a-bruise kind of hard. He grunted, and then let out a long breath while rubbing his thigh. After that he stayed silent and kept his eyes straight ahead.

I looked up at Lily, and she had a smirk curving one corner of her mouth. It looked really good on her. I couldn't believe it. I was holding Lily's hand for the second time in a week and, once again, she didn't pull it away.

# Chapter 36

The day after the funeral, Sam picked up Big and me in her Jeep so we could visit Lily. It was Sunday, and I had spent the morning counting the minutes until I could see her. I sat in the tiny back seat thinking about whether I'd be able to hold Lily's hand again with Big and Sam there. That made me think about how Lily punched Chuck at the funeral.

"What are you grinning about, brah?" Big asked. He'd turned around to look at me. His customary gigantic smile seemed a little smug, like he knew exactly what I was grinning about.

"What? Me? I don't know. No reason, I guess." I hadn't even realized I was smiling until Big pointed it out.

"I bet I know why, yeah?" Big said and nudged Sam with his elbow.

Sam gave me what must have been an attempt at a smile, but it was more of just a tired-looking tightening of her lips. It made me feel guilty for being happy only one day after her brother's funeral.

Right then, my phone rang. I pulled it out and saw Lily's name.

"Hey, Lily," I said.

"Hey, twerp." I could tell she was trying to sound cheerful, but there was a heavy note in her voice.

"What's wrong?" I asked as a pit formed in my stomach.

"I was just calling to let you guys know I can't hang out tonight."

I could hear people talking in the background and some random commotion. "You're at the hospital," I said.

"Wow, smarty-pants, how'd you know?"

"What's wrong? I thought things were going fine."

"They were, and they are—for the most part. I just got some blood work done, and it wasn't great, so they want me here for a few days while they sort it out. It's nothing to get excited about. Just a minor setback." She was trying to make it sound like she wasn't worried, but I knew better.

"Can we come visit you up there?"

"Not today, no. Maybe tomorrow. We'll have to see how it goes, and I'll let you know."

"Oh . . . alright."

"It's okay, Paul. Don't worry. I'm pretty tough, if you haven't noticed."

"I've noticed."

"Then quit sounding like someone kicked your puppy and cheer up."

We were both silent for a moment.

"How can I help?" I asked.

I heard Lily take a big breath and let it out. "You are, Paul. Just keep caring."

"I do care. I really do."

"I know you do. You might even love me, remember?"

"I remember."

"I'll call you tomorrow."

"Okay, bye."

"Bye."

I waited for a few seconds until she hung up.

By then, Sam had parked in Lily's driveway.

"She's not here," I said and told Big and Sam what Lily had said on the phone.

One of the Smalls' trucks was parked next to the road with a "For Sale" sign in the window, but all the other cars were gone, and it didn't look like anyone was home. We got out anyway and knocked on the door, just in case. Of course, no one answered. I'm not sure what we expected. Maybe we thought one of Lily's brothers would be there, and we could get some more information. Since we didn't have anywhere else to go, we hung out on the porch. Sam sat on the swing and Big sat in a rocking chair. I was too restless and paced back and forth instead.

"Lily said it was no big deal?" Big asked.

"Yeah, but I think she was downplaying it," I said.

Big nodded.

We were quiet for a while. I listened to the creaking of Big's rocking chair and the wind in the cottonwood trees. The wind sounded almost like a river splashing over rocks. If I hadn't been so worried about Lily, I might have commented on how beautiful it sounded. Big was really starting to wear off on me.

Sam said something I couldn't hear.

"What's that, Sam?" Big asked.

"I was wondering what we could do for Lily."

"I don't know," Big said.

"I'm sick and tired of not being able to do anything," I said.

"I'm not sure there's anything we can do," Big said.

"There has to be something."

"Poor Lily," Sam said.

I was so frustrated, I felt like smashing something. I'm not usually like that, but right then I wanted a baseball bat and a room full of china to destroy. After my big idea to take Lily climbing at Indian Creek failed miserably, I was more eager than ever to do something meaningful. To *show* Lily I cared, not just say it.

"You can't cure cancer," Big said.

"I know," I said. "I just wish I could take away some of her pain or give her some of my energy so she's not so tired all the time. But I can't do anything." I flopped down onto the porch swing next to Sam and sent it swaying crookedly.

"I think you've made Lily happier than anyone else has lately," Big said. "That's doing something, yeah?"

"That's not enough." I let out a long sigh. To be honest, Big's words helped. Still, I wanted to make a grand gesture. I wanted to do something *big*.

I stared out at the yard where bikes and toys were scattered in the shade of the cottonwoods. Out at the road, I could see the pickup truck with the "For Sale" sign. I was pretty sure it was Lily's dad's truck because it was the nicest and newest of all the vehicles.

"Why are they selling their truck?" I asked.

Sam shrugged.

Big said, "Money's probably tight, yeah? Lily's medical bills must be expensive."

Then an idea hit me. I don't know why it took me so long. I jumped up and said, "That's it. That's what we'll do."

"What?" Big asked, but then I saw the light turn on in his

eyes, and his mouth grew into a gigantic smile. "That is a beautiful idea."

"What?" asked Sam. "Are you thinking of a fund-raiser?"

"Exactly," I said. I felt so good it was almost like I was holding Lily's hand right then.

"I don't think Lily would like that," Sam said.

Big's smile shrank a little. "That's true. Lily doesn't like a lot of attention. She might kill us if we tried to do something like that."

For a moment, I thought they were right. Then I thought about Conor. "Too bad," I said. "Lily's going to have to deal with it. I'm going to help her whether she likes it or not. She might hate me for it, but I'm not going to stand by and do nothing. I can organize a fund-raiser for Lily and her family, so that's what I'm going to do. Are you two going to help me?"

Sam and Big looked at each other, then at me, then back at each other.

"I'll help," Sam whispered with a half smile.

"Me too," Big said. "I'll just be sure Lily knows it was all your idea, so she'll only hurt me a little." He laughed and then added with a huge smile, "But you, brah—you're going to be in trouble."

# Chapter 37

We brainstormed for over an hour sitting on Lily's front porch. It was getting close to Halloween, so we talked about doing a corn maze or a haunted house. We considered doing something at school like a Halloween party or a dance. We also talked about doing some kind of online social-media event. But everything made me cringe when I thought of how Lily would react. For all my brave talk, I really was afraid of what Lily would do when she found out about our idea.

It was Sam who finally suggested a Halloween climbing competition and party at the Ogden Climbing Center. Instantly, all three of us knew it was perfect.

Big said he thought he could get local businesses to donate prizes, Sam said she would make posters and flyers, and my job was to get the gym on board and organize the competition.

After school on Monday, I told Andy about our idea.

"Absolutely," he said. "That's a great idea."

We planned the event for the weekend before Halloween, which was three weeks away. Andy said the gym would let people climb for a discount if they wore a costume and that most of the money would go to Lily's family. He also thought he could get a local band to play for free as part of the party.

As for the competition, we decided to do it the traditional way where everyone competed individually. Andy said he would advertise it on the gym's website if I would get flyers out to all the climbing and outdoor shops. He said climbers would come from all over the valley for something like this, and all the entry fees would go to Lily's family.

Just before I left, Andy grabbed me by the arm. "This is a great thing you're doing, Paul. You're a good friend. Lily and her family are going to be so grateful."

"Well, it's not really me. I mean, you're doing most of the work here, and Big and Sam are helping, too."

"It wouldn't be happening at all without you. You're a good man."

*Man?* Had Andy just called me a man? I tried to think if anyone had ever done that before. Nope, not ever.

"Thanks," I said.

The next day, Big, Sam, and I went to visit Lily at the hospital. I was nervous about what she would say. On the way up the elevator, I mumbled, "Lily's going to kill us."

"No, brah," Big said with a smile that was more mischievous than sunshiny. "She's going to kill *you*."

When we got off the elevator, we ran into Chuck staring into a huge saltwater fish tank in the hall. Big said, "Hey, Chuck. How's it going?"

Chuck turned around and, like everyone else, his face lit up when he saw Big's smile. "What's up, my brother?" They hugged each other, and then Chuck stepped back, looking at us with unconcealed amusement. "You guys are so dead."

"It was all Paul's idea," Big said.

Chuck shook his head. "Well, it was nice knowing you, bro." He laughed.

I did not laugh. I was genuinely scared, and Chuck's stupid jokes weren't helping. I was pretty sure Lily wouldn't actually hurt me physically, but she might be angry enough to no longer want to hold my hand, speak to me, or even see me.

Chuck turned to Sam. His eyebrows came down like he was trying to remember who she was. Then they shot up, and he said, "Sam, right?" His quiet voice trembled a little.

Sam nodded and looked at her feet.

"I'm sorry about your brother," Chuck said. His voice was tight, and his face scrunched up like he was fighting off emotion.

Sam continued to look at her feet. "It's okay."

"No," Chuck said, "I mean, I'm sorry about . . . I'm sorry I didn't treat him better."

After a long five seconds, Sam whispered in a voice that was quiet even for her, "I know."

There was another long five seconds, and then Chuck stepped forward and hugged her tight. Sam let out a surprised squeak as she disappeared into his huge arms.

"I'm so, so sorry," Chuck said.

One of Sam's skinny arms patted Chuck's huge back. "It's okay," she said again.

I wasn't sure who was comforting whom. I looked at Big, who nodded and mouthed the word, "Beautiful."

After a moment, Chuck let go of Sam and stepped back. He turned to the fish tank, wiping his eyes. He sniffed and said, "Lily's in room eleven, down there on the left. Just listen for the mooing."

Big put a hand on his shoulder and said, "Thanks, Chuck."

We started down the hall, where, ahead of us, a kid was walking with a nurse. He was pushing one of those IV bags on a pole with wheels. As he passed a room on the left, he mooed. Instantly, there was a whole variety of realistic-sounding moos as if a herd of cows was sitting just inside the doorway. The kid grinned and giggled. The nurse smiled and waved at the source of the mooing, and they kept walking.

When we reached the room, Big poked his head in and said, "Hey, there, kaikuahine."

"Hey, Big," I heard Lily say. She sounded drowsy.

Big went in, and Sam followed him. I went in last and hid behind them.

"Hey, Sam," Lily said. "Thanks for coming to see me."

The room was packed. It wasn't so much that there were a lot of people in it, but more that the people in it were so *big*. Lily's dad and Junior half-stood and half-sat, leaning against a windowsill. Lily's mom was in the only chair.

Lily was in the bed, which was too short for her long body so her feet hung off the end. Also in the bed with her were her little brother and sister, Jason and Carol, and a big stuffed cow. Colt stood in a corner and, once Big and Sam had shuffled in, there was no more space at all. Except for someone as small as me.

Everyone exchanged greetings, and then Lily said, "Hey, twerp. You going to come out from hiding back there and say hi to me?"

I stepped around Big, standing right next to the bed. Carol giggled, and Lily gave her an elbow.

"Hi, Lily," I said. I tried to meet her eyes, but failed. She looked so worn-out it made my chest ache.

"You're in trouble," Carol said to me, drawing out the word "trouble" to emphasize just how bad it was.

"Yeah, he is," Lily said. "What should we do to him, Carol?"

Carol considered for a long time. "Put him in time-out?"

"I don't think that's painful enough," Lily said.

"Does he need a spanking?"

Everyone laughed, and I felt my face heat up.

"I think it needs to be worse," Lily said. "Much worse."

I dared to glance up and saw Lily giving me that crooked smirk of hers. As tired as she was, she was clearly enjoying this.

"I know," Jason said. "Let's hold him down while Lily *kisses* him."

Now everyone was really laughing, and even I couldn't help but smile.

"You better be careful," Colt said. "If that's the punishment, Paul might organize a dozen fund-raisers."

Lily shot him with her death ray, and he cut his laugh short, which only made everyone else laugh harder. "Yeah, just keep laughing it up," Lily said. "One day soon, I'll get better, and then you'll all be sorry."

Mr. Small crossed the room and held out his hand to me. "In all seriousness, Paul, thank you for doing this. We truly appreciate the help." He looked me straight in the eye while he shook my hand. "Thanks to all of you," he said and shook hands with Big and Sam as well.

Mrs. Small got up from her chair and gave me a hug. "We'll never be able to thank you enough." She let go of me and gently pushed me toward the head of the bed. "Lily, quit teasing the young man, and thank him properly."

"For what?" Lily said. "For letting everyone know I have

cancer after I worked so hard to keep it a secret? For making me into a charity case and embarrassing me in front of everyone?" It was hard to tell if she was kidding or not.

"Oh, stop that," Mrs. Small said. "Thank him for being a good friend, and for being the angel God sent to help us when we needed it most."

"Alright, fine," Lily said with a melodramatic groan. She was smirking again, so I hoped that meant she wasn't too mad. "Thanks, Paul," she said, and she almost sounded sincere. Then she shot her death ray at Big and Sam. "And thanks a lot to the two of you. I know you had a hand in this as well. You're not escaping punishment. I just don't have the energy to make you suffer right now."

"Oh, Lily," Mrs. Small said in exasperation.

"Will you be able to come?" I asked Lily.

Everyone in the room was quiet. Lily's family exchanged uncomfortable glances—the kind when they have bad news they don't want to share. My stomach knotted up.

Mr. Small finally answered, "We don't know right now. We hope Lily will be able to attend, but we'll have to see how the next few weeks go."

What was that supposed to mean? He didn't sound like he was talking about how tired she felt. He sounded like, well, I didn't want to even think about what he sounded like.

"But the rest of us will be there, for sure," Colt said.

"Yeah," said Junior, "we wouldn't miss it for the world."

They were trying way too hard to be cheerful. I felt woozy and grabbed the edge of the bed to steady myself. It got hard to breathe, and I worried I might start hyperventilating right there in Lily's hospital room in front of everyone. Then I felt a hand on mine. I looked down. Lily squeezed my hand. I looked up at her face. She smiled. It was a weak smile, but it was nice, and I felt like I could breathe again.

"I heard you're holding a climbing competition as part of the fund-raiser," Colt said.

"Yeah," I said.

"Are you going to enter?" Carol asked me.

"Of course he is," Lily said. "And this time, he's going to win it for me."

# Chapter 38

The next few weeks went by in a blur. It was exhausting but very satisfying. Sam designed the flyers and posters and got them printed. We hung them all over our school, the nearby university, and in every climbing shop, gym, and sporting goods store in the valley. As we drove around with the flyers, we also got a dozen different businesses to donate prizes and money.

We spread the word in other ways, too. Big talked about the fund-raiser on our school's daily broadcast. The university radio station added it to their announcements and included the fact that a local band would be performing. Ogden's local newspaper added it to their calendar. Katie and her friends helped share the word through social media.

It seemed like I was always on the phone—texting or emailing someone about something to do with the fund-raiser. I'd never had so much interaction with other human beings in my entire life, and the effort it took to communicate with people was the most exhausting thing of all. Somewhere in the middle of all this, I realized I hadn't been fumbling my way through every conversation.

We also assisted Andy with planning and preparing the decorations, and helped him set up the routes for the competition. I helped him with the women's routes and Sam helped him set up the men's. That way, we wouldn't have an unfair advantage in the comp.

Almost every evening, my dad displayed his Zen-like patience belaying me on Bildungsroman. I got used to cheating past hold number eight, and I focused on the rest of the route. I had all but the last few moves to the top dialed. My dad and Andy both thought I'd be able to do the whole thing, but I knew they were wrong. Unless I suddenly grew six inches over breakfast one day, I was never going to make that height-dependent move.

I'd fall asleep as soon as my head hit the pillow every night, and sometimes before. The weird thing was, I'd never felt better.

Lily went home from the hospital at the end of the first week, but she seemed more and more tired all the time. She wasn't always up for having us visit, although we tried almost every night. We still brought her homework to her, though sometimes she fell asleep right in the middle of an assignment. On a few occasions, her mom shooed us away, saying, "How's she ever going to get better if you three won't let her rest?" As far as I could tell, all Lily ever did was rest, and it didn't seem to be doing her any good at all.

A few days before the fund-raiser, I finally had to accept the fact that she was not going to have the energy to be there. After that, I almost didn't want to go through with it. I wanted her to see all the work we'd done. Maybe it was selfish, but I wanted her to see my grand gesture of love. If she couldn't be there, what was the point? I mean, I knew the important thing was for Lily to get better, and for us to help her and her family to make that happen, but I also wanted to impress her. Like any guy who might be in love would.

On the Friday night before the fund-raiser, I checked to make sure we had everything ready to go. I was proud of what we had accomplished but also extremely nervous about the whole thing, and I was pretty sure I'd given myself an ulcer. But it looked like we were really going to pull it off. That is, as long as people actually showed up.

That night, we were all sitting in Lily's room watching a really boring movie Big had insisted was nothing short of amazing. Lily looked like she was about to doze off when Big asked, "What are you guys going to dress up as?"

Sam and I shared an uneasy look.

"What do you mean?" I asked.

"You know, what costumes are you wearing tomorrow night?"

"I'm not going to wear a costume," I said.

Big looked at Sam, and she shook her head to indicate that she, too, had no intention of dressing up. I was glad to see she was with me on this.

"You have to dress up," Big said. "It's a Halloween party. Lily, tell them."

"What?" Lily mumbled, blinking her eyes open.

"Oh, sorry," Big said. "I didn't mean to wake you."

"What are you guys talking about?" Lily asked.

"These two don't want to dress up tomorrow."

"You have to dress up," Lily said. "It's a Halloween party."

"That's what *I* told them," Big said.

Even as tired as Lily was, I could see a smirk sneak onto her face. She knew perfectly well I hated costumes. They were embarrassing, made you stand out, and provided way too much of an opportunity for bullies. I'd come a long way in fighting off my desire to stay invisible over the past few weeks, but that didn't mean I wanted to give people an excuse to pick on me. Besides, what would I go as? An Oompa Loompa? No way. I would look stupid no matter what I wore.

"Sam and I are going to be competing, remember?" I said. "A costume would get in the way."

Sam nodded in agreement.

"Really?" Lily said with a fake pout. "You won't dress up even for me?"

Big smiled, "Yeah, you guys. That's just cold. *I'm* dressing up for you, Lily."

"Thanks, Big," Lily said. "At least *somebody* cares enough to dress up for my Halloween fund-raiser." She started to fake cry.

Big patted her on the shoulder as if consoling her and said, "Hey, kaikuahine, it'll be okay. They'll dress up, won't you, guys?"

When we didn't respond right away, Lily let out a theatrical wail.

"I just . . . I really don't want to, you know—" I couldn't finish because Lily wailed even louder in an attempt to hide her laughter.

Big continued to pat her shoulder, shaking his head. "I'm sorry, Lily. Some people just have no heart, yeah?"

Mrs. Small burst into the room. "What on earth is the matter? Are you okay?"

Lily wasn't able to disguise her laughter. She and Big laughed for a few seconds before Lily managed to phase back into her fake crying. "Mommy, Sam and Paul won't dress up for my Halloween party."

"Oh, for heaven's sake," Mrs. Small said. "You scared me nearly to death." She rolled her eyes and left the room.

"I could maybe dress up," Sam mumbled.

I shot Sam a look of betrayal. She only shrugged.

"But what about Paul?" Lily said through more fake sobs. She covered her face with her hands as if to hide tears, but I could see she was hiding a grin. "All I ever wanted was for my dear friend Paul to dress up for my fund-raiser." She peeked at me through her fingers.

I shook my head no.

"Did I mention I have cancer?"

What was I supposed to say to that? Lily was exacting her revenge on me for starting this whole fund-raiser business, and there was nothing I could do about it. I let out a disgusted groan and gave a very reluctant, "Fine."

# Chapter 39

For the first hour of the fund-raiser, Sam and I manned the registration table. Our job was to catch the climbers as they came in the door, help them with the paperwork, and answer any questions. It sounded easy enough, but the place was a madhouse. People were everywhere, the band was loud, and Sam and I weren't exactly good at getting people's attention.

I'd been apprehensive that no one would show, so it was a huge relief when people started filing in. But then they kept coming and coming and coming. The actual competition hadn't even started yet, and the gym was more crowded than I'd ever seen it. I was glad the fund-raiser was a success, but I also felt overwhelmed.

I saw Hunter and Anne walk in and waved them over.

"What do you want?" Hunter asked, annoyed. He was wearing a tank top and had his arms folded, showing off all his muscles. I swear he was flexing on purpose because they bulged out all over the place.

"You need to sign in if you're going to be in the comp," I said, trying hard to be heard over the noise.

"Hi, Sam. Hi, Paul," said Anne with a little wave. She was dressed as Wonder Woman.

"Hey, Anne," I said, making a huge effort to ignore Hunter the hyena looming over me. "Just sign right here next to your names. Sam has the release forms. You'll need a parent or guardian to fill them out."

"Okay," Anne said as she signed her name. "I'll go get our dad." She ran off into the crowd.

Hunter signed the paper and then sneered down at me while he waited for his dad and Anne to come back. "Are you in the comp?"

"Yeah."

"You can't," he said. He sounded like a spoiled kid who doesn't get his way.

"What do you mean I can't?"

"I saw you helping Andy set up the routes," he said. "You already know all the moves. That's cheating."

"I only helped with the women's routes," I said.

"Bull." He spat the word at me.

"Sam is the only one who helped Andy with the men's routes. I don't know any more about them than you do."

"So you're saying Sam is cheating, too?"

"No, of course not," I said with growing anger. "Look, go talk to Andy if you have a problem. I haven't touched any of the men's routes, and Sam hasn't touched any of the women's."

"Whatever." He shook his head like he didn't believe me. "What are you supposed to be dressed up as, anyway?"

I had on a red plaid shirt, black beanie, blue jeans, my dad's old hiking boots, and a plastic axe I'd found at the Halloween store. I'd drawn on a fake beard and spray-painted one of Lily's stuffed cows blue. It looked more like a zombie cow than a blue ox sitting on the table next to me, but still. I was clearly Paul Bunyan.

"He's Paul Bunyan," Sam said loud enough for Hunter to hear.

Hunter looked at Sam. I think it took him a minute to recognize her. To be fair, I didn't recognize her when I saw her in costume either. She was just so completely . . . *not* Sam. She wore zebra-striped spandex pants, a weird tutu-like, frilly skirt thing, a red leather jacket, lacy, fingerless gloves, and bright makeup, with huge 80s rocker hair.

"What are you supposed to be?" Hunter asked "A crackhead ballerina or something?"

Before either of us could respond, Anne came back with her dad. He looked a lot like Hunter only slightly shorter and slightly less muscular. He didn't look like a man who smiled much.

When he noticed Sam, though, his eyes softened. "How are you doing, Sam? Holding up okay?"

Sam looked at her lap and whispered, "Yes, I'm okay."

"And your parents?"

"They're good. They should be here soon."

"Oh, good. I haven't seen your dad since the funeral. I was wondering if he'd like to start climbing again. Maybe we could all go."

Anne's face lit up. "That would be so cool. Wouldn't that be fun, Sam?"

Sam shrugged.

Mr. Bouda said, "Did you have some release forms I need to sign?"

Sam slid the forms over to him, and while he signed, Anne

said, "You make a really cute rock star, Sam. I wish I would have thought of that."

"Thanks," Sam said softly.

Mr. Bouda handed Sam the forms, but looked at her for a second before adding, "Hang in there, kid. Things will get better."

The three of them turned to leave, and Anne called over her shoulder, "Good luck in the competition. You, too, Paul."

"Thanks," I said and waved.

After Hunter and Anne walked off, I turned to Sam. "Your costume *is* awesome. Don't listen to Hunter."

"It was my mom's idea," she said, looking at her lap. "She did the whole thing. She was so excited, I couldn't say no."

"Really? Well, she did a great job."

"I just wanted to put on a red-and-white-striped sweater and be the 'Where's Waldo' guy," she said. There was a longing in her voice.

"This is definitely cooler."

"I guess."

Right then, a cheer broke out from where the band was playing. We both looked to see what the commotion was about. The crowd had formed a circle around something, so I stood up to get a better look and, when that didn't help, I climbed up onto my chair.

Big was in the center of the circle, wearing a grass skirt, flower lei, and coconut bra and dancing like a madman. The crazier the music got, the crazier he danced, and the louder the cheers became. It was quite possibly the most hilarious thing I'd ever seen.

"That's something you don't see every day," I said.

Sam laughed next to me. It was the first time I'd heard

her laugh since Conor's death, and it was beautiful. Then she snorted.

She clamped her hands over her mouth and looked around to see if anyone had noticed. We made eye contact for a second, and then we both started laughing again.

"If only Lily could be here to see that," I said.

"What did her dad say? Is there any way she still might make it?" Sam asked.

"No. He said she's had a pretty bad day today."

Suddenly I didn't feel like laughing anymore and sat back down. Sam did the same.

"Samantha? There you are." I turned to see Mrs. Dolores coming toward us. She was dressed as Alice in Wonderland. "You look fabulous, honey." Her huge, unnerving grin looked like there were invisible hooks holding the corners of her mouth up in the shape of a smile. "Doesn't she look fabulous, Ted?"

Mr. Dolores walked up beside Mrs. Dolores. He looked exhausted. There were dark bags under his eyes, and his face was almost gray. He was dressed in a fancy three-piece suit with a pocket watch. I didn't know who he was supposed to be.

When Mrs. Dolores saw him she said, "Where are your ears? No one will know who you are without your ears, Ted."

Mr. Dolores sighed and put a pair of floppy rabbit ears on his head. While Mrs. Dolores took a second to straighten the ears, I saw Mr. Dolores wink at Sam and Sam smiled.

Right then, Andy's voice came over the band's PA system. "All climbers report to the bouldering area."

The competition was about to start.

# Chapter 40

The competition was a lot different than the high school one we'd done with teams. There were five bouldering routes set up right next to each other—five for the men and five for the women. One woman and one man climbed at the same time but on separate routes. That meant the whole audience was watching as just those two climbed. I wished I wasn't competing. I did not want a few hundred people staring at me as I fell off some easy hold or stuck my butt out in the air to do some awkward move.

We had four minutes to climb each route. The routes got progressively harder until the fifth and final route, which was the toughest of all. Points would be awarded for each hold we reached. Tara, the lady who'd helped me when I passed out at the sight of Lily's blood, was the women's judge and Andy was the men's.

While Andy explained the rules, I looked at the other climbers. I knew Hunter, Anne, and Sam, and I recognized a few others from the gym, but many of them were total strangers from all over northern Utah. They looked hard-core. I felt out of place and out of my league. Several of the climbers gave me strange looks like they thought I was lost or something. I knew I was going to be the laughingstock of the whole place. For the first time, I was glad Lily wasn't there to see me be humiliated.

When the competition began, Sam was one of the first to climb. She looked nervous, but determined. She no longer wore the weird tutu-dress, the leather jacket, or the gloves, but it was still pretty funny to see her in zebra-striped spandex tights, a black tank top, and her huge hairdo.

I heard her mom screech, "There she is!"

I looked at my dad, who was exchanging a nervous look with Big's mom. Even Andy glanced over at Mrs. Dolores when she started cheering. I think we were all on edge waiting to see if she could hold it together.

Sam flashed the first route. I couldn't believe it. She didn't fall once. In her slow, controlled style, she worked her way systematically to the top and jumped off looking almost embarrassed by her success. She walked away from the climb with a shy smile as everyone cheered.

The best part, however, was Mrs. Dolores cheering along with the rest of us. Admittedly, she cheered a little louder and shriller than anyone else, but she didn't get too carried away.

After a few other climbers went, I heard my name called. I walked up to the waiting area. Sitting behind the table was the guy who'd been working the front desk on the day I'd skipped school with Lily.

"You can't stand here," he said. "This is where the competitors wait."

I said, "I know. I'm competing."

"*You're* competing?" He gave me the up-and-down look, then down at his paper. "You're Paul Adams?"

I rolled my eyes. "*Yes*, I'm Paul Adams, and, *yes*, I'm competing."

"Whatever you say," the guy said. He called out, "Lisa Ross." A lady with her face painted as a Day of the Dead sugar skull walked up to wait beside me. She looked even stronger than Lily. "You two are up next," he said to us.

My dad, Big, Sam, and all the Smalls cheered as I walked out. I overheard someone in the audience ask, "Why is that kid going out there?" and another one said, "Whoa, he's so tiny. Is this a joke?" I tried to block the comments out, but it was hard not to let them get to me.

As it turned out, the first route was practically custom-made for me. It was all overhanging big holds with gymnastic moves perfectly suited to my strengths.

I fell off it five times.

I couldn't stop thinking about all the people who were watching me and wondering why a little kid was competing with the grown-ups. Well, technically they were watching me and Lisa, the sugar skull lady, but still. There were a lot of people.

The fifth time I fell off, I only had thirty seconds left. Unlike the high school comp, as long as you were on the route when time ran out, you could keep climbing and have it count. I knew this would be my last try, so I shook out my hands, breathed slow and deep, and rested as I watched the clock count down.

I heard a huge cheer when Lisa completed her route. That meant there was no one else to watch but me. Not good. I wanted to run to a dark, quiet place where I could forget about competing and be alone.

I was about to get back on the route when I heard Big call my name. I turned around and saw him in his hula girl costume.

"You got this, brah," he said.

I tried hard to believe him.

With only a few seconds left, I got back on. I heard the buzzer that indicated my time was up. If I fell now, that would be it. I hung on the bottom holds for a second and tried to calm down. I breathed and listened.

Finally I heard it: the rain. Now I could climb.

I swung, dangled, and launched myself from hold to hold in my usual dynamic style. It was hard, but I made it. Hanging from the top hold, I turned around to be greeted by a few hundred cheering strangers and a hula-dancing Big. I spotted my dad at the back of the crowd, standing with the Small family. He was smiling, and I smiled back. Maybe this wouldn't be such a horrible competition after all.

Sam and I were comparing notes on our routes when she got called up for round two. I walked with her up to the table, still chatting.

Then I heard Hunter say, "Are you anorexic or something? You look like a zebra carcass in those tights."

I turned to see Hunter smirking at Sam. "Knock it off, Hunter," I said, trying to sound tough.

Hunter laughed. "What are you going to do about it, half-pint?"

I was saved from coming up with a retort when the guy at the table said, "Hunter, Sam—you two are up."

Hunter jogged out to climb the second route. Sam followed after him at a walk. She had her eyes on the ground and her arms wrapped around herself in her usual shy way. Stupid Hunter. For a moment, I thought about asking the rhinos to make him behave. Then I remembered Conor. No, there had to be a better way.

This time, Sam looked far less sure of herself as she climbed. I knew the route was harder than the first one, but I also knew it was within her abilities. After all, I'd helped Andy set it up. She fell three times before she finished it.

I glanced at Hunter. He hadn't completed his route, and his time was about up. As the buzzer went off, Hunter fell from the second-to-last hold. He was by no means out of the running for the win, but he'd definitely lost a few valuable points by not completing the route. As much as I disliked Hunter, he really was a good climber. I wondered if I'd be able to climb this route. As he walked away, he shot me a look that rivaled Lily's death ray.

Two other climbers went, and then it was my turn. I was not feeling confident. Only about half the men had been able to finish the second route. Some of them were bulging with muscles and bristling with facial hair. Others were long and wiry. None were short and scrawny.

As I jogged out, the crowd cheered. They cheered for everyone, of course, but I swear they were cheering a little louder and longer for me. Was that possible?

The route was steep and edgy and required a lot of balance. It was the kind of route that was all about footwork and hope. It was about finesse. There was no way I could leap from hold to hold, that was for sure. I understood why Hunter had struggled with it. He was all about strength and power, both of which were virtually useless on that route. It was a slow and delicate process, but after three tries, I made it to the top.

Once I got back down, Sam found me. "That last climb was amazing. I can't believe how well you did. You could actually win this if you . . ." Sam's voice trailed off, and her eyes looked at something over my shoulder.

I turned around to see Hunter and Anne striding up to us. They both looked angry.

Hunter stood over me with his hands on his hips. "You two are cheating."

He said it loud enough to draw the attention of some of the other climbers around us.

"What are you talking about?" one of them asked.

"I'm talking about these two being cheaters," Hunter said in his high-pitched voice. "They helped set the routes. Obviously, zebra-girl here told him all about the men's routes, and he told her all about the women's. Otherwise, there's no way this *shrimp*"—he poked me in the chest with a thick finger—"could have done that last route."

"Is that true?" Anne asked me.

"No, it's not true," I said. "I already told Hunter, we didn't give each other any information on the routes."

Anne looked doubtful.

"Is there a problem here?" someone asked. Lisa had her arms folded across her chest. She looked pretty intimidating with her sugar skull face.

"No," Hunter said. "There's no problem . . . if you don't mind *cheaters*."

"You need to relax, kid," Lisa said to Hunter. "This is a fund-raising competition, not the world championships."

Hunter mumbled, "Whatever," and walked off.

Lisa said, "Some people just need to chill." Then she turned back to the competition along with most of the other climbers.

Anne was the only one who stayed behind. "You two are

good climbers," she said, "but it does seem like you're climbing unusually well."

"We're not cheating," Sam said.

Anne stared at Sam for a few seconds. "If you say so." Her face told me she'd decided not to believe us.

# Chapter 41

Sam stood beside me, staring at her feet, until it was time for her third route. I knew Hunter and Anne had gotten to her. I said, "Don't listen to them. First of all, you look great. Really. And, second, everyone knows we didn't cheat."

Sam nodded, but I knew I hadn't helped any.

The third route was hard. Sam seemed to be climbing with her customary focus, but she still fell three times. After her third fall, she looked at the clock. Forty-five seconds remained. Instead of jumping right back on the wall, she studied the route and massaged her forearms. With five seconds left, she got back on. If she fell now, she wouldn't get another chance.

Only Lisa and Anne had finished this one. If Sam made it, she would be in the top three. She worked her way up to her former high point with no problem, but then she got stuck. She tried reaching up with her left hand to a big sloper and then changed her mind. She awkwardly dropped back down to her former hold. She tried with her right and moved back down once again, causing her foot to slip. She almost fell, and the crowd gasped.

I knew what she had to do. She needed to reach out with

her right foot and hook her heel on a high red hold. I held my breath and screamed in my thoughts for her to do it. She must have gotten my telepathic message, because she stretched her leg up and out and hooked the hold. The move was almost easy. Sam finished the route with no other problems.

Big was so excited by Sam's success, he leaped in front of the crowd for another hula dance. The crowd cheered. I was laughing so hard, I almost didn't hear my name called.

The third route made me feel like I almost was cheating. It consisted of a series of one- and two-finger pockets on a slightly overhanging wall. Watching the other climbers do it looked like torture. They had to stab their middle fingers into the pockets and then crank on them with nearly all their weight. I kept waiting for someone to blow a tendon or tear a finger right off. It looked excruciating.

For me, however, all those single-finger pockets were two-finger pockets, and all the two-finger pockets were three-finger pockets. I could tell this route was designed to narrow the field. Andy did not expect many climbers to get past it. I flew up it. Unfortunately, so did Hunter. I was still in the lead, but only by two points.

Sam's fourth turn came. This was the point where the women's routes really started to get hard, and Andy had set up the fifth route on his own. When I asked him about it, all he said was it would be "interesting." In Andy terms, that meant "painful and scary."

Lisa and Anne had both finished it with ease. Everyone, including myself, assumed the real contest was between those two, and Sam's only hope was for third place.

Then Sam practically strolled up the fourth route, and the

crowd went wild. I leaped onto a nearby chair and cheered at the top of my lungs. I never guessed Sam would do so well.

As Sam tried to walk off, Big wrapped her in a big hug and swung her around so her feet came off the ground. When he let her go, she was blushing and smiling. Her mom was jumping up and down, and her dad had a huge, proud smile on his face.

Then I was falling. Someone bumped the chair I was standing on and sent me sprawling onto my face. Luckily, the chair was next to the thick pad below the routes, and I fell forward onto that. Otherwise, I might have broken my neck. I looked up to see Hunter standing there with his ugly, gap-toothed grin.

"Oops," he said.

I jumped to my feet in an instant, ready to charge him. At the last moment, I stopped. A few weeks ago, I would have held back out of fear. But this was different. I almost felt pity for Hunter. Like he was the weak one, not me. That was a sensation I'd never experienced before.

A voice called, "Hunter and Lisa, you're up."

As Hunter passed me, he sneered, "Klutz," and laughed.

It was immensely satisfying to watch Hunter get shut down by the fourth route. He barely got off the ground before his time ran out. Maybe he was tired from the first three routes, but more likely it was because the route started out in a crack before angling left onto a face full of huge black slopers. Hunter would have handled those slopers fine, but he never got the chance. He had no idea how to climb a crack.

When my turn came, I felt confident. I didn't think I would do very well on the slopers, but I knew I could float up the crack, and all I cared about right then was getting higher than Hunter

had. I slotted my fingers and toes into the crack and almost enjoyed the pain.

In only seconds, I was moving onto the slopers. They looked
like a series of black beach balls hanging half out of the wall. They
were extremely hard to hang onto, especially if you're sweating,
which I definitely was. I thought for sure I would fall off the first
one, but I didn't. I didn't fall off the second one either. Or the rest
of them. It wasn't skill or anything. I guess sometimes you just get
lucky. The next thing I knew, I was at the top.

When I walked off, Andy waved me over to his desk. I figured he was going to congratulate me. I mean, I had just flashed
one of the hardest bouldering routes of my life. I waited for the
compliments to pour out of Andy, but he stared at me like I was
a difficult math problem he was trying to solve.

"What?" I asked. "Didn't you see me crush that thing?"

Andy motioned me closer and whispered, "I saw it, and you
crushed it all right. You almost crushed it a little too well."

"What do you mean?"

"I mean, that was some amazing climbing . . . even for you."

"I know, right? I seriously have no idea how that just happened."

"Paul, some of the other climbers have been complaining. I
need to know—did Sam help you with that route? Did she tell
you the moves beforehand?"

"What? No. Did Hunter tell you that? He's been saying we
cheated all night, but it's not true. You don't believe him do you,
Andy?"

"Paul, even I couldn't have flashed that route. I'm not sure
what to believe. And it's not just Hunter who is suspicious. There

are other people, too. Sam seems to be climbing a lot better than I expected as well."

"Look, I just got lucky. That's all there is to it. I promise, Sam and I are *not* cheating."

Andy nodded like he believed me, but he still frowned.

"What?" I asked.

"If you and Sam both take first place, there's not a person here who won't think you cheated."

I was having trouble processing what he was saying. "I don't understand."

"It's my own fault," Andy said. "I shouldn't have let you guys help set the routes. I didn't think it would be a problem, but . . ."

"What do you want me to do?" I asked.

Andy sighed and leaned back in his chair. "I want you go out there and win this thing." He tried to smile at me.

"Andy . . ."

"Hey, I believe you," he said, and I could tell he meant it. "I know you're not cheating. I'm sorry I doubted you. Who cares what anyone else thinks. Go out there and show them what a real man can do."

"Okay," I said. I wanted to tell Sam everything Andy had said and ask her what she thought we should do, but I didn't get the chance. She was up next for the fifth and final route.

Unfortunately, Sam was climbing alongside Hunter again. As the two of them headed out, I saw Hunter lean over and say something to her before he jogged over to his route. Sam froze in her tracks.

The four-minute clock started to count down, but Sam still didn't move.

"Sam?" I heard Mr. Dolores call out. "Are you okay?"

Sam had her back to me, but I saw her reach up and wipe her eyes. Was she crying?

"Sam," I yelled, "the clock has started. You have to get climbing."

Finally, she took a deep breath and jogged to her route. Everyone broke into a loud cheer.

Despite the support from the audience, Sam was rattled. She fell off almost as soon as she got on. She tried again, made it a few feet, and then fell. She put her face in her hands, and I could tell she was trying not to cry. She shook her head and lowered her hands to study the route. With only two minutes left, she composed herself enough to try again.

She made it almost halfway before reaching the two tufas— long, skinny holds that looked like dripping candle wax—that Andy had bolted vertically only an inch apart. Lisa and Anne had pinched one tufa in each hand and powered their way up with lots of loud grunts and flexing muscles.

Sam tried the same thing but quickly fell. Only thirty seconds remained. She put her face in her hands.

A cheer broke out as Hunter finished the fifth route. He let out a victory cry and pumped his fist in the air. Technically, he was now in first place, but I wasn't worried because I only had to make it halfway up the route to win.

I turned back to Sam. She still stood at the base of her route, looking miserable.

The clock ticked down to ten seconds.

With only three seconds left, Sam stepped back on. The clock hit zero. This was her last try. She dipped for chalk, and started up the route. She made it to the pair of tufas with no problem, but then stopped. She tried several different ways of holding them, but wasn't having any luck. She dipped for chalk with first one hand and then the other. She was stuck. It was a matter of seconds before she fell. The whole place went silent.

Then a woman's shrill voice started to chant, "Samantha! Samantha! Samantha!" It was her mom. Then I heard Big start chanting, too. Pretty soon I heard other voices join in. It sounded like Chuck and Colt, but I couldn't be sure. Then more and more people joined in until the whole place was chanting her name over and over and getting louder and louder. Soon, the whole gym shook with the thunder of the name of the quietest girl I'd ever known.

Sam reached up for one of the tufas with her left hand. She fumbled around again, and then she froze. What was she doing? She had to move quick or it was over. Finally, she switched hands, reached up with her right, and jammed it between the tufas like she would a crack. None of the other climbers had thought to make that move.

It looked hideous and painful, but it worked. She moved up with her left hand and jammed it above. This one looked even worse. The crowd's chanting turned into astonished cheers. Sam repositioned her feet higher on the wall and then let out a fero-cious growl. I'd never heard Sam make a noise like that. It was a battle cry. She hung off her left hand and reached up with her right. The crowd went wild.

Sam had to do one more hand jam in the "crack" formed by the tufas, and then she was back to the normal holds. Three moves and she'd be at the top. This is where Anne had fallen, but Sam pushed through to the next hold and then the next until she was at Lisa's high point. One more and Sam would win.

At this point, Lisa had made a last, desperate lunge for the final hold and missed. Sam looked like she was setting up to do the same thing. She matched both hands on the big, sloping hold and hiked her feet up. She had to be exhausted, but there was no doubt she was preparing for a dyno. The gym itself seemed to hold its breath. She stared at the finishing hold, squatted on her footholds until her arms were almost straight, and then sprang.

Sam looked like a bird taking flight. She spread her wings and soared to the finishing hold. She caught it with her right hand, and her feet swung so that, for a moment, she dangled by one skinny arm. Then she matched with her left hand, replanted her feet, and turned around to see the crowd explode.

At first, Sam appeared more confused than excited. She looked over the audience with wide eyes, and her mouth fell half open. She almost seemed scared to come down. Finally, she let go and dropped to the pad.

She was greeted by countless high fives and slaps on her back. Her dad gave her a hug, and her mom planted a kiss on her forehead that left a red lipstick mark. Big picked her up and swung her around again and, when he set her down, she was laughing.

I only wished Lily could have seen it.

# Chapter 42

When it was almost my turn, I started getting pretty excited. I imagined myself hitting the top hold just as the band starts playing "We Are the Champions." Lily, miraculously cured, comes walking through the door in time to see my victory. I drop to the ground, and she greets me with a very, very long kiss while the crowd goes insane. As a finishing touch, I imagined confetti falling from the ceiling and Hunter slinking off alone to cry. I just knew it was going to be the greatest moment of my life.

Then I remembered what Andy said. If I won, everyone would think Sam and I cheated. It looked as if the other climbers were willing to accept that Sam could pull off an upset, but not me. In their minds, someone as small as me could never beat a brute like Hunter. Not without cheating. And if they were sure I cheated, then they would assume Sam cheated.

I stared up at the ceiling and sighed. I had to face the truth: by winning, I would take Sam's victory away from her. I couldn't let that happen. Plus, how long would it take for climbers to trust an OCC competition again? This gym—Andy's gym, my favorite place on the entire planet, the place that was doing all of this for Lily and her family—might actually lose business if I won. I couldn't let that happen either. But why did I have to lose to *Hunter*?

"Paul Adams, you're up," the guy called.

I walked out to the final route. There were some cheers from the crowd, but most of the climbers were pretty quiet. Some of them were whispering to each other and shooting me suspicious looks. What was I supposed to do? Forfeit? Just announce I was quitting? Wouldn't that look suspicious, too? I had to climb. I just couldn't win.

Hunter was leading by six points. I counted up to the sixth hold. It was a bright-red, crescent-shaped edge. I made a mental note not to touch it under any circumstances. I chalked up my hands and took a few deep breaths. I had to make it look like a legitimate effort.

I stepped up to the route and tried to grab the starting holds. They were too high. I heard a few people laugh as I reached for them. That was embarrassing. I took a few steps back, ran up to the wall, planted a foot on a low hold, and jumped. The starting holds were both small, sharp edges that cut into my already raw fingertips, but I held on. A cheer went up from my friends and family, but not the other climbers. I was already blowing it. They would wonder how I knew to do that running start. But when you're as short as I am, you have to do it all the time, so it becomes second nature.

I pretended to struggle with my footwork and let myself fall off. The crowd let out a collective groan. I took another running start and caught the sharp holds. This time I got my feet on and looked for the next move. It was crazy hard, so when I fell, it was for real. I had to do that stupid running start three more times before I stuck the next move.

The fourth hold looked good, but it was pretty far away. Normally, I would just dyno for it and be done. Instead, I forced myself to find a way to do it without jumping. It took a while, but I managed to do it by doing the splits out to a tiny chip. It was way harder than just jumping, which was good because, once again, I didn't have to put on an act.

Hold five was right in front of my face, so I didn't have any choice but to grab it. I looked up. The red crescent was pretty stinking far away. There was no way I could hit it without jumping for it. Good, if I couldn't reach it, I could try as hard as I wanted and not have to worry about winning.

I sweated and grunted and growled and fell right as the buzzer went off.

# Chapter 43

The party was in full swing. People danced, climbed, and talked. Sam was practically glowing with her victory, and Big got an honorable mention in the costume contest. The fundraiser had turned out better than I could possibly have hoped. And I was miserable.

Don't get me wrong, I knew I'd done the right thing. Just seeing Sam, dressed as a rock star, standing on the top of the podium between Lisa's sugar-skull face and Anne as Wonder Woman, made it all worth it. Anne had even congratulated Sam with a hug and didn't seem to be harboring any hard feelings. It also helped when Andy gave me a nod and a smile that said he knew exactly what I'd done, and he was grateful. But I still wanted to sneak away and go home.

Big came barreling out of the crowd, sweating and breathing hard, his smile cranked up to full capacity. "This is the best fundraiser in the history of the world!"

I couldn't help it, I smiled back. Sam fluttered out of the crowd behind him and landed like a bird at my side. She gave me a shy smile.

I looked at her and felt better. "Yes, it is."

"Here, I saved you something." Big handed me a half-eaten cookie.

"Thanks." I inspected it. "It's beautiful."

Big laughed. "Indeed, it is. You know what else is beautiful?"

"My blue ox?" I asked. I gestured to the spray-painted stuffed cow sitting on the table next to me.

Big cocked his head at it. "Is that what that was supposed to be? I wondered why you had a zombie cow. But, no, that is definitely not it."

"I give up, then. What else is beautiful?"

He looked around like we were conspiring to rob the place. When he was satisfied no one was listening, he said, "When a man is willing to give up something he desperately wants, so others can have something they need."

"Big, I have no idea what you're talking about," I said.

"I mean you, brah. You could have won, and you didn't."

"What do you mean? I tried as hard as I could. You think I wanted to lose?" I was looking around like a conspirator, too. I thought I had fooled everyone but Andy.

"We saw the way you climbed that last route," Big said. "Normally you jump from hold to hold like a rabbit, but this time you didn't, yeah?"

"So? I was tired."

"No, you weren't," Big said.

"By not dynoing," Sam said in her soft voice, "you made it so there was no way you could reach the holds, and you were guaranteed to lose."

"Or I was just really tired, and I fell off," I said.

Big shook his head. "At first, we couldn't figure out why. Then

Sam told me about how Hunter said you were cheating, and I told her that I saw you and Andy whispering together before the final route. Give it up, Paul Bunyan, we're onto you, yeah?"

"You two can believe what you want, but I legitimately fell off that last route." It wasn't exactly a lie.

Big smiled down at me. "Whatever you say, but we know you could have won, and you chose not to, and it was beautiful."

"Why would Paul choose not to win?" a man's voice said from behind me, causing all three of us to jump. I turned to see Mr. Dolores approaching with his wife on his arm.

Mrs. Dolores asked, "Who chose not to win what?"

"Apparently Paul chose not to win the competition on purpose," Mr. Dolores said. "I thought it was strange the way your climbing style changed so abruptly. I assumed you were getting tired."

"You intentionally lost?" Mrs. Dolores said far too loud.

"No," I said, looking around again to see who might be within earshot. "I was just tired, and it was a really hard route."

"Why would you intentionally lose?" Mrs. Dolores said even louder. "Did you throw the competition to win a bet or something?"

"No, no, nothing like that. I lost, that's all. Can we just drop it?"

Sam whispered, "Some of the climbers thought Paul and I were cheating. They thought we'd told each other all the key moves on the routes. Paul lost on purpose so people wouldn't be suspicious of my win."

"That's absurd," Mrs. Dolores said in her shrill voice. "You won fair and square." Then she whispered, "You did, didn't you?"

"Of course she did, honey," Mr. Dolores said. "No one thinks she didn't." He looked at me like he was putting the last few pieces of a puzzle together and finally seeing the complete picture.

It was time to change the subject and maybe make a hasty exit. "It's amazing what Sam did. Those were some tough competitors." I started backing away. "Anyway, I gotta go check on something with my dad, so—"

The next thing I knew, I was on the ground.

I looked up to see Hunter laughing as he walked by. "Watch where you're going, loser," he called over his shoulder, but then he ran smack into a brick wall. It was actually Colt, but it might as well have been a brick wall.

"Maybe *you* should watch where you're going," Colt growled.

I scrambled to my feet right next to them. What I wanted was for Colt to start beating the tar out of Hunter, and then let me get in a few kicks once he was on the ground, but instead I said, "Hey, Colt, it's alright. Just let it go. Let's not ruin the fund-raiser."

Hunter said, "Why are you standing up for this pathetic little gnome?"

"His name is Paul, and he's Lily's boyfriend, and he's my friend, and this whole fund-raiser was organized by *him*."

Wait, whoa. What did he just say? I didn't want a fight to break out, but my head was spinning. Had Colt just said I was Lily's *boyfriend*?

Hunter laughed. "Oh, man. You totally had me going there for a second." He punched Colt in the shoulder like they were pals sharing a joke.

Colt folded his arms and didn't laugh.

"Wait. You're serious? This dude, right here." Hunter pointed at me. "*He's* Lily's boyfriend? He's like four feet tall."

"I'm practically five feet," I mumbled, but I don't think anyone heard me.

"He's more of a man than you'll ever be," Colt said.

Hunter gave a loud, fake laugh, but he was angry underneath. "Yeah, right. He's the size of a kindergartener."

"He's a better climber than you," Mr. Dolores said, stepping up beside me. Big, Sam, and Mrs. Dolores all stepped up beside me, too. I had my own little protective herd surrounding me.

Hunter turned from Colt to Mr. Dolores. "I don't know if you noticed, old man, but I won the competition, not him." Hunter looked around at all of us and shook his head like he was disgusted with what he saw. "I'm out of here." He started to walk away.

"No, you didn't," Mrs. Dolores said.

Hunter stopped. "No, I didn't what?"

"*You* didn't win," Mrs. Dolores said, tapping him on the chest with a long, red fingernail. "Paul *let* you win."

Hunter laughed again. "Are you people insane? I finished the last route. Shorty here couldn't even reach the first holds."

Mr. Bouda walked up with Anne. He seemed oblivious to the tension in the air. "You ready to go?" he asked Hunter. When Hunter didn't answer right away, he asked, "Is everything alright?"

"Everything's fine," Mr. Dolores said. "How are you, Colin?"

"Good, Ted. I saw that Sam won tonight. You must be very proud. I guess you noticed Hunter won as well? He might even be better than you were when you were his age," he said and gave a little laugh. It sounded just like Hunter's fake laugh.

"I must admit, Hunter is a very good climber," Mr. Dolores said. "But I'm not convinced he was the best here tonight."

Mr. Bouda narrowed his eyes. "I would think that winning

the entire competition would put to rest any suspicions you have to the contrary."

"Hunter is very talented and very strong, but I wonder if maybe he just got lucky on that last route," Mr. Dolores said.

"Are you kidding? He flashed it." Mr. Bouda said. His voice took on a warning tone. "Luck had nothing to do with it."

Mr. Dolores put his hand to his chin like an idea had just occurred to him and said, "Would you like to put your convictions about your son to the test?"

"Are you suggesting a bet?" Mr. Bouda said as if that was beneath him.

"I wouldn't normally suggest such a thing, Colin, but what if it was for a good cause?"

"Go on."

"I'll bet you a thousand dollars that my friend, Paul, here"— Mr. Dolores put his arm around my shoulders—"can outclimb Hunter on any route in this gym. The loser donates the money to the Small family. What do you say?"

Mr. Bouda gave me the up-and-down look. "What do you think, Hunter?" he asked, as if bored by the idea. "Want to do one last climb"—he stared hard at Mr. Dolores—"for charity?"

Hunter's eyes darted around like he was a cornered animal, searching for an escape. "Uh, I don't know, Dad. I'm, um, pretty tired after winning the competition."

"Don't be silly, son. He's just a little kid. Besides, I'd be the one writing the check, not you."

"I don't know," Hunter said.

"What about you, Paul?" Mr. Dolores asked me. "Are you in?"

I faced Mr. Dolores and whispered, "Are you sure? That's a lot of money."

Mr. Dolores knelt down so he could talk to me face-to-face. "I don't care about the money, Paul. In fact, if you win, I'll donate two thousand. I just want to repay you for everything you've done for Sam." He paused, took a deep breath, and whispered, "If you want to know the truth, Sam told me Hunter was the one who bullied Conor the most at school." Mr. Dolores swallowed hard. "I *really* want to see him lose."

"Okay," I said. I turned back to Hunter and Mr. Bouda. "I'm game," I said. "Come on, Hunter. It's for a good cause."

Hunter suddenly didn't look as nervous anymore. "Only if I get to pick the route."

"That's fine with me," Mr. Dolores said. "That okay with you, Paul?"

I thought about it. I looked around at the gym. I couldn't think of a single route Hunter could outclimb me on. If he thought I'd legitimately fallen off the last route in the competition, then I guessed that would be the one he'd choose. It would be hard, but I could do it. "Sounds good."

"Just to be clear, I don't have to finish the route, right? I only have to get higher than Paul?"

Wait. If he'd already climbed to the top of the fifth competition route, there was no reason he'd be worried that he couldn't do it again. I started to feel sick.

"Yes, that's right," Mr. Dolores said.

"Okay, I'll do it," Hunter said.

"Well? What route is it going to be?" Mr. Bouda asked.

Hunter sneered down at me with all his gappy little teeth. "Bildungsroman," he said.

# Chapter 44

How could I have been so stupid? Hunter knew I was too short to make the move to the eighth hold of Bildungsroman. All he had to do was climb to hold number nine and he'd have me beat. I was going to lose again, and there was nothing I could do about it.

"What's this I hear about a rematch?" my dad asked as I was putting on my harness.

I shook my head and tried to swallow the lump forming in my throat. "Mr. Dolores bet Mr. Bouda I could outclimb Hunter on any route of his choice. The loser will donate a thousand bucks to the Small family."

"Oh, wow. That's really generous of them. What's the problem?"

"He chose Bildungsroman," I said.

"Oh," my dad said. "But that's okay, right? I mean, even if you lose, the Small family gets the money. That's worth it, isn't it?"

"Yeah, I guess."

"Hey, look at me," my dad said. "I am so proud of what you've done here tonight. All of the Smalls, and Lily in particular"—he gave me a corny wink—"will be grateful no matter who wins this bet." He stepped back, folded his arms, and looked up at Bildungsroman for a few seconds. "Besides," he said with a Zen smile, "you can do this."

Right then, Andy's voice come over the PA system. "Can I get everyone's attention, please? It turns out, the entertainment is not yet over. I've just been informed there's going to be a rematch between the first- and second-place winners of the men's climbing competition."

No. Not this. It was bad enough I was going to lose to Hunter again, but everyone in the whole place would see it—again. I wanted to dissolve into the crowd.

Andy continued, "Hunter Bouda and Paul Adams are going to see who can get the highest on Bildungsroman, the hardest route in the gym. For those of you who don't know, this is the lead route on the center of the prow that has yet to be completed by anyone. Feel free to come cheer them on."

Everyone started gathering around the base of the prow. They were looking at Hunter and me with curiosity and chatting excitedly. I fought the urge to throw up.

"Well, this is an interesting development," my dad said.

I groaned.

"Look," my dad said, "you hate crowds and being in front of people, I get that. But this isn't about *you*. It's about Lily. If it means you have to feel embarrassed to get an extra thousand bucks donated for her, I'd be willing to bet you're man enough to deal with that. Am I right?"

"Yes," I grumbled.

"And here's the thing," he said. "I've belayed you on that route almost every day for the last few weeks. You have it dialed.

Andy told me the other day he thought you had a good chance of being the first to finish it. You can do every move."

"Except for one," I said.

"Yes, except for one." My dad paused and looked up at the move I couldn't do. He studied it for a moment and said, "Paul, you of all people know that small things often go overlooked. They're invisible to most people. Or if people do notice them, they think they're worthless."

I rolled my eyes. Why was he going all Zen-dad on me *now*?

"But sometimes," he continued, pretending not to notice my impatience, "the small things are what matter the most, right?"

I thought of Big and how he was always noticing beautiful things no one else did, and how some of them really were small, like the ant on the stairs or the dandelion in the courtyard. "Right," I said, "but what does that have to do with Bildungsroman?"

"Everything," he said.

"Paul," Andy called over to me. "Everyone's waiting."

"Okay," I called back to him.

"No matter how you do, I'm proud of you," my dad said. "And if your mom were here, she'd be proud, too."

"Thanks, Dad." I walked over to the prow before I started getting all teary eyed and embarrassed myself even worse.

Hunter was waiting with the rope. "Ladies first," he said, holding the end out to me.

"I don't think so," I said. "You picked the route; you go first."

"Fine, whatever." He shrugged and tied into the rope.

I secretly hoped that, by some freak accident, he would fall before hold number eight, and I could keep what little pride I had left.

Andy agreed to belay us both. He gave me a reassuring smile as he put Hunter on belay, and I tried to smile back.

Hunter powered up through the moves in his customary style until he came to the first dyno up to hold number five. Even he had to jump for that one. He paused as he prepared himself. I held my breath and hoped he would slip, but it was only a little hop for him, and he stuck the move without incident.

I almost got lucky on the next section, though. He stabbed two fingers of his right hand into the next pocket when he should have used his left. Unfortunately, Hunter had strength to spare. He reversed the move and switched to his left, so he could set himself up to hit the next hold with his right.

Hunter clipped the rope through the quickdraw and turned to smile down at me. The next move was the one he knew I couldn't make, and it was obvious he wanted to rub it in. He turned back around, reached out, and grabbed hold eight without even having to stretch much.

I let out a long sigh and felt all my energy drain out of me.

Hunter continued to power up the wall. Once he made it to the third clip, he casually sat back and lowered to the ground as the crowd clapped.

I noticed the crowd seemed to be clapping more out of politeness than excitement. They had to be wondering why he just stopped not even halfway up the climb. If this was really a rematch, why wouldn't he push himself until he blew off the wall? The smug look on his face probably appeared pretty odd to them. Well, they would know why soon enough when I fell far short of his high point.

"That should be more than enough," Hunter said as he untied from the rope and handed it to me.

As I tied in, Andy said, "Paul?"

I looked up at him. I'd been avoiding eye contact with him up until now.

"You can do this," he said in a quiet, confident way.

"Probably not," I said. "But I'll tell you one thing, when I fall off this thing, it will be a real fall. I'm not going to give up."

"Good man," Andy said with a smile.

I chalked up and took a moment to close my eyes, breathe deep, and listen for the rain. Nothing. Only the sounds of the huge crowd at my back. I had never wanted to disappear so badly in all my life, and that was saying something.

"On belay?" I asked Andy.

"Belay is on," he replied.

"Climbing," I whispered.

"Climb on."

I had the first few moves so dialed, I could have done them in my sleep. Even without hearing the rain, even drowning beneath the eyes of the crowd, I flowed right through them on muscle memory alone. Hearing the crowd cheer when I made the dyno to hold five helped too.

Unlike Hunter, I knew to go with my left hand for the two-finger pocket—three for me. In less than a minute, I hit the baseball-sized seventh hold and clipped my rope through the second quickdraw. There were more cheers from the crowd, and they sounded more sincere than they had for Hunter, but they didn't know I was done. That was it. A dead end for someone as short as me.

Then something made me turn around. Maybe I heard the door open, or maybe someone whispered her name, or maybe I just sensed her presence, but I looked over my shoulder and scanned the crowd. I saw Andy belaying, my dad smiling at me, Big in his hula dancer costume, Sam the rock star, the Small family grouped together, standing head and shoulders above everyone else in the place, and at the very back, having just come through the door with her mother, the tallest, toughest, most beautiful Maasai warrior in the world.

"Lily." I only whispered her name, but the whole crowd turned as if I had shouted. The audience's reaction was slow. It started small with an intake of breath, then a dozen gasps and whispers. Then the noise and commotion grew like a wave until it crashed down in the form of a huge cheer. Even from across the gym, I saw Lily's eyes go wide at the unexpected greeting.

She stood in the doorway, leaning on a long black spear that was as tall as she was. She carried a white-and-black shield shaped like a football and had a blood-red sheet draped over her shoulders. Her head was shaved, she was draped in hundreds of beads, and she wore leather sandals. A Maasai warrior had wandered right out of Kenya and into the climbing gym.

I made eye contact with her, and she smiled. It was a tired smile, but it warmed me even more than the most powerful of Big's happiness rays. "Don't look at me," Lily called out. "Climb!"

Everyone laughed, including me. Then I stopped laughing. Lily had arrived just in time to see me fall off Bildungsroman and lose to Hunter. No, I couldn't let it happen like that. I turned back to the climb.

I refocused myself and tried to study the move from a fresh perspective, pretending like I'd never seen it before. My eyes went to the tiny, worthless blue chip a foot below hold eight. Was there *anything* I could do with that? No way. It was too small.

I looked down to see if there was something different I could do with my feet. I had a huge foothold—hold five, the big black bucket—but because it was slightly to the left, I couldn't put all my weight on it. There was also the two-finger pocket, but it was too high for a foothold and too sloped on top to step on anyway.

What if I stabbed the tip of my right toe into the pocket? I tried it and realized immediately it was a terrible idea. My balance shifted to the right and made it impossible to move.

Frustrated, I took a second to breathe deep and slow. Okay, what else? What about stabbing my left toe into the pocket? It seemed crazy to take my left foot off the huge black bucket, the best foothold on the entire wall, but I didn't have any other ideas.

It was the most awkward move I had ever done. It required me to hang off hold seven, the baseball, with both hands, one over the other and scrunch my body up into a little ball with my butt out in the air. I hoped everyone was still looking at Lily and not at me. It was a desperate move, and I barely managed to stay on, but I carefully poked the tip of my left shoe into the pocket.

Hopeful, I looked up to see how close hold number eight was.

Not. At. All. Now what?

I was about to make a desperate slap for the hold anyway when I noticed something small and blue out of the corner of my eye: the worthless chip. Maybe it wasn't so worthless after all. I reached out and grabbed it. It was like trying to hold on to the edge of a matchstick. Impossible. And yet I didn't fall.

I heard my dad say in his Zen-master voice, "That's it."

Then I heard another voice say, "Turn your hip into the wall." The second voice was me. I turned my left hip into the wall and, suddenly, there it was: the move opened up like a flower blooming in my mind. I leaned sideways off the baseball and pushed harder than I would have thought possible off my foot wedged in the pocket.

It hurt. My toes were crushed, and I felt like I was going to tear the muscles in my back and shoulders. Inch by inch, with my cheek pasted to the wall, I crept slowly upward like I was levitating with willpower alone. Somehow, I knew the exact moment my fingertips were going to pop off the not-so-worthless blue chip. At the last second, I slapped for hold eight. It wasn't pretty, but I caught it and hung on.

The crowd cheered. I guess they weren't just looking at Lily after all.

Hold number eight was a pathetic, sloping edge, but after clinging to the blue chip, it felt great. Now I was on familiar ground. I grabbed the fin, leaned off it, and easily reached hold number ten, a big, in-cut, two-handed hold. I was so happy to hit it, I'd forgotten that had been Hunter's high point until I heard him yell, "No!" in his high-pitched voice while the rest of the crowd cheered me on.

I clipped the third quickdraw and looked up at the next hold, which looked like someone had bolted half a basketball to the wall. It was another big dyno in which I had to jump to catch the hold with both hands. If I stuck it, I had Hunter beat, but I was surprised to discover I didn't care. I didn't want to just beat Hunter. I wanted to complete the whole route!

I shook out one hand, then the other. I chalked up and breathed deep. I listened close, and there it was: the rain. About time.

I launched for the basketball and caught it. Somewhere in the back of my mind, I heard the faint sound of the crowd going wild, but it didn't really register. There was only room in my thoughts for the next move and the rain.

I grabbed hold twelve, heel-hooked the basketball, and clawed my way up a long rib to the fourth quickdraw. After that, the universe narrowed down to the essentials. Getting my foot placed exactly right on a small edge, positioning my fingers in the right way to get maximum purchase on a tiny crimp, finding my balance by hooking my toe around the corner of a sloping hold.

It's what I found most beautiful about climbing: it made you focus only on what matters most at each moment. I knew my muscles were screaming, I knew my fingertips were worn raw, I knew there were a few hundred pairs of eyes burrowing into my back. I knew I was sweating and grunting and growling and huffing like a steam engine. But none of that mattered. Only the next move, that single pinprick in the universe, was important. Each one got me one step closer to the top; each one got me one step closer to Lily, waiting at the bottom.

And then I was staring at the brass bell at the top. The final hold was huge, and normally I could have hung off it for hours, but I was completely spent. A pair of quickdraws dangled next to the hold, but I didn't bother to clip them. I reached for the bell and then stopped. I turned around, smiled down at my dad and Andy, and put on a big show of pretending to stretch and yawn like the climb had been so easy it was boring. My dad shook his head, and Andy laughed hard and loud. I patted my mouth with one hand and, as casually as I could, I reached out and rang the bell.

Then I jumped.

# Chapter 45

"Tell me about something beautiful, Big," Lily said. Her long body was stretched out in the fall sunshine below the boulder called Mother's Womb. Her shaved head, now covered in a soft fuzz, rested in my lap. We were watching as Sam tried to traverse the boulder.

Big, who a moment ago had looked close to dozing off, grew suddenly animated by Lily's request. He opened his eyes wide and sat up straight. "Oh, I don't know. There's so much to choose from, yeah? Do I have to pick just one?"

I watched an amused, closed-lipped smile stretch Lily's face.

Not waiting for an answer, Big asked, "For instance, did you notice the way Sam was humming to herself all soft and unselfconscious-like as we hiked in?"

Sam laughed and fell off the boulder. "I didn't think you could hear that."

"That's partly why it was so beautiful," Big said. "And did you see the psychedelic pattern the fallen leaves made on the trail? Some of them are yellow and orange and brown like you'd expect, but a lot of them are still mostly green, and it made me almost dizzy to look at them, yeah?" He cocked his head and looked off into the sky like he was savoring the memory of the leaves.

"I can't imagine why anyone would think he's on drugs," I whispered to Lily.

"I heard that," Big said.

"Sorry," I said.

Before he could get upset with me, Lily came to my rescue and said, "Keep going. Tell us something else beautiful."

Of course Big couldn't resist. "Well, there was this moment, Lily, when you stopped to rest, and that alone was kind of beautiful because, for once in my life, no one was waiting on me, but that wasn't what I was going to say." Big took a deep breath. "What was beautiful was that moment when you stopped to rest, and I saw you put your hand on Paul's shoulder to steady yourself." He closed his eyes as if to remember it better. "Your beautiful black hand on Paul's shoulder and Paul's arm around your waist."

Lily groaned, "Oh, gag. Don't make me throw up. I do way too much of that these days."

Sam and I both laughed, while Big looked mildly offended. "Hey, you asked what I thought was beautiful," he said. "It's not my fault if it makes you barf."

"Okay," Lily said, "if you could only pick one thing, what would it be?"

"For today, or does last week count?" Big asked. "Because a few days ago, I saw a friend of mine, the one and only Fantastic Fainting Rabbit, leap from the top of a climbing wall the size of a skyscraper and soar through the air, smiling as he fell like I've never seen anyone smile before."

Lily laughed. "That *was* beautiful."

"You know what I think was beautiful?" Sam said. "Hunter's face."

Lily and I laughed, but Big didn't. He formed one of his frowns that wasn't really a frown, and he said, "I felt kind of bad for Hunter. He seemed really upset." His face lit back up, and he smiled again. "Hey, I know. Maybe we should take Hunter some cookies, yeah?"

"No!" Sam, Lily, and I all said at the same time.

Big looked at us like he was confused as to how we could possibly *not* want to take cookies to Hunter. "Well, if you guys don't want to join me on a covert cookie-delivery mission, that's your loss."

Lily said, "Sorry, Big. You're on your own for that one." Then she looked at me and asked, "Why *did* you jump from the top of Bildungsroman? Why didn't you just clip the quickdraws at the top?"

I thought about it for a moment. "I don't know. It just felt right." I thought about it more and then added, "I guess I was sick of being afraid to fall, and I just wanted to jump for once."

Everyone was quiet, and I started to feel awkward, so I said, "Okay, Big, if you had to pick just one beautiful thing from *today*, what would it be?"

"That's easy, yeah?" Big smiled one of his biggest and warmest smiles. "It would be hearing your read your paper in Language Arts class."

"What? Me?" I asked.

"Yes, you."

"No fair," Lily said. "I wasn't there. I didn't get to hear it."

"I don't remember exactly how it went," Big said, leaning back in his chair and closing his eyes, "but the gist of it was that

Paul thought the way George shot Lennie at the end of the book was totally messed up. Paul said that George should have stood beside Lennie and did whatever he could to help him, not give up before the real battle started, yeah?"

"I agree with that," said Lily. "But I'm not sure Paul reading a paper in Language Arts is all that beautiful. No offense, Paul."

"None taken," I said, remembering the way my hands shook and my voice trembled when I spoke in front of the class.

Big cracked his eyes open and studied Lily and me for a few seconds. "Well, Paul also talked about being a warrior, yeah?" He paused until he saw Lily nod like she understood. "He said warriors have to value every moment and focus on what's most important in that moment because they don't know how many moments they might have left."

I studied Lily's face. I saw the little mole on the side of her chin, and smiled. Then I met her eyes, and neither of us looked away.

"Paul said you don't just give up on a friend because they might have a long, hard battle ahead of them. A real warrior will fight alongside them right to the end. Did I get that about right, brah?"

"More or less," I said.

"Now that," Lily said, "is beautiful."

# Acknowledgments

Thank you to all the Ogden climbers who have inspired me for the last twenty-five years and who continue to inspire me.

Thanks to my alpha readers, Stacy Atkinson and Derrick Keibler, who endured without complaint the earliest version of this book when it was much, much, much too long.

Thank you to everyone at Shadow Mountain who played a role in making this book come to fruition. In particular, thank you to Lisa Mangum, my editor, who, before she ever knew who I was, taught me some hard truths I needed to hear when she spoke at a writing conference years ago. And a special thank you to Heidi Taylor Gordon and Chris Schoebinger, who championed *Paul, Big, and Small* through the entire publishing process.

Thank you to my good friend, Gary Davis, for listening to my endless rants during our countless adventures in the mountains. And thank you to my many other friends who have given me so much love and support over the years.

Thank you to my family for cheering me on every step of the way, especially my two sons for all their input, feedback, and inspiration. I'm not sure I could have done this without knowing you all were behind me.

And, most of all, thank you to my amazing wife, Ruth. There are no words adequate to express my gratitude for your sacrifice, support, and patience. I love you more than I can possibly say.

# Discussion Questions

1. The title, *Paul, Big, and Small*, refers to both the names of the characters in the story and attributes of Paul himself. In what ways is Paul small? In what ways is he big? Which characteristics change over the course of the story? Which do not?

2. Near the end of the book, Paul's dad tells him that sometimes the small things are what matter most. What are some small but important things that go unnoticed in your life?

3. Big is a connoisseur of beautiful things. He can see miracles where others see only the mundane. Do you see any miniature miracles around you right now?

4. There are several references to *Of Mice and Men* by John Steinbeck. What parallels do you see? How are the characters similar? How are they different? What situations and events in the plots are similar? How are they different?

5. At the end of *Of Mice and Men*, George kills his best friend, Lennie, in what he sees as an act of mercy. He feels he is saving Lennie from suffering. Paul disagrees with George and thinks that George should have stood by his friend despite

his suffering. Who do you agree with? George or Paul? Explain.

6. When Chuck and Colt confront Connor, they don't think of it as bullying. They think they are protecting and defending Lily. At what point does defending someone become bullying? If a bully is being bullied, does that make it okay? Why or why not? Can you think of a time when you were bullied? What did you do? Can you think of a time when you were the bully?

7. Paul sees people as either predator or prey. How is his viewpoint simplistic and flawed? Does Paul ever realize his perspective is distorted?

8. A "bildungsroman" is a coming-of-age story that tracks the protagonist's development from youth to maturity. How did Paul change and develop over the course of the story?

9. Rock climbing is an inherently dangerous sport. It is all about taking risks and facing fears. Outside of climbing, what risks did Paul take? What fears did he face?

10. Paul is struggling to come to terms with the death of his mother and the possibility of Lily's. Connor's suicide forces him to confront these realities. How does this change him?

11. When Paul sees Connor's mother break down in the grocery store, his reaction is profoundly emotional and surprises even him. Why do you think he reacts that way? When have you had an unexpected emotional reaction to a situation? What did you learn about yourself from the experience?

12. Paul has to choose between a life of "safe" solitude or risk having friends and falling in love. Are these relationships worth the risk? Why or why not?